It had always been my fantasy to be part of a biker gang. Ever since I first saw Hell's Angels riding around with their greasy leathers and body decorations, the idea of being apprenticed to such a biker had turned me on something rotten. When I saw the film *Mad Max III*, the idea got stronger, for there were these guys in the film who were clearly the slaves of the other bikers, chained to the bikes, doing what they were told and nothing else. And then I saw a TV documentary about a bikers' gathering in small-town America.

One scene really struck me hard and has never gone. There was a prospect, an apprentice, basically a guy who wanted to be a full member of the gang and who had to serve his time doing just that—serving. Of course, the full details of his servitude and initiation weren't shown on the programme so I'll have to fill in the details by telling you what happened to me....

Also by KYLE STONE:

The Initiation of PB 500
The Citadel
Rituals
Fire & Ice
Fantasy Board
Bizarre Dreams (Ed. with Stan Tal)
Hot Bauds (Ed.)
Meltdown! (Ed.)

HOT BAUDS 2

Edited by Kyle Stone

BADBOY

Hot Bauds 2
Copyright © 1997 by Kyle Stone
All Rights Reserved

First BADBOY Edition 1997

First Printing February 1997

ISBN 1-56333-479-8

Manufactured in the United States of America
Published by Masquerade Books, Inc.
801 Second Avenue
New York, N.Y. 10017

Acknowledgments

Thanks to Jorge and Allan, the sysops at The Connection BBS, (http://www.the.connection.com) for their generous donation of time and technical help in launching the original Kyle Stone's Back Room onto the web. :)

HOT BAUDS 2

INTRODUCTION

They're back! Those steamy studs of cyberspace are at it again, getting off to the sound of one hand clicking out hot words on the computer keyboard. You'll find a few names familiar from the first *Hot Bauds* collection, as well as lots of hot new talent that'll keep you hard and hungry for more.

Maybe this is your introduction to the on-line world of gay fantasy. Maybe you've heard about it, but don't know a baud from a badger. In that case, these pages should give you a good feel for what's out there in phosphor land, from the big commercial services to the small local gay BBSs and all the way to the newsgroups like alt.sex.bondage. Just remember that the rules are different here. Some of these guys write on-line, just letting those creative juices flow, so to speak, making liberal use of capital letters, Gs for grins and exclamation marks to get the idea across, since there is no way to show italics or underlining in on-screen text. Others compose off-line, giving themselves more time and space to develop the narrative, which they upload later. And then there's spelling. I've left spelling variants (U.S., British, etc.) as they were, to let the flavor come through, as well as the usual short forms that reflect speech.

If you read the first book, you'll know I like to mix the stories all up together in one steamy mass. In *Hot Bauds 2*, heavy kink is followed by a tender scene between lovers; a British fetish story about cigars and SM precedes a gentle tale of a medieval knight and his young squire. This time I've included the Internet addresses of the writers who agree, so you can let them know your reactions!

Several writers were so enthused about this project that they E-mailed me reams of stories, each hotter than the last, which made my job very hard indeed <G>. Other goodies I know you would have loved I had to leave on the boards, unable to contact the writers for permission to print them.

So here they are, gathered from sites in the United Kingdom, the United States, Canada, and Australia. Cruise the fast lane of the information highway with us, without any hardware but what's built in! This way, you won't melt your hard drive!

Kyle Stone, Toronto, 1995
Internet address: stone@io.org
homepage: Kyle Stone's Back Room:
http://www.io.org/~stone

TITLE: My Fantasy Man
BY: Ajay Vanden
FROM: big tedd's—Melbourne, OZ

Man, he was so kewl, you broke out in a sweat just
lookin' at 'im! I wanted to jump up on the stage and lick
'im like an ice cream, except that would make me hotter
still! Ohhh, I think I'm crackin' another one just remembering him again! His name is Jon Stevens, and he had a
rock-music career before turning to the stage. He put
out a coupla albums both on his own and with a group,
and I was thinkin' 'bout tracking 'em down after seeing
this guy and hearin' him sing! It was lust at first sight!

Long black hair, dark brooding eyes that can see right
thru you. He'd be about six foot, broad shoulders, and
the pecs…hard, firm and round! I was practically drooling over the pecs, with large, round nipples that begged
to be nibbled. I'd give his pecs a thorough cleansing and

11

those hairy armpits of his as well, before following that trail of hair down over the abs into the nether region. I know at one stage I was thinking that this guy must work out at a gym to have such well-shaped pecs and abdominals. I'd imagine he had a personal trainer, and I was wondering what it would be like to be that trainer. I'd give his muscles a workout, including the one between his legs. <GRIN> Lots a massage required there. And when I have him nice and hard, I'd take him slowly between my lips, inch by inch, all the way down to the pubes and just hold him there, feeling him hard and throbbing. Then I'd let him fuck my face, my hands on his hips and feeling those hard muscles working to give me all he's got! He'd lay his hands on my head, holding me lovingly while I took all that he gave. A cry of joy would issue from his mouth as he flooded me with his love juice. I would pull back a little to savour the taste of that spurting fluid.

When the last drop dribbled down onto my waiting tongue, he would kneel down with me and give me a long hard liplock as his tongue mingled with mine to taste both our fluids. One hand circled round my back to pull me close to him while the other grabbed hold of my hard-on and began jerking me off to a climax of my own. And it didn't take long! Feeling him mouth to mouth, chest to chest, and hard-on to hand brought me to a land where my body erupted with sensation. The feeling was so explosive that the first spurt from my dick hit us in the mouth, adding to the taste and enticing Jon to seek out some more.

His head bobbed down over my dick, while my love juice continued to shoot into his mouth. Then he took me all the way to my pubes and held me there till I begged him to let me go. Man oh man! What a feeling that was! And all this happened before the first song! So I guess I had a lot more in store before the night was thru. <GRIN>

Well, you DID ask for my fantasy.

Cheers, mate,

Luv ya hard on!

* Internet address: mindmeld@geocities.com

TITLE: Briefly Stated
BY: Han Solo
FROM: STUDS BBS—San Francisco, CA

How about this scenario, stud:

You arrive home from work worn and sweaty, definitely horny!!! I'm there, a burglar, rifling through yer drawers and laundry, cuz my target is your underwear.... I've been watching you and fantasizing about you for weeks.... I intend to have something of yours!

I surprise and overpower you enough to get your hands tied to your bedposts, you spread-eagled on your back...and I kneel on your chest, pressing my packed crotch, lump growing noticeably, onto your face. You smell man smells...dick...balls...sweat...stale piss and even a note of something else. I press my rounded crotch more forcibly against your nose and mouth and force your lips open to lick me through my Levi's.

In the meantime, my hands are roaming your body, tugging your shirt buttons open, your shirt outta your trousers....

I stand up and look at you, unzipping my Levi's and parting the fly to show a white package with a long tube-shaped mound above a rounded pouch.... I begin tugging your shoes off slowly, and proceed to lick and chew your stockinged toes, then tug your socks down your hairy ankles and off...placing one over your nose. My hands roam up your thighs, with quick gropes at the crotch, then over your exposed stomach, tugging and tangling in the hairs there...then up your chest to pinch your nips and move into your hairy armpits lost in the shirtsleeves. They're wet, and with one hand's fingers, I drag the wetness over your nipples. The other hand's wet fingers dab your sweat on your upper lip and onto mine.... I shrug off my T-shirt.

My Levi's have slipped to mid-thigh, and you see there's a rampant boner pulsing in there.... With each pulse the wetness at the head of my cock makes a wider and wider stain in the material.... You focus on the wild dark hairs hanging out the legholes of my FOLs at the pouch...and the trail of dark hair disappearing at the waistband....

I part your thighs and kneel between, Levi's around my ankles now...and put my hands on the tops of both your thighs and massage, each circle getting closer to the tented fly of your trousers.... I lean forward and lick your nipples one at a time, finally trailing my tongue slowly down your stomach and abdomen, tongue-fucking your belly button till there's a pool of spit there, then moving down to mouth at your skin and stick my tongue into your trousers waistband and lick back and forth, tickling.... Then I open your belt and with my lips I tug down the zipper of your fly, struggling to get it over the mound of your own dick...and enjoying how there is a huge wet spot in the material of your trousers.....

When the fly is open, I part it. You can tell by my stare how hot I think you look with your briefs exposed, your nuts outlined and your dick pulsing.... I stand up and look at you, rubbing the boner trapped in my own stained briefs....

I drop my Levi's off me completely and again move to kneel on your chest, pressing my worn, crotch-damp and vaguely piss-scented white cotton against your face...the smells of my cock and nuts are nearly overwhelming.... You have the impression I've worn these shorts awhile....

"Stick out yer tongue, fucker!"

You comply and I move the leg band of my briefs onto it so that there's half hairy flesh and half damp cotton on your tongue...and I move so your tongue swabs that area...moving again so your tongue disappears into my leg hole and contacts the salty, hot, wrinkled skin of my ballsac...and its hairy covering.... My hands are grabbing and massaging your aching nuts

17

and you'd give anything for me to touch your dick...but I only tease over it lightly with my fingers....working the wet spot against your sensitive dickhead...then again I back off till our briefs pouches are against one another, me kneeling upright, and I grind my balls against your balls, the cotton catching and pulling from the friction, the heat of my nuts warming your already-glowing pouch....

"Lookit this, asshole!"

I lower the waistband of my briefs just enough that the top of my bush hangs over...and I put my fingers in the fly, working at tugging out through it a fat-shafted, plum-headed dick, very wet at the parted piss-slit, and a strand of clear juice hanging in the air....

Yeah...

You moan a little...there's concern in your eyes...but your boner does not shrink....

"Wonder what's coming, li'l boy????? Gonna get serviced by a man-sized cock!"

Yeahhhhhhh...

My fingers play around the juncture of your dick and nuts, playing into the fly, parting the material.... I pull back a bit and begin to rub my wet cockhead over your cotton-covered nuts, wetting the material...the shaft rubs against the lower portion of your cock...and in one thrust I insert my dickhead into your fly and suddenly it's in that area and my shaft is bare-skinned against your shaft...wetting it where your own seep hasn't...sliding along the wetness...and I lean forward, fucking into your briefs and rubbing my cock along your cock...my abdomen pressing my cockhead against yours and yours against your abdomen.... You feel a pool of precome on your flesh and hanging in your pubes...and then I kneel up again, my hard boner pulling the material of your briefs up with it.... You see into the waistband...our two dickheads are stuck together with precome, swollen, pulsing, huge, drooling...as I fuck again into the cock-ring your material forms, my piss-slit flares on the stroke toward you...and leaks more clear prejizz all over your own head.... Then I pull back entirely, your Jockeys like demanding lips pulling at my shaft, then the loose skin below the head, then the corona itself before my cockhead finally plops free and the shaft stands in swollen red assertion.

I have to struggle to get it back in my own Jockeys' fly...but I do and it looks like the material is going to fuckin' BURST, but it holds. For the first time you notice old stains in the material along with the wet new ones that make it almost transparent the last 2 inches of my cocklength...you don't have to wonder what's next...immediately I'm back on the bed, but this time I hoist your thighs over my shoulders and bury my face behind your nuts...whiffing your scents and pressing with my nose so the cloth is pressed against your hole...and my tongue starts licking up your cotton-covered crack...slow laps, sometimes along the edge of your leg holes, little fucking motions inside the seamed material. I press my wide-open mouth over the place your hairy asscrack is deepest and begin to tongue there insistently, able to tell where the hot pucker of your hole is...enjoying the scents and tastes of clean man-ass...licking, tongue-fucking the cloth...making it hot with my lust-crazed breathing and wet with my mouthjuices...your writhing is really getting me hot....

Yeah...

Again I kneel upright, one hand working the wet cloth at your hole, fingers probing and teasing...the other hand is working your cock...seriously, insistently...it's obvious that I'm going to make you come right now...and my hands both go to work to do just that...one hand tugs and grips your aching balls, the other moves up and down the trapped shaft in its cotton ridge...my fingers play with your dickhead through the transparent wet material...I tug at the loose skin below your notch, rub the pinched flesh and cotton there, then take the whole shaft in a juicy cotton sheath and hand-fuck it...my free hand wreaking havoc on your nuts and your nips and your chest, tickling, scratching...prob-ing...bearing your armpit sweat, your dickjuice, your ass-moistures up and into your sucking lips...and when you taste your own tastes your body stiffens and I know you're gonna blow and I step back so there's no contact at all.... With hypnotic fascination, I watch you writhe as your nuts draw up in the cloth and your dick starts beating on its own, the head swelling as your spew starts to shoot out.... Your arms strain to touch your cock to help, but there's nothing they can do for it, your shaft and head fuck against the damp, crusty cotton for sensation, and the sensation that you feel gets you over the edge and WHAM you spew, WHAM you spew, WHAM you shoot, WHAM your nuts feel like they're gonna follow your load up your dicklength and SHOT after SHOT leaves your wide piss-slit to soak into your shorts, coming so fast it makes a creamy icing on the white material…you're in a fuckin' ecstasy of coming in your briefs, man, and I'm watching the whole damn show kneeling over you and rubbing my own bulge…your shooting settles into weaker pulses, your spew into a stream of jizz…and my hand moves into the heat of your thighs to work once more back against your hole…and before your orgasm is completely spent, while your head is lost and your breath is staggering, I once more lift your thighs onto my shoulders and move my head against the now-sweat-soaked seat of your briefs, tearing a hole there with my teeth and moving my tongue into it and against, then into your asshole, a wet hard hot probe opening the space of that hole…making you move down onto as much of it as you can, wakening sensations that transfer to your balls and then your cock, whose dwindling is halted and which now lies in the hot cummy wetness of your destroyed briefs pouch.

The smell of come is rich in our nostrils. You watch

as if from a distance while I pull my pecker out the fly of my briefs once more…even more swollen now, the head purple, the shaft red and angry looking…the veins stark on the shaft…and then I press the head against the little wet hole in the cotton and there's a ripping sound as it passes through, the cloth like delicate lips on my shaft…. My wet head meets your spit-slicked hole and presses there. You think there'll be pain, but you're too far gone from your orgasm to resist and my fat hawg-head slips into the wet tight darkness of your opening… and then you feel it, heat and hardness and…size…thick hard size spreading your asslips, pulsing wetness, size, hardness sliding in farther, I lean onto you and my body weight moves the size, the hardness, the hot wetness into you farther…your legs must part. My cotton briefs are pressing against your nuts again…my hands start massaging your nuts, working the spunk-loaded slimy cotton over your sensitive dickhead and you feel yourself swelling, getting longer and unbelievably thicker…my own thickness increases its penetration and soon I'm impaled in you and my abdomen works your nuts and my hands are working your new fat hardness and aching dickhead and you feel the corona of my cock doing an intense flicking dance over your prostate and your dick aches and I free your hands and they grab the waistband of my Jockeys and caress and slap my cotton-covered hard butt muscles. You pull me into you as far as possible and I begin to lose myself in the ride, in the

22

sensation of your assheat gripping my dick, the sight of our briefs nearly blending, and the emotions on your face…drool running outta yer hot fuckhole of a mouth, eyes half-lidded, rolled back. You tug and rip at my briefs trying to pull all of me, briefs and all, into your hole and into you and the feel and look of our underwear-clad bodies and the grinding of me up your ass and my hands on your cock tugging it into my own tight briefs fly, ripping it in the act, your boner pulled tight and painfully against my upright stomach, buried and pulsing in my underwear while I'm fuckin' into yours and then we both go over and over and fuckin' OVER THE EDGE AND BLAST AND PULSE AND I TRY TO FUCKIN' PUSH OUT YOUR MOUTHHOLE WITH MY DICK AND SHOOT AND MY PULSING DICK AGAINST YOUR NUTS AND YOU SHOOT AGAIN AND I WRANGLE YOUR DICK TILL IT FEELS LIKE I FUCKIN' *AM* GONNA JERK IT RIGHT OFF AND MY OWN WILD COCK HOT AND SPEWING GEYSERS OF COME INTO YOU AND PULSING AND RUBBING YOUR PROSTATE AND THE SMELL OF COME AND SWEAT AND ASSFUCK AND

YEEEEEEEEEAAAAAAAAAHHHHHHHHHHH-HHHHHHHHHHHHH

OVER WE FUCKIN' DAMN ***GO*** BUDDY O'MIIIINE!!!!!!!!!!!!!!!!

!!!

The fuckin' stars themselves shower heat and rain down come and light and gentle cotton and I collapse on you in a tangle of cock and come and briefs and we both glide down the long slope of abandon into deep, contented, briefs-dreaming sleep...connected, tangled, wet, stickin' and smelling of each other and lost...

* Internet address: Han.Solo@studs.com

TITLE: Surprise
BY: Beartrap
FROM: The Vault—London, U.K.

I'm standing in the middle of the playroom, naked except for a head harness, waiting for the Boss to enter. I can smell stale poppers, sweat, piss, come and cigars. Each smell merges into the next. Even without seeing the straps hanging on the wall, the ropes hanging from beams, or the sling in the middle of the room, there is no mistaking that this room's function is to provide a space for sex. I don't know how long I've been here. I just wait. I try to keep as motionless as I can: there have been times when he's entered the room and I haven't known he was there until he's belted my arse for moving.

As usual, I have no idea of what he has planned for tonight. When he told me to come in here and get myself ready, there was no clue as to what he wanted.

Not that I had time to check for anything out of place. He might have intended coming into the playroom immediately after me. I've been caught like that before: I wasn't ready for his immediate use when he followed me in. My punishment that time was to hold a large enema for two hours. Two hours of keeping my sphincter clenched and keeping silent while my guts cramped and he ignored me.

Even if I didn't hear the door creak, I'd know someone had opened it: the blindfold on the head harness isn't entirely lightproof. I stand absolutely still listening to him moving around the room. I manage not to flinch as I feel something around my head: another blindfold. I lose what little vision I had. He is standing behind me. He reaches round in front of me and takes a nipple in each hand. I can feel his leather jeans pressing against my ass, the hair on his chest against my back, his breath on my neck. He squeezes my tits gently, massaging them between his finger and thumb. My dick swells.

He increases the pressure slowly until it hovers on the edge of pain. I'm breathing more deeply now and find myself beginning to press myself back against him, not caring that I could be punished for my presumption. My Boss is holding me and making me hurt. My dick stiffens.

He makes some sort of odd movement with his head, and as I'm trying to figure out what's going on, something hot and wet surrounds my dick. Someone is sucking my cock. It's been a while since I've had my dick in someone else's mouth, and I push forward as the Boss increases the pressure on my tits. I cry out in pain and the mouth pulls away for a few seconds.

Now the mouth is holding just the head of my cock, and the Boss's pressure on my tits is just enough to hurt. I push forward slightly and, as I expected, the pressure increases again. I pull back. I want to grab the head at my crotch and shove my dick into the throat, but I know the Boss doesn't want that. So I remain where I am, with the Boss pulling on my tits, and the unknown mouth torturing my cock with its promise of what the Boss won't let me have.

The Boss signals again, steps away from me, and the mouth is gone. I'm standing alone in the darkness. I wait, not daring to move. Nothing happens. I begin to wonder who the other boy is, trying to remember if the Boss has given me any clues beforehand.

They each grab one of my arms, and I'm pushed back against the wall. One wrist is expertly cuffed and fastened to a chain on the wall, while the other is cuffed and fastened by someone less practised. So the Boss was on my right. My ankles are bound: the Boss hasn't changed position. The first words are spoken.

"Plug his arse."

There is a bottle of poppers at my nose. I inhale greedily: I don't know which buttplug he wants in me, so I might need all the help I can get. As the poppers begin to hit, a greased finger pushes into my arse, only to be withdrawn and replaced by the tip of the buttplug. I can't tell yet which plug it is, so I continue to inhale. The buttplug's pressure increases, and I rock slightly to and fro to help it in. I want my arse filled. The Boss is pulling on my tits again: I push against him, hoping, needing him to hurt me. I feel my arse stretching, pulling the plug in. Suddenly, the widest point is passed and it feels as though it's shot into me. My dick dribbles precome, and the Boss lets go of me.

I stand spread-eagled against the wall with my arse full. From what I can hear, I would say that the other boy is being tied up. The effect of the poppers is still there: my arse seems to suck on the buttplug, trying to pull it farther in. My cock is hard and aching. My tits remember the Boss and want him back.

The Boss removes both the blindfold and the eye mask of the harness. Although the playroom is dimly lit, I've been in total darkness for long enough for what little light there is to dazzle me. The other boy is tied to the wall opposite me: mid-thirties, fairly smooth, 'stache and beard framing a mouth that begs to wrap itself around a dick. The Boss is leaning over in front of him. When he moves away, I see that he has tied a boot to the boy's balls. Judging by the look on his face, it doesn't look as though he's used to having his balls pulled like that, but his cock seems to like it.

"Watch carefully. Next time you come here, this will happen to you."

The Boss turns away from the boy and picks a larger buttplug from the shelf. Another hit of poppers, and he squats down in front of me, pulling out the first plug. This next one is a struggle. I need it in me, but I'm afraid that I can't take it. The Boss continues to push, holding the poppers up to my face again. The playroom disappears as I concentrate on filling my arse. The widest point passes in, and my arse clamps around the plug tightly with such force that I cry out.

"Stop that fucking noise!" He slaps one thigh hard enough to leave the mark of his hand.

I'm trying to catch my breath and maintain the silence he requires of me. My attention shifts to the other boy: in his face I see fascination, fear, and lust. A slight rattle shifts my attention back to the Boss: the clothespegs.

He starts with a line from each armpit to the nipple, then a line up the tender flesh of the inner arm. Before moving to my belly, he passes his hands lightly over the pegs on my tits. The extra pressure of their movement makes me pull in my breath sharply. In another minute or so, those pegs will feel like they're on fire. After my belly, he starts on the inside of my thighs. The line of pain along each arm and across my chest keeps changing from a single line to a series of individual sharply defined points.

The Boss stands in front of me, moving closer so that his body presses on the pegs, and holds the poppers up to me. I inhale frantically, knowing that the poppers will help me deal with the pain. He grinds his crotch against my dripping cock. I can't help but try to thrust against him. He pulls away, wipes my precome off his leathers and pushes his fingers into my mouth for me to clean.

More pegs. He builds a wooden halo around my scrotum and then places a line up the underside of my dick. I concentrate on keeping my breathing regular as each wave of pain passes through me. He moves away from me. Immediately I need him back: he's the one making me hurt like this, and I need his physical presence to get me through the pain.

Instead he goes to the other boy and releases him from the wall. He sets the boot swinging, slaps the boy's cock and orders him to get me into the sling. I move slowly, each movement sending fresh waves of pain through me. When I don't move fast enough, it's the other boy whose arse gets belted. As I lie back in the sling, the Boss runs his hands over all the pegs: this time I can't hold it back and I scream.

"I told you to keep quiet!"

As my wrists and ankles are fastened to the chains holding the sling, he belts my arse. This pain is a relief from the pegs: somewhere else hurts and distracts my attention from the pegs. Once I'm secured in the sling, he holds the poppers to my face and then moves away out of sight for a moment. He removes the head harness and pushes my head down. I see that he has removed the boot from the boy's balls.

"Stuff your balls in his mouth and then remove all the pegs above his waist."

The boy's cautious. Of course he is: I've got his balls in my mouth. The last thing he wants to do is give me cause to hurt him. He picks off the first few pegs individually. There is a crack of leather against flesh, and I feel him jerk. My mouth pulls on his balls.

"Faster, asshole!"

The boy pulls the pegs of three or four at a time now. The pain makes me jerk around in the sling. Although I try to keep my head as still as I can, I'm obviously hurting him, but not as much as he's hurting me.

"Over here."

The boy removes his balls from my mouth and goes to stand between my legs.

"Take the plug out and then use this on him."

The large dildo.

The boy complies immediately, pulling on the plug. My arse does not want to let go. Again, the poppers: my arse dilates and the plug creeps out, only to rush when the widest point is passed.

The Boss stands back to watch and lights a cigar. The boy begins pushing the dildo into me, unaware of the significance of the cigar.

"Play with his dick: I want him desperate."

The boy slips his free hand under my dick, avoiding

the pegs, and rubs my precome around the head. At the same time, he's pushing the dildo farther in. I watch the tip of the Boss's cigar.

I'm being fucked slowly and deeply, my cock and balls feel like they're being pulled apart by all the pegs, and the head of my dick is harder and wetter than I ever remember its being. The Boss inhales on his cigar, knocks the ash off the end, and moves toward me. I can't take my eyes off the orange glow.

The boy obviously remembers what the Boss said about the next time he comes here: he stops wanking and fucking me and watches in disbelief. The Boss looks at him. "If you don't want the cigar now, get back to working on his arse and dick." The fucking resumes, but he's going more slowly on my dick now. I could come very easily at this point.

The Boss returns his attention to me and slowly brings the tip of his cigar toward my chest. I don't know which I am more scared of: the pain he's about to cause, or letting him down by being unable to take it. He places his free hand on my chest, finger and thumb on either side of my left nipple. The boy continues fucking me, but is barely moving on my dick.

The cigar moves closer. I think I can feel the heat of it and moan.

"Shut it."

The heat increases as the cigar slowly moves closer. I'm breathing quickly, almost hyperventilating. I must keep control. I must remain silent. I turn my eyes away from the cigar and watch the Boss's face. He's staring intently at the cigar, and just beyond it, at my nipple. The heat becomes painful, but I know there is a way to go yet. The Boss's face remains impassive.

The cigar touches and I scream behind closed lips, trying to jerk away from the pain, but unable to move. He withdraws the cigar and inhales on it. I catch the smell of my own burned flesh. I relax back, barely aware of the dildo in my arse and the hand on my dick, and watch the tip of the cigar as it glows brighter.

"Keep the dildo in his arse and get rid of the pegs. And you"—he turns to look at me—"keep quiet."

The boy starts with the pegs on my dick. The blood rushes in and all the pain the pegs have caused is concentrated in one burst. I manage to remain silent by exhaling forcefully through my nose, almost—but not quite—grunting. I try to count the pegs on my balls as they come off, a way of distracting myself from the pain. It doesn't work. I forget my burned nipple as the universe contracts and focuses on my scrotum. By the time the last peg is removed, I'm panting heavily, but I didn't cry out.

"Keep fucking him and use your hand on his dick. Don't let him come."

His hand on my chest again, this time framing the other nipple. I tell myself that this time won't hurt so much, that it hurt so much before only because I was afraid of the pain. It doesn't work. A few moments ago, I was close to coming. Now I can hardly feel the hand on my dick.

The cigar comes down. I breathe faster and faster, only to hold my breath at the moment the cigar touches. It burns. The Boss holds the cigar against me a little longer this time before withdrawing it. Still I don't cry out.

My attention is so concentrated on the pain in my tits that I don't notice the dildo being removed. When I finally take notice of what's going on, the Boss is standing between my legs with his erect cock pressing against my arse.

"Suck him off."

The Boss holds my thighs and pulls me onto his cock as the boy takes my dick in his mouth. He quickly increases the speed and force of his thrusts. I look into his face and our eyes meet. As he comes, he pulls the boy's head down on my dick so I'm fucking his throat. It's too much: I come immediately. He pushes the boy away and stands for a moment, with his cock softening in my arse, looking into my eyes.

He frees me from the sling, orders the boy to clear up the mess, and pulls me to him. As he stands there with his arms around me, I decide it's worth the risk of disobeying his order to keep silent and whisper, "I love you, Sir."

* Internet address: beartrap@vault.posnet.co.uk

TITLE: The Biker
BY: Ray Cornett, aka Writer@seattle.com
FROM: Rendezvous—Seattle, WA

It was a warm day, and I had to drive from Seattle to Olympia to see some friends. My car did not agree with that plan. Just south of the city limits, it crapped out on me. So, with the warmth and all, I donned my shorts and stuck out my thumb.

I had walked just south of the airport when a guy on a motorcycle pulled off the road. He removed his helmet, revealing waist-length almost-white blond hair (quite beautiful actually) and asked me where I was headed. I told him I was going to Olympia. He just handed me a helmet and told me, "Mount up." Once he told me just *how* to do it, I got on and we went. He showed me how to hold him and how not to overcompensate when we turned—all the simple stuff I knew nothing about. I held him firmly just above the belt line, probably a little too tight for comfort. He didn't seem to mind.

"Mind if we take the scenic route?" he asked. "I just want to take some of the back roads and go down through the tide flats."

Since he was driving, I didn't care which way we went. So we pulled off onto Dash Point Road and settled back for the ride. I soon discovered it's not too easy to talk while riding a motorcycle. I just watched the beautiful countryside pass and thought about the man who picked me up. He certainly was good-looking. Besides the long blond hair, he had the blue eyes and tall, slim body that makes a man irresistible to me (or most people, for that matter).

Once we got back off the main highway, I could feel him relaxing, leaning against me and putting his feet up. My hands kept wanting to drift down to his crotch (where my mind already was), but I didn't want to cause an accident or lose my ride.

Once I got a little more comfortable with the movement of the bike, I relaxed some, too, putting my hands down onto his thighs. It was very pleasant. He smelled wonderful with the heat, and there were all the sounds, the beautiful view....

Without thinking much about it, I put one hand in his crotch. He reached down to it, but didn't push it away. Instead, he held it and cupped it there. He had a wonderful bulge, too! I squeezed it gently, couldn't tell how he reacted, but he didn't complain or ask me to stop. Instead, he reached behind himself, and returned the favor. The man had great hands...I was hard in no time at all.

I noticed he was trying to tell me something. Couldn't quite make it out...the roar of the engine, the wind....

"Have you ever fucked someone on a bike?"

Of course I hadn't, never having ridden one before.

"Like to try?"

Since I'm always game for new things, I agreed.

He asked me to undo the buttons on his pants. I was more than happy to comply.

"Okay, I'm gonna stand a little here. Pull them down as far as you can. Just don't pull too hard or jerk me off balance." Again, I did my best to help. He sat back down, and the feel of his bare ass against me was nice; I knew how to make it better, though. I undid my pants quickly and tried to pull them off a little. Luckily, the roads were pretty dead. That would have been a tough one to explain.

"Now, move forward a little when I stand again. Don't try to get inside me just yet, though."

I did as he asked, and he sat back down on my thighs and crotch. This was getting to feel better all the time! He came up with a small container of lube from some-where, and told me to apply some to the head of my cock, which I did gladly. He stood once again, coming down this time on my rod. Very slowly, he sat down on me.

With the bike vibrating beneath us, it was a wonderful feeling! Once he got down on me, he didn't move much. He simply let the bumps and movement of the road do the work. It was doing a fine job, too! I reached up to his chest and gave a nipple a squeeze. Searching for the other one, I found a small ring. (Something *else* I had never tried before.) I squeezed his left nipple hard while pulling gently on the ring with my other hand. He seemed to enjoy this, but I couldn't tell if he said anything about it.

We drove around the back roads between Federal Way and Tacoma for quite a while. Every corner and hill in the road brought new and more intense sensations. After what seemed like a *long* time, the feelings in my groin were getting too strong. I assumed he couldn't do a lot to help, though. It's not like you can just bounce up and down on a hard cock while trying to control a motorcycle. I just enjoyed the intensity of these feelings and waited for things to get to the point of making me come.

It took quite a while, but I finally did! The feeling was incredible! After waiting all that time to come, when I did, I about exploded! All the while pulling on that little ring in his breast, clinging tight to his body, and screaming. What the heck, who was going to hear me out here?

Once I had relaxed a little, he stood up high enough for me to come out of him. He motioned me to move back. I pulled his pants back up a little and tried playing with him a bit.

"Sorry. Can't do that while driving. If you'd like to stop at my place, though, I'd love your help in finishing it off."

"Sure, if you don't mind me calling my friends when we get there."

He said, "No problem," and I sat back, buttoned myself up, and enjoyed a *very* pleasant ride around the sound.

I called my friends to cancel our plans, and looked forward to a very interesting long weekend with Jerry the Biker.

When I returned to the living room, my new friend was standing at the bar. "Would you like a drink?"

I accepted gladly, and we sat down on his huge leather couch to talk. The bulge in his pants told me we weren't going to be talking long.

"I have to ask, what made you stop and pick me up? People don't do that much anymore."

"Well, I was curious as to why you were hitchhiking, and I found you very attractive," he said with a slight blush creeping into his face.

Jerry suggested we take a shower to wash off the sweat of the ride. I got a *real* surprise when he took off his shirt. His entire chest and stomach were covered in soft blond fur. It was so thick, it looked rather like a blond rug. Quite beautiful, actually. As he got more naked, I discovered his fur covered his entire body.

(Note: Furry men make me *melt!*) It surprised me that I hadn't noticed his fur earlier. Guess I was distracted. :)

Jerry stepped into the shower and set the temperature. The water made crazy patterns out of his body fur. Though I was a little timid about my own bare body, I got undressed and stepped in with him. Jerry was just a little taller than I. I had to reach up a bit to give him a timid kiss. He returned it with great zeal. I leaned back, relaxed and left him in control of things. My hands roamed his beautiful hairy body, coming to rest on his furry butt.

Jerry grabbed some soap, lathered both our bodies, and held me close. His fur felt wonderful as our bodies meshed. Our cocks grew to full erection and rubbed between our bodies as we moved together. Jerry directed the flow of water to rinse our bodies and whispered in my ear, asking me if I'd like to move into the bedroom. I agreed gladly, and he shut off the water. Once I stepped out of the shower, he grabbed a towel and dried every inch of my body. Then he motioned me to sit while he dried himself very seductively.

We left our clothes in the bathroom and moved into the bedroom and onto his king-size water bed. I lay there a moment, relaxing. I looked up at his ceiling to drift a little and noticed a couple of very sturdy looking hooks. I asked about them, and got another wicked little smile as I watched him blush like mad.

"Well, those are for a sling. I use it occasionally when I'm playing. It can be a lot of fun."

I admitted that I had never used one, but agreed that it would be fun to try it sometime. Without missing a beat, he reached into one of the drawers and pulled out a leather contraption that looked like a big net. Within a couple of minutes, he had it hooked to his ceiling and was sitting in it.

"See, pretty simple, and it gives great access to everything," he said, showing me just what he meant.

I went over and gave him a long kiss. "I can see that," I said as I caressed his butt through one of the holes in his sling. Jerry moaned and kissed me again. When my finger found and probed his asshole, he leaned back into the sling and groaned out loud. I had to pursue this.

I replaced my fingers with my mouth, fingering the hair on his ass while my tongue dived and played with his sphincter. After about a half hour of tonguing his ass, I needed to give my jaw a break. I moved up and took his cock into my mouth. His cock was almost as long as my 8 inches, but I managed to get most of it down my throat. Jerry groaned and forced me the rest the way down on his cock. I had to suppress my gag reflex, but managed to get him all the way down. It was *fantastic!* And Jerry screamed his agreement. Apparently, my gag reflex and all the ass licking was just enough to get him off! Feeling his come shoot down my throat was great. I had to pull off, though. Too much of a good thing, I guess.

All this licking, sucking and watching Jerry's body

writhe under my torturing tongue was more then I could stand. My raging hard-on ached to be somewhere deep within him!

I found his lube on the headboard of his bed. Without hesitation, I lubed myself and plunged into him all the way to the hilt. Jerry arched his back and let out a little scream, but didn't resist my efforts much. I *did* notice that his cock went hard again when I took the plunge.

With Jerry at about hip level in the sling, it was real easy to fuck him without moving much. So I concentrated on playing with the rest of his body while I gave him an internal prostate massage. I started running my fingers through the hair on his chest and stomach, parting it with my nails, and watching him enjoy my touch.

Jerry's nipples grew hard and pushed his nipple ring away from his body. I ran my nails over his breast, tightening his nipple even further. When it looked like I was going to drive him nuts with my fingers, I changed tactics. I leaned down and put my mouth over his breast, applying suction to it and pulling his nipple into my mouth. Using my tongue, I pulled, pushed, and generally drove him crazy playing with that nipple. I could feel his cock pulse under my stomach. When I pulled back up to stretch, I noticed the come all over our stomachs. I massaged it gently into his stomach and cock as I continued to fuck him. His cock was still very sensitive from coming and, as I played with it, he jumped around.

The motions did wonderful things to his ass. Our screams filled the house as my cock finally exploded.

Out of sheer exhaustion, we crawled back into bed and collapsed.

The next morning, I woke early. Not wanting to disturb Jerry, I went out back and lay down on his hammock to watch the sun rise. Lying on my stomach (for reasons that still escape me), I threaded my cock and balls through the mesh in Jerry's hammock. It felt good. A little tight, but pleasant.

I lay there for quite a while, totally engulfed in watching the sun rise through the trees behind his house. Apparently, I was paying more attention to the sunrise than I thought. Before I realized it, Jerry had come out and moved under me, gently taking my soft cock into his mouth. I looked down at him through the mesh.

"Umm, good morning. How're you feeling?"

"Hungry." Jerry returned to sucking my cock. The rope of his hammock tightened rather uncomfortably around my cock and balls as I hardened from his expert sucking.

"Sorry, Jerry. This is getting a little uncomfortable. I've got to pull out of this rope."

Jerry released me reluctantly, and I pulled myself back up through the ropes.

"Ah, that's better."

Jerry got up off the ground and joined me in the

hammock, snuggling up close. He took my cock in hand and stroked it until it hardened again. Jerry *(carefully!)* moved down and took my cock into his mouth, slurping it down with little effort and running his tongue all over my shaft. He was driving me nuts, and he knew it. He kept getting me just to the edge of coming, then pulling back. I knew I wasn't going to be able to take much more when he pulled his mouth off me completely.

Without saying a word, he got up and straddled my hips. He positioned my cock at the opening of his ass. And pushed. I have to admit, it hurt a little having him push down on my cock without lube, but things were too good to stop and worry about that. With all the sucking, it took me only a couple minutes before I was more than ready to come. My nails clawed into his back as I shoved my cock up into his ass. Once my spasms stopped, Jerry lay down on me. I played with the fur on his chest as we lay there, drifting back off to sleep.

A little while later, Jerry squeezed my cock a couple of times to wake me back up. "Good morning again. Would you like some breakfast?" he said looking down at me.

I agreed. He pulled himself off me (reluctantly), and we stumbled into the kitchen to *get cooking*...(:

* Internet address: Writer@seattle.com

TITLE: True Love
BY: Rudette Stratocaster
FROM: The Connection BBS —Toronto, CANADA

Here is a story as confessed to me by a close friend about the woman he loves. And love is the word here, as it helps him overcome his notions about what love is supposed to be. Maybe we can all learn a little lesson from him as he tells his exciting tale about his beautiful little lady Micela.

My life is now complete. I have found the most wonderful human being in this whole wide world to share the rest of my life with. This is how my story goes.

I lived an uneventful life making a living in the city like so many other countless souls, always hoping to meet a woman to love who would love me and make me feel cared for and important.

Bring some meaning into my life. This finally did happen, but not the way you would think it would.

I met her through a family in the apartment building where I lived in 1982. When I first saw her I was shy, but I smiled at her and soon was saying hi. As time went by, we started talking.

We had very little in common, but still got along very well. She was Catholic and Spanish. I was just plain old nothing. She always looked beautiful when she went to church, and I couldn't stop myself from thinking about sex with her. Her body was built amazingly. When she wore jeans, her ass would give me a hard-on just imagining how it looked naked.

She was seldom allowed out for much because her family was strict. Usually it was in the laundry room that I would get to talk to her for any length of time. When she took out the garbage, too. After about a year of this, she got really friendly with me and we began to push each other playfully when we joked, or touch each other's shoulder or arm when we were talking. Soon I had to kiss her, or I would never forgive myself! It was perfection. Her soft lips excited me so. We started kissing as often as we could after that. I began to hope for more and touched her firm breasts through her clothes. She responded by pushing her chest toward me and kissing me deeper. In a few days, she put my hand under her top, and she had no bra on. I had never felt breasts so firm and warm! My dick was like a rock in my pants, and she rubbed her body against me.

She told me we couldn't have sex because she was

Catholic and it wasn't allowed until marriage. She shed a tear when she told me that and said she wished it wasn't so. We began to touch each other all over and she put her hand in the pocket of my dress pants and began to rub the tip of my cock. I ran my hand between her legs and began to rub her crotch right along the seam of her jeans.

She moaned as I pressed my fingers to feel her meaty pussy through her pants. My dick was really enjoying her fingertips, and I creamed myself after 20 minutes of her hot little hand. She came, too, and pulled me real tight as she did. I enjoyed giving her so much pleasure and saw nothing wrong with what we were doing.

One night I heard a big fight in their apartment and was worried about what was going on. I heard the door slam so I went into the hall to take a look. I found Micela sitting in a stairway crying her eyes out.

"What happened?" I asked.

She told me to go to my apartment and leave her alone. "Everything's all right."

I asked her a few more times, and she assured me everything was okay, so I started back to my apartment.

Then I saw her brother. "You stay away from that fucking whore!" he shouted. "I'll kill you!!"

This freaked me out and I just left it at that. I figured it was a family squabble. I know how excitable Spanish people can be. I saw her again in a few days, and she said that everything was fine and to ignore her brother.

About a week later, I heard another fight coming from

their apartment, and again I went to investigate. This time she had a black eye, so I didn't even listen to what she tried to tell me. As I turned around to go to her apartment, I caught a glimpse of her brother with a bat in his hand. I ducked and spun around, caught his arm, and wrestled the bat from him. It was an all-out struggle, and I knew if he got away from me, one of us would end up dead. I pinned him with the bat on his neck and kneed him in the balls to put him out.

I took Micela to my apartment and began to look after her eye. About five minutes later, her brother pounded on my door. Her whole family was yelling in the hallway, shouting at her to never come back, that they never wanted to see her again. I called the police, and they helped sort things out.

Micela was very upset about her family not wanting her. I was happy in the back of my mind that we were together, but wished it could have been in better circumstances.

Five weeks later, her family moved out of the building, but those five weeks were hell on earth. They were always banging on my door, name calling. My car got trashed, my mailbox destroyed, everything. I even had to pull a .45 on one of them when they didn't want to let me into the building one night. I'm glad they knew I was sick enough of their shit to blow the asshole away, or I'd never be telling Rudette this story. Micela quit her job because of her eye but got one at a different doughnut shop a few weeks later on.

Our life together now was really great. She still stuck to her guns about no sex, but began to walk around with her top off when she felt like it. My sex life consisted first of her jerking me off while I kissed her and sucked her tits; then she began to give me the best head you could imagine. She was a perfect angel, but when she sucked my cock she was like a whore high on some kind of drug. I begged and begged for her to let me suck her pussy, or at least finger her, but she always said no. One night I got pretty depressed about her not letting me at her pussy. We got into a fight and she cried.

"It's okay," I said. "It's really okay. I'm being too selfish."

She told me I wasn't and asked me over and over if I really loved her for who she was as a human being. I assured her that I did because it was true, and because I hoped to make love to her the way we should be.

Finally she said, "Let's celebrate!" and poured us rum and Cokes, her favorite.

After we got pretty happy, she said it was time to make love in the bedroom, where it should happen, so we crawled into bed and she turned out the lights. She said she still wanted to be a virgin when she married me but was willing to let me make love to her ass instead of me going without anymore. After trying to reason with her for five minutes, I agreed and got on top of her as she lay facedown on the bed. She pulled her panties to one side and reached back to guide my cock into her ass. She moaned how good it felt.

49

I had never fucked anyone in the ass. The feeling was unbelievable. It's not like a cunt that is all slippery and wet. It's more creamy and tighter, giving a wild sexy friction sure to drive one crazy.

She got onto her knees, and we fucked like dogs for a while. Then she sat on top of me and I lay on my back and held her firm bouncing breasts while she pumped herself up and down on my rod. Then she lay on her side while I drove myself into her hole, which seemed to be getting a bit wetter from her natural juices up there. She reached back to grab my hips and pull me with her as she lay facedown again, moaning into her pillow. She must have began coming because she started saying things like "Fuck me through the mattress. Cream in my ass. Rip me apart." She went nuts.

I came like crazy. It was the best orgasm I ever had! It excited me so much my dick didn't go soft and I fucked her ass full of my come until I shot off again. She was crying, but told me it was because it felt so good. She told me to go and clean up so we could talk and that she would sit and wait for me to get back while holding my hot come deep in her ass. What a sexy bitch she was turning out to be!

When I got back to the room, she had two more drinks ready and we talked about why her family didn't want her to go out and be with boys. We talked about why she didn't want to let me fuck her pussy. We talked about why she let me fuck her ass. But most of all, we talked about how much we were in love with each other. Then she took off her panties to show me—her cock. To say I sobered up would be an understatement!

I walked around the apartment stunned out of my mind. I was TOTALLY blown away! I had just fucked someone with a dick in the ass. Someone I loved. Someone beautiful, caring, sexy, kind, giving. Someone with a cock! I was stunned. I couldn't even talk. I felt sick. I wanted to cry; I wanted to laugh; I wanted to slap her. I didn't know what I wanted to do. But I didn't walk out on her. We stayed up all night and talked about it. I kept thinking of all the things she had done with me, how good she made me feel. I kept remembering how my imagination saw what her pussy must look like—and then I would look between her legs and see her cock.

That was the family secret. They had left Spain to get away from everything that was happening there over Micela. She had been a very cute little boy until reaching the age of eleven, and then her breasts began to grow. I listened to a very interesting and sad story that was touching me deeply and confusing me more and more about what to do next.

I decided to do nothing. I couldn't leave this person I had fallen so deeply in love with, but I was having a really hard time with the idea of her having a cock. I had sucked and had my dick sucked by boys when I was too young to know better, but now this was a big decision. I knew that no one would ever suspect her, she was so beautiful. We would never be able to have our own children. But I loved her and stayed with her.

We started to have sex again about six weeks later. We started all over again from scratch. I learned that she could come from my rubbing the tip of her cock just like I do to myself, but she never gets fully erect. Sperm flows out of her cock when she comes, but she comes only after she gets really excited, which is about once a week. There is usually quite a load because she gets off only once in a while, and I enjoy rubbing it all over her body as much as I enjoy rubbing mine all over her. She can usually come when I fuck her ass and rub her cockhead with some kind of cream or oil. After a few months, I even got horny enough to suck her off. We go 69 quite regularly now, and I'm beginning to enjoy the taste of her come.

Generally, she wants me to treat her like a woman and fuck her bottom. She starts off giving me awesome head and then pulls me on top of her and guides my saliva-covered cock into her gripping ass, taking everything I have until she has satisfied me, as well as herself, and her need to be with me.

And so my story goes. I am loved and cared for the way I wanted to be, and so is she. I am on top of the world because of her, and because our love made me see that some things don't matter one bit at all.

* Internet address: rudette@the.connection.com

TITLE: Masked Encounter
BY: Bandana Boy
FROM: SM Board—U.K.

You pull into the secluded car park and park your motor-cycle at the far end under a tree. You stand by the machine and wait.

Within a few moments, another motorcyclist arrives, pulls up beside you, and dismounts.

You are both dressed similarly in leather jacket, jeans, and boots. Motorcycle scarf and gloves complete the total motorcycle mummification/bondage. The crash helmet is darkly visored, and your faces are concealed by a coloured bandanna mask. The eyes are barely discernible.

You eye each other appreciatively. There is no mistak-ing that both of you have found the man you have come to meet. You stand watching for a while, taking in the details of the masked stranger before you. Leather-gloved hands start squeezing leather-covered cocks. Leather-covered bulges grow.

The other motorcyclist turns and walks away into the bushes. You notice a bandanna hanging out of his back pocket. You have one there, too. When you reach a clearing, you stop and stand a short distance away, facing each other. The place is safe and secluded, and there are no people anywhere to be seen.

You both, in unison, unfasten the front of your jeans and pull your now-hard cock and balls out into the fresh air. You fix each other with your eyes, getting turned on by the image of someone you cannot really recognise. But that doesn't matter, for it is the disguise, the motor-cycle clothes, the masks, that excite you.

You work slowly at your cocks, getting them harder. At a given signal, you pull the bandanna out of your back pocket and wank furiously into it, fixing the other man with an excited stare as your back arches and you come. You fasten the come-soaked cloth over your face and watch as your companion does the same.

Doubly masked, you return to your machines and ride in your different directions, sniffing the scent of your experience on the way.

* Internet address: bandanas@dircon.co.uk

TITLE: Gothic
BY: davis trell
FROM: STUDSnet—San Francisco, CA

"An eye for an eye, a tooth for a tooth…"

After the humiliation, I swore revenge. A youth, paltry, whose gates had been stormed and pillaged. A tear-stained pillow the only witness, the stained sheets the only evidence, long since destroyed. A temple, desecrated, debased, degraded, debauched.

I lured him back—the lunking hulk of the man he'd become—with promises of honey.

To the top room, up the stairway, with its lighthouse window, an aperture opening onto the roiling sea of humanity below, a view of beached whales, porpoises, lobster and dolphin, tuna and trout. I closed the curtain so none could see in.

I had grown, in body, brain and cunning.

I hadn't recognized him at first, at the Hesperion Restaurant o'er looking the bay. Where ships that pass in the night meet, unload after docking, replenish and leave for newer shores.

I'd gone to borrow a pen from the bar, to note the address of one Thom Barth, a tourist from Sarajevo, sitting at the table across from me. I glanced at the mirror to tidy my hair and saw the face I'd learned to loathe in the dark-dewed glass. A scowl disguised as a grin creased his bull-like face. His eyebrows grunted a flicker of recognition. A hand slapped around my thigh, gripping buttock, vulgarly, uninvited and unwelcome.

"It's cocksucker Matt! Haven't seen you in a dog's age. My, but you've fleshed out your sorry scrawny frame. Grown a pair of man's tits since last I saw you. How's your cock—grown, I hope?"

"Fletcher! How utterly fabulous to see you! Handsome as ever, I see." The lying response came easy to my lips. Like a poker player playing stud, I hid my true feelings, of disgust, of deception.

But first a feint.

I made my excuses, to say farewell to Thom, but alas, he had gone. My chance to flavor East European peccadilloes, stanched. I returned and now could pay full attention to my reclaimed foe.

He sat at the bar, alone. His body big, shirt-opened to expose black-haired chest, leathered muscle, a bead of sweat trickling along the pectoral ledge to a cavernous armpit that smelled of temptation.

"How long has it been?" I asked.

"Since my dick grew down to my knee."

I picked up the pink cocktail he bought me, pulled out the plastic umbrella, rolled the swizzle stick end on my tongue, twisted my torso, rested an elbow on the counter and brushed my ass against his bulbous lap. The buttons of his fly strained to contain the enormity it held secret.

I pressed my left-hand palm against his jaw, feeling the quivering masseter muscle, and he turned his head and licked the flat underside of my wrist.

"Still a cocktease, you little fucker."

"Still a horsecock, you big man, you."

The flirtation continued thusly, for an intemperate length of time. The compliments becoming coarser, closer to the gutter, the language of love twisted into sadomasochistic romance.

All the while, my mind formulating the plot of my revenge.

The stratagem simple—seduction.

And so he was here, all six feet-three, two hundred ten pounds, a body full of expectation and impatience, his lust forming an aura of sensual libidinous emanations, striated with sexual anticipation.

He had an eagerness to bare my body, expose my carnal orifice, impale me with ferocity, give no quarter, leave me bleeding, as he had done before, at the dawning of my innocence. I would be revenged.

You might think me insane to invite the luggard into the very environs of my home, where I had slept peacefully only the night before, with the kindly married tax accountant who had shared my flowers and sowed the sweet seed of man, at harmony with the universe. He'd left quietly, leaving a small token of his admiration and of my enterprise.

Fletcher paid a passing compliment that he liked the size of my room, glad to see there was a lock and barred windows. (A recent spate of neighborhood robberies making this inevitable.)

The bed with strong headboard had been made, freshened sheets laid thereon, the pillows fluffed, the duvet turned down. An invitation for lovemaking, a rose in the center, now out of place, poisoned by his presence, contaminated by his decadence.

His raven-colored hair, his face a mask of red passion. He made one grand movement and emerged from his clothing, cock hard.

"Whaddaya say we skip the foreplay? Grease your butt—it's gonna get a lot of friction."

"No. No, we musn't forgo the pleasantries, you have to suck till I come; then you may have your anal way." I pirouetted away, but not before teasing him, displaying my ass.

In the bathroom cabinet I found what I was looking

for. A form of laudanum, or so my doctor tells me, an opiate for insomnia as I have difficulty sleeping, awakened as I am by wet dreams that come in the night, violent in their fantasy, luxuriant in their imagination; but the nocturnal emissions make me look haggard at work, and I need to keep my scrivenly job.

I pour the potion into the K-Y jelly, and return to my saturnine guest. He lies abed, idly flopping his engorged cock, and working up his cannonballed testicles into boiler rooms of sperm production.

I clamber up and kiss him full and languorously on the lips, and he tells me to quit with the sissy stuff. So I flaunt my too-aroused dick, and press it close to his face, bouncing the shaft against his nose, so he can smell, and rub the pink head against his mouth, so he can taste my succulent stick.

He pounces on and savors full, boysweet flesh, yummy delicious, straight and true; not like my heart, black, telltale of my soul.

He sucks greedily, like a faster breaking a hunger strike. His lips warm and wet, noisily greedy, his tongue —sandpaper rough clutching my penis like a trowel, swishing it inside his mouth, nipping with his ivory-white teeth, grazing and almost bruising my intimate extension, Jonah in the belly of the whale. My buttocks clench as I plunge inside his face, slurped and epiglottised, churning my lower abdomen, harpooning in a sea spray of saliva and precome.

It tasted sweet, I know it did, as I had lubricated my cock with the embrocation that would produce stupor, even before I could ejaculate. But I did anyway, and my pearl-white come splashed and oozed on his snoring face, not waking him up. I sat down in his heavy-breathing lap, and licked off my comesnot and tasted him, mixed with me, and drank the concoction of sweat and sperm matted into his chest hair like beads of milk-dew.

While he slept I tied him up, gagged and chained him with handcuffs and fisticuffs, manacles and rope.

His body was heavy as I pulled him up to a sitting position, his head hanging down as if he had been rabbit-chopped, and turned him over, his torso on the bed, his knees on the floor, legs spread wide, restrained to the bed. I found the extra-large dildo, a joke present from friends, and jammed it into his hole and buried it deep between his buttcheeks and waited for him to wake and for my testes to refill. I pushed and pulled on the way-too-far-inserted dildo, playing with it as a gearshift, changing from forward to reverse and park in no particular order. The smell of brimstone and excrement filled the soft air, like atop the Himalayas, rarefied and heady.

A murmured grunt arose, stopped, became a wail, painful and excoriating, like I had felt, lo those many months before.

My captive awoke, and the gag forced his protestations into a garble of Joycean nonsense.

I ran to the other side of the bed and rubbed my ass in

his face, slipping the tip of his nose into my anal rose, forcing his nostrils closed, engulfed between my asscheeks, and let him smell my unclean hole, letting wisps of flatulence gag his sensitive nasal membranes.

His eyes blinded by buttocks, gouging his eyelids, the gag shouting entreaties to my nonlistening scrotum. I climbed over his back, scissor-gripping his head with my thighs and gained easy access to the giant barber pole stuck far up his ass. I gave it a turn, to produce an Indian burn on his sphincter, that winced at the pucker, groaned under the strain. Some measure of compassion flitted through my brain, so I pulled out my mimetic cocksword, stained with shit, and threw it away. I pressed open his globular gluteals, clamping hard with my hands, and filled in with tongue, the winging whimpering calyx, and breathed fiery venom into the echoing walls.

A fist, I thought, was bigger than a hand, so I delved deep inside, until only wrist was exposed. I should rip out his prostate, and bury his gonads in his duodenum, but compassion won out. I relented.

So I slid down and everted myself to sandwich my manhood 'twixt cushiony flesh, meaty and tense, and grabbed hold of his shoulders, a fulcrum for the force as I dipped my dick in. With Trojan protection, polyurethane armored, I crossed the portcullis and forced my way in. A maelstrom of boiling man-eating man, I fucked his bronzed ass, with self-indulgence, and allowed poetic license as I sawed, and jackhammered, with lumberjack frenzy, a steelworker in hell, like Vulcan's smithy, smelting ore into gold.

The bed groaned and creaked as I fucked him with due anger, lunging and plunging, giving no quarter, until the wet explosion spurted within, cockthrobbing, spending its load. White vengeance, slick with slime, his cobwebbed interior, clammy-walled posterior, sore with my exertions. A volcanic rumbling ensued, and he started to come on the covers. I put a stranglehold 'round the base of his dick, and he humped it, bleaching the paisley pattern with hot fetid come.

I rolled on my back, stroked my rod, strong warrior, now soft soldier, pulled off the condom, and wiped away the excess. He lay beside me, furious with anger. You could read the indignation as I slapped his ass hard.

At last I took off the gag so he could speak.

The vein in his temple turned white as he let out the invective, unsuitable for human consumption, filled as it was with bloodcurdling oaths, threatening my extinction.

I was highly amused.

He spluttered on, until his vocabulary weakened, as he ran out of words. He struggled awhile; the bonds held him firm. He posed no danger, so I kissed him full, and a twinkle shone in my eye.

I feed him daily with nutrient protein gleaned from the health-food store. I want him to stay fit.

* Internet address: davistrell@aol.com or davist@dsp.com

TITLE: lighter.txt
BY: Leatherbear
FROM: The Vault—London, U.K.

All events described here are real. Bill's name has been
changed as his lover doesn't know what the horny little
bastard has been up to. Persons of a nervous disposition
may feel more comfortable if they read the message
entitled FOLLOW-UP first (at the end of the story).
Persons with nasty wicked minds will simply continue
from here.

Well, guys, there's nowhere worth going to of an
evening in London anymore, and I've cleared up the
backlog of mail that I've been struggling with for the
past couple of weeks, so now I've time to tell you a bit
about Bill. I was just thinking how you can wander
along through life with a secret fetish, and suddenly you
meet someone who, in the heat of passion, admits to

feeling the same and you're not a freak anymore. It doesn't happen very often, but here's an instance when it did.

I'd met Bill a few months earlier on an evening out at The Block. For a couple of hours, we played eye-contact games intermittently: he looked like the stereotypical (to British eyes) American boy next door. Slightly taller than me, short—but not cropped—brown hair, slim, neatly trimmed 'stache. He was obviously comfortable in his leathers, wearing them like the second skin they are. To me, it seemed like the only thing missing was the accent. He was with a taller, heavier guy who seemed to be his lover. Certainly they were never apart for very long in the bar.

Toward two in the morning, I was sitting with one foot on a small table near the entrance to the club enjoying one of the Maduro No. 10s that had arrived in the post from L.A. a few days previously. Bill and the other guy seemed to be about to leave. I watched them have a brief discussion and the big guy disappeared in the direction of the toilet. Immediately, Bill walked round and stood at my shoulder. After a few seconds' pause, he began inching closer. It was obvious what he wanted, but I don't make the running. I like to make my boys work for it, so I let him sweat a bit. As he stood there with his crotch almost touching my shoulder I could feel his tension.

I took pity on him. "Does the boy have a name?"

"Bill," he replied as he moved round to face me and knelt by my raised thigh.

"And what does the boy want?"

"I've been wanting to talk to you all evening, Sir, but I wasn't sure if you were interested." He tried to maintain eye contact, but his eyes kept straying to my cigar.

I inhaled deeply on it, held the smoke for a few seconds, and exhaled the smoke into his face. He pressed himself closer to me.

"I don't have much time, Sir. I'm here with my lover—he's just gone to the toilet, and then he wants us to go."

I took another pull on the cigar and held the smoke while I reached into a pocket for an address card. I handed him the card in a cloud of smoke. "You'd better phone me later."

Just then Bill's lover returned, and Bill got to his feet hurriedly to follow his obviously angry lover out of the club. Bill phoned the next day. His lover would be working late the following evening, so I told him to come to my flat and we'd talk further. I warned him that there would be no sex on this visit: it was purely to establish whether or not we thought sex would work.

He arrived promptly, and although he wasn't wearing his leathers, he was dressed presentably in Levi's and T-shirt. As we talked, I learned that he was relatively new not only to SM, but to the gay scene, too, having been out only for a year or so. He was in his first gay relationship. Although he enjoyed sex with his lover, he felt that there was something missing, but he couldn't say what.

I liked the way he automatically sat at my feet while we talked, and the way his eyes followed my cigar. He was honest enough to tell me what he knew of what he wanted. I decided I could do something with this boy. He was to visit again the following evening.

When Bill arrived the next evening, there was a slight edge of nervousness in his manner. I had already prepared the playroom, setting the lighting to a fairly low level, using mainly floor-level lights to emphasize the beams and to disorient him with the unexpected angles of the shadows. A CD of electronic music, slow and monotonous, was playing gently, set to repeat. I started the scene with what became a ritual with him: while I sat in the living room, he went into the playroom and brought me a cigar from the box on the shelf. Then, kneeling in front of me, he clipped the end and passed the cigar to me. I lit it, and my first few lungfuls were blown straight into his waiting face. I ordered him to go into the playroom, strip, kneel, and wait. I smoked perhaps a third of the cigar before I entered the playroom.

He jumped when he heard me come in. Good: I'd left it long enough to unsettle him. I explained the rules to him: since this was the first time I'd played with him, he wouldn't be completely restrained. I didn't insist on being called Sir, but most people did in the end. His safe word was to address me by my first name. When he had said that he understood this, I got things under way.

Very basic, very slow, and watching his responses constantly. A little tit torture to start with, and then into the sling. I restrained his ankles, but not his wrists, emphasising that this was because it was his first time with me. I pulled on his balls and slapped his hard dick around, noticing that every time I pulled on my cigar, his eyes watched it intently and his dick got stiffer. The only negative response I had from him during this first session was when I started to finger his ass: that was only for his lover.... All in all, it was a pretty run-of-the-mill first scene. There was enough there that I could see that I could make something of him, especially with his interest in my smoking.

Throughout following sessions, I pushed at his limits, partly by encouragement and partly by force. Each visit brought further improvements and became increasingly exciting for both of us.

One evening a couple of months ago, I had him strapped securely into the sling, and with a boot tied to his balls and swinging freely. I'd already worked his tits well with my hands and now put clamps on them. I was on my second cigar of the scene and ordered him to watch me while I brought the glowing end of the cigar closer and closer to his nipples. Breakthrough. As the threat of his tits being burned became more real, he lost control of his mouth. The guttural sounds of his pleasure were replaced by a monologue, at first almost incoherent—I caught only a few words.

"What did you say, boy? You know what I want from you: what do you want from me?"

"I want to be tortured, Sir. Really tortured."

"Explain, boy."

He fell silent, so I brought the cigar even closer to his nipple.

"Sir, I have fantasies about heavy torture."

I freed his left hand. "So tell me about them. And jack off at the same time. All the time you're talking, I'll be getting this cigar closer to your flesh. I'll stop that only when you come."

Three fantasies spilled out. One became the story "Bound," which some of you will have read: an everyday story of Master, slave, cigars, and a shotgun. The second involved bondage and two lorries moving slowly in opposite directions, both drivers smoking cigars, of course. The third fascinated me: this one I could do something with. He had fantasised about being tied to a chair to be interrogated, being tortured in various ways and then having not supplied the information required, being soaked in petrol...

I'd really got to him: he came more intensely than he had before, and left my flat that evening with the proverbial shit-eating grin.... I wanted to explore this heavier side of his urges further. That third fantasy wouldn't be very difficult to run. A little misdirection and sleight of hand were all that would be needed, and he need never know he'd been conned. Well, not until afterward...

When Bill arrived for our next session, he was unaware of my plans for him. I could hardly contain my excitement. I'd turned it over in my mind for a week, and even run the vital part of the scene alone to make sure that it would go exactly right. I let him into the flat and sent him to the playroom as usual to get me a cigar. Had he noticed the full can of lighter fuel next to the cigar box? He could hardly have missed it, especially as he knew I don't use a petrol lighter. I moved quickly through the opening ritual and got him into the playroom. With almost no preparation he found himself restrained in the sling, wrists strapped, ankles strapped and belts round his waist and chest. He couldn't move. For this to work, I had to take things quickly. He mustn't have time to think. I needed him confused and excited. I took a deep drag on my cigar, pinched his nose, put my mouth over his and forced my secondhand smoke into him. I repeated this several times, knowing that this would help disorient him as he didn't smoke.

His head was hanging off the back of the sling. I started fucking his face while getting his tits receptive with my fingers. Abruptly, I stopped and took two g-clamps from the shelf. He barely had time to deal with the sudden cessation of pain in his nipple before the g-clamps forced a different pain into the underlying muscles. I pulled my dick out of his mouth and stood away from him for a few seconds, before moving to the other end of the sling. With no chance to prepare for it, he found his balls being pulled up and away from him. I had looped a bungee cord through his cockring and attached it to a hook on the wall. He started groaning: he was moving into the state of mind I wanted him in.

I went back to his tits, again making him watch me as I heated the flesh around his nipples. He started mumbling. Now I had to take a calculated risk. I reached up and freed his hand, telling him to start jerking himself off. He had to come by the time I'd counted to ten. I touched my cigar to one of his nipples so gently that he would never have felt it had it not been lit as I counted quickly. By the time I reached six, he was screaming, begging me to fuck him…. Ten.

He hadn't come. Good!

I clenched the cigar between my teeth, removed the g-clamps and the bungee cord, and then removed all the restraints. I sat down in the heavy wooden chair and watched him. Despite the music, the silence was deafening. He was completely confused: he didn't know what to do or say. I gave him no clues; I simply sat looking at him.

"Sir, I'm sorry, Sir."

"Why are you sorry, boy?"

"Because I didn't come, Sir. I'm sorry, Sir."

"Not half as sorry as I am, boy. Get out of the sling." I had to keep him off balance: "Don't piss about with me, boy. I told you before, you want a pretend master, you go to the bars and find one. I'm sure you'll have a fun time licking boots and sucking cock."

"I'm sorry, Sir."

I stood up. "Get in the chair."

Thirty seconds later, he was once again immobile, and I was applying heat to his tits and watching his dick twitch and jerk. I took a fresh cigar from the shelf and lit it slowly, gaining pleasure from the act of lighting the smoke and listening to him repeat over and over again, "Fuck me, Sir."

"Why didn't you come when I told you to, boy?"

"I couldn't, Sir."

"You couldn't or you wouldn't?"

"Couldn't. Honestly couldn't, Sir."

"You disobeyed me, cunt."

"Sir, I couldn't help it, Sir. I just couldn't, Sir. Please, Sir, I'm sorry, Sir. I didn't mean to disobey you, Sir. I couldn't help it, Sir. Please, Sir, I'm sorry, Sir"

I began shouting, "Shut the fuck up!"

"Sir, I'm sorry, Sir."

"I said, 'Shut the fuck up or I'll shut you up.'" I took the cigar butt I'd been smoking earlier and pulled on it until it was glowing brightly and stuck it in his mouth. "Wanna smoke, do you, boy?" I pulled hard on my cigar, inhaling deeply. "Now let's see you do that, boy.... No? Need a little encouragement, do we, cunt?" I reached behind him, fumbled slightly, and grabbed the tin of lighter fuel, removing the cap as I recovered myself. Even before the smell of petrol spread about the room, the look of terror in his eyes told me that he'd seen the

71

can earlier: he knew what it was too quickly. He bit on the cigar, afraid of letting it fall onto his naked body and too bewildered at what was happening to think to spit it out to one side.

"Fucking worthless cunt!" I screamed as I took a step back away from him. I pointed the can at him and squeezed, spraying the fluid over him, starting at his feet, moving upward quickly. He tried to scream through his clenched teeth as the come exploded from his dick...

FOLLOW-UP: Whilst you were reading the previous message, you were as unaware as Bill was of the following facts: <GRIN> The primary ingredient necessary was to make him think I was out of control.

I reached behind him, fumbled slightly, and grabbed the tin of lighter fuel, removing the cap as I recovered myself.

This sentence is the key: as I fumbled behind him, I opened a small container with sufficient petrol in it for the smell to be obvious. The lighter-fuel can had been thoroughly washed out and contained only water. To make doubly sure, I had used water from the can of "lighter fuel" to PUT OUT a small fire. The "calculated risk" was the countdown to coming: I know how fast he can come, and I was *reasonably* sure I was counting too fast for him to be able to come.

When we talked about it later I asked him what he

had thought when I sprayed him with "petrol." He replied (and this is a verbatim quote): "I didn't know what to think, but underneath I knew I was safe." And that was the shit-eatingest grin I've ever seen....

TITLE: For My Lover
BY: Ray Cornett, aka Writer@Seattle.com
FROM: Rendezvous—Seattle, WA

It's that magical time of evening. There's a little sunlight still filtering through, the heat of the day is beginning to fade and (most importantly) the sexual juices are starting to flow. Watching my beautiful lover pounding away at our computer is always fun. This was NOT the fun I wanted this evening, though....

Without a word, I walked over and took him by the hand and tugged gently. Since I'm 8" taller, and about 60 pounds heavier than he is, I usually don't have to pull hard to get his attention. He looked up at me with his gorgeous innocent blue eyes questioning. I just tugged at him again and headed back toward the bedroom.

Since Gene doesn't wear clothes often around the house, getting rid of his clothing wasn't a problem. I met him on my knees as he came into the bedroom. He was already half-hard, anticipating what was in store. I didn't disappoint him.

I sucked the cutest little five-incher all the way down without hesitation. Gene groaned and leaned back against the bedroom wall to stabilize himself. Since he's always had tons of precome whenever we play, I got a good taste of him from the very start. My fingers roamed through his furry chest, taking time to play with his pierced tit as I sucked his cock.

After a few minutes of sucking his little hard-on, I (hesitantly) released him from my mouth-grip. Running my tongue down the shaft of his cock. Stopping at his fremming pierce, sucking and biting at it for a moment. His moans echoed off the walls of our bedroom.

From there I moved down and sucked both his balls into my mouth, using my tongue to probe and play with them. Again he groaned. Though I didn't want to, I released his balls. Taking his hand again, I put him down on the bed and climbed on top of him. (He's ALWAYS been the best little Bottom Boy I've ever had!) Starting at his neck and shoulders, I licked, kissed, and sucked my way down his spine, stopping at that spot just above the asscrack (one of my hubby's many erogenous zones) to suck. He started squirming under my torture.

Finally, I reached the next stop on my tour of his body—his ass. I've always enjoyed rimming Gene. He has an ass that BEGS to be sucked and probed. I complied, taking my time and lapping slowly at his butt, occasionally sucking or nibbling at his asshole while he groaned beneath my tongue. All this was making my own 8" cock stand at attention. I could feel the blood flowing through it. I wanted to fuck him but had to wait. Just sucking his ass was intensely pleasurable. His groaning told me Gene was having a good time, too.

With one final thrust, I rammed my tongue into his ass as hard as I could. He arched his back and almost screamed with pleasure. At that I knew I couldn't take any more. My cock was throbbing and ready to plow him.

I laid myself down on him, my cock riding the crack of his ass. I could feel his anus constrict as I rubbed against him. "Fuck me," he whispered.

I didn't keep him waiting long.

I grabbed the lube off the nightstand, applying just a little to my hard shaft. I probed his ass with a finger while I got ready for the main event. Without hesitation, I plunged my cock into his tight little ass. He screamed again. I wasn't sure if it was out of pleasure or pain, but he didn't try to pull away. The warmth of his ass was incredible! Slowly, I started moving up and down on him, pulling almost all the way out before thrusting back into him. I searched the fur on his chest, finally finding his nipple ring. I played with it gently, twisting it as I fucked him. He grabbed at the sheets, groaning loudly at the pleasure I was giving him.

Without warning, Gene started constricting his ass around me. He worked with remarkable speed. I could do little more than lie there and let his ass jack me off. Then the spasms started. I could tell from his moans and movements that I was making him come. I'd done my job well.

This was more than I could take. My own cock started throbbing as I gushed come deep into him. I clawed his back and screamed as he kept up the feverish pace of fucking. As the spasms subsided, I laid my weight on him, taking a moment to catch my breath. I pulled his long blond hair out of the way and kissed the back of his neck.

"Well done, boy. Well done," I managed to gasp as I lay there. He gave my cock another squeeze in response.

After a few minutes, my cock softened enough to slide out of his warm asshole on its own. I reached down and gave his ass another kiss.

Rolling him over on his belly, I was greeted by a mass of come in the fur around his cock. I slurped and licked at it greedily, tasting his seed as it slid down my throat. I had to torture him a little more. I sucked his still-hard cock into my mouth and felt his little body shudder beneath me. Once I'd had my fill of his juices, I climbed up and draped myself over him, making patterns in his chest hair as we dozed off for a little nap....

* Internet address: Writer@seattle.com

TITLE: The Bear and the Blade—A True Story
BY: Captain Midnight
FROM: The Pig Pen—Ottawa, CANADA

It had been a dull night at the bar. Most of the regulars had come and gone, and from the looks of things, most of them would come alone tonight. The only outstanding feature of the bar had been The Bear. Or at least that's the way I had referred to him all evening.

He had arrived with his friends about 11:00 P.M. and spent the whole night standing in a corner talking with the same crowd. He made no attempt to move around the bar and almost looked like it wasn't even interesting to him. On the few occasions that his friends moved away to get another drink or take a leak, I had gotten brief opportunities to check him out.

The Bear stood about 6'4" and might have weighed in at 220 pounds of solid beefy man. Broad shoulders filled out a red-and-black flannel lumberjack shirt that was unbuttoned just enough to reveal a forest of thick dark hair. The same dark hair covered his head but was cropped short and had begun to recede at the temples. Deep blue eyes looked out at the room and his lips were half-hidden by a bushy mustache that I wanted to have mix with certain hairs on my body.

His torso narrowed to the waist (there was obviously no excess flesh on this animal) where black suspenders held up his 501s. Though I wanted desperately for him to turn around and let me see how they fit his ass, I was satisfied from the front view that what this guy had to offer would stock the cupboard for a long winter. The vision ended at a pair of work boots, casually pulled on without tying the laces and whose tongues curled forward like a pair of hungry bottoms reaching for their Master's balls.

I wanted this man!

As the evening wore on, it became obvious that The Bear was paying attention to no one but the people he had arrived with. Their conversation was animated and involved and offered no opportunity for me to catch his eye or even to break through the group as I moved around the room. But I didn't stop looking, or checking out the situation. You know what they say about stripping a guy with your eyes? Well, you can do it. I had The Bear down to his fur coat in no time and knew that my vision of a man with hairy chest, arms, legs, ASS, cock and balls was not only accurate, but HOT.

I had wandered into another section of the bar for a while and watched as two tops began the slow process of finding out which one would switch his keys and allow the other to have control. It was absorbing, and usually I would have watched with interest, but my mind was on The Bear. I headed back to the main part of the bar.

He was gone. At first I thought that maybe he was wandering around and looked through the rest of the bar to find him, but soon realized that he and his friends were nowhere to be seen. I resigned myself to the fantasy I had created and began to look for a substitute to satisfy the bulge that had been growing in my jock-strap all evening.

The night wore on, but to no avail. As it happens, I left the bar alone, but with a friend. Part way down the street on the way to our cars, a rather attractive blond caught up with us and threw his arms around our shoulders.

"Where are you heading, boys?" he asked.

"Home," my friend replied.

One thing led to another, and despite the fact that I offered to take them both back to my place, it was obvious that the blond had his eye on a duet with my buddy. I loaded them into the blond's truck and headed off, not sure where I was going. All I knew was that it was 2:00 A.M., I was horny, and not ready to give up.

I cruised the streets for a while thinking that I might run into somebody from the bar in the same condition who needed a little action. But the night had been cool, and most of the guys had come by car. There were very few people around.

Then it hit me. Horny and in need. The baths! Not my preference, but certainly functional enough on a cold night. I didn't figure I'd be there long—a fast blowjob or a quick fuck, and I'd be on my way. But at least I'd be happy and contented and able to sleep. I headed across town.

At the door, I was told there were no rooms or lockers, but it was bar night, and for a $4 charge, I could just go in and wander around. Who needed anything more than that? There were dark corners to do things in, and others had rooms. Why spend a fortune on getting laid? I paid and headed in.

There were obviously a number of guys from the bar who had decided to do just the same thing. The halls were busy, and the rooms, though their doors were closed, echoed with the sounds of people having a good time. I rounded a corner into a hallway that seemed to be a gathering place, or at least a cruising place.

There he was. The Bear! Leaning against the wall, casually watching the crowd pass by and obviously looking for action. I was not going to lose out a second time. I walked in his direction and as I passed, our eyes made contact. The corner of his mouth twitched as if about to smile.

This was too good to be true. Not only had I seen him again, but I had the distinct impression that he was interested. I chanced a look back. Now my adrenaline was racing. He was following me down the hall. At the top of the stairs he passed me and whispered quietly, "Later, I hope." Then he disappeared down the stairs and into the lobby. Who says that fantasies don't come true!

With thoughts of all the things I wanted to do to that Bear running through my head, I strolled around the halls for a little while longer. There wasn't much of anything to look at anymore.

The hour had grown late, and many of the guys had either left or gone to sleep. Once more I turned into the hall where I had first seen him and saw his red plaid shirt disappearing down the hall and into a room. At first I thought that he had been cruising and had decided on that room, but soon realized that the door had not closed. Even if he was with someone else, I wanted to at least watch, even if they didn't let me join in. I headed down the hall.

As I neared the room, I was aware of movement. Not the kind that two guys make when feeling each other up. Rather the kind that lets you know someone is undressing. I passed the room and caught sight of him removing his pants and hanging them on a hook. It was his room. He had placed his name on the waiting list and gotten a room after the last group of departures.

I didn't want to seem too anxious, so I made the tour around the halls and soon found myself approaching his room once more. As I passed, I looked in.

He had removed his pants and jockstrap and stood there in sweat socks and open shirt. His hand held the most enormous cock I had ever seen; long, veined, and hard. He smiled and stepped forward until he was framed in the doorway.

"I thought you might have left," he said. "I'm glad you didn't."

As he spoke, he reached into the pocket of his plaid shirt and pulled out a pearl-handled straight razor. He held it out to me and smiled even more.

"Please, SIR," came from his lips more like a groan than words.

As I took the razor with one hand, I ran the other over the forest of hair on his chest, down over his thighs and across his hairy ass. This would be no quick job. I would make it last, and this bear would lose his fur until he looked just like Daddy's little man—smooth and hairless.

He pushed the door closed, turned up the light, and removed his shirt.

"How do you want me?" he asked.

"Spread your legs, place your hands on the wall, wide apart and lean into it, boy."

"Yes, SIR."

His back, though not as hairy as his chest, was still a challenge. I opened the razor and ran the back of the blade down his back. A low moan emerged from his lips, and his head rolled back in pleasure. I placed my hand at the top of his spine, across his left shoulder, and applied the blade at the top of the hairline. With two or three swift strokes, I made a three-inch path right down to the top of his butt. The hair fell to the floor and was soon followed by more as I worked on the left side of his back. When I had finished this, I stood back and looked at the contrast. One side dark and hairy, the other white and smooth.

My cock had gotten increasingly harder as I worked. Now it pressed against the buttons of my 501s. There was a good long time yet before this Bear was done and before my cock would get released to do its work. I finished his back, making sure that no stubble remained. The effect was as if he had removed his shirt. Just below his waist, the hair that covered his ass and legs resembled a pair of pants not yet removed.

"On your back on the cot, boy," I ordered. He responded quickly.

"Now lift those legs and grab your ankles. I want that ass up and ready."

His thick thighs flexed and his legs rose into the air, to be held there by the grip of his hands. What a view. Furry butt, tight hole, his balls hanging down big and low. His cock was hard. It lay flat on his stomach and seemed to reach halfway up his chest. Two and a half hands at least, and thick. Veins curled their way up the length of it, and the head, big and purple, would have been hard to cover with my hand.

I ran the blade backward down the middle of his

chest, letting it rise over the length of his cock and balls, lifting the balls from beneath so that they hung over the dull side of the blade. I played with them for a while and then resumed my work.

I started behind one knee, taking the hair from the back of his leg and upper thigh. I told him to let go of that leg and let it rest on my shoulder so that I could work on the front of his thigh. Then, moving to the other leg, I repeated the process. Now, if he had stood up, the hair pants that he had seemed to be wearing had been reduced to shorts. A few strokes of the blade took care of the hair that covered the top of his feet and toes.

He still lay on the cot with his feet held in the air. I pulled over the small table that stood beside the bed and sat between his legs. Working very slowly so that he would feel every movement of the blade, I started working on his butt, removing the hair in strips that moved ever closer to the crack of his ass, alternating sides so that the strip of hair was being reduced until all that remained was a pair of hairy balls hanging at the top of a thin strip of hair that lined the crack of his ass.

"Get those hands down here and spread 'em."

"Yes, SIR."

Leaving his legs in the air, his hands grabbed the cheeks of his ass and pulled them open. Would I be able to wait to get at what lay exposed in front of me? The buttons on my 501s were strained to the limit.

Lifting his balls, I started between his legs, narrowing

the line of hair until it disappeared and revealed that seam line that a lot of guys have that leads down toward the sphincter. Then I worked the other end of his crack, cleaning it of any hair until all that remained was the areas immediately around the Bear's hole.

I laid the blade carefully against one side and, with short strokes, worked my way down until he could feel the cutting edge knocking at the opening itself. I blew away the hair and changed my position to work on the other side. With even more deliberate slowness, so that every stroke of the blade could be heard scraping away the fur, I worked on the hair here until all that was in front of me was the soft pink pucker of his ass muscles, twitching with anticipation.

That ass was so inviting. I wanted to rip open my jeans and plunge my shaft into that warm, moist muscle. But there was much work yet to do. It didn't mean that I couldn't have a little fun along the way, though.

I stepped back. "Turn around on the cot so that your legs are up the wall and your head is at the edge near me." As he obeyed, I pulled off my boots and removed my jeans and jockstrap.

Sitting again, this time with my cock hanging only an inch from the top of his head, I told him to hold his left arm in the air. From wrist to shoulder, the hair came off as if I were pealing back a protective layer. I changed hands, and while I worked on his right arm, his left moved to his cock and began to play with the head and shaft, running his finger slowly up the underside and around the head. The hair of his other arm peeled back, and now there lay before me a man wearing only the front half of a hairy tank top and briefs.

I had noticed that another razor lay waiting at the foot of the cot and took up this new blade for the rest of the job.

I put my hands under his arms and pulled him toward me so that his head was off the bed and bent down, looking up at my cock. "Now put your arms around my waist and clasp them together there."

As he reached around I drew him even closer into my crotch and dropped my balls into his open and hungry mouth.

"Now you treat them very carefully, boy. Remember, I've got a razor in my hand."

"Yes, SIR!" came the muffled reply.

With short strokes, I cleared a straight line of flesh across the middle of his stomach. I'd save the rest for the finale. Then I cleared a line right up the middle of his torso, dividing the two halves of his chest with a clean white space.

Starting on the left again, I began to edge the line up across his stomach and lower chest until I reached his pec. I shaved around the nipple carefully, and worked my way into the armpit. All the while, the Bear's hungry mouth was sucking and licking my balls gently. He was good. A hot load was being stirred up that would eventually reward this naked cub. But for the moment, I was happy letting him work.

Several more strokes removed the hair across his pecs and I started on the other side, following the same pattern while he continued his work on my balls.

All that remained here was a line of hair around his neck, the part that I had first seen earlier in the evening poking up from under his shirt.

I pulled away from him, removing my balls from his mouth, and pushed his head farther down so that it was pressed against the side of the cot. I moved back into place and let my cock slip easily into his mouth so that it pinned him against the cot and held his neck stretched for me to work.

"Don't move your head, boy. I don't want to do any damage. But I do want to feel good, so you use that tongue and throat, but don't move your head. You understand boy?"

He nodded as much as he could and then went still. I felt his tongue began to move around in his mouth and he swallowed, tightening the back of his throat against the head of my cock.

I placed the razor against his throat. "Don't swallow," I said.

Then, with four or five quick strokes, the line of hair disappeared. I stopped. He resumed his tonguing, and I pushed my cock deeper into his throat.

I sat there for a while, slowly pumping in and out of his mouth and listening to his muffled moans of pleasure. His cock throbbed now, rising above his body from the only hair that remained (other than on his head), and I wanted to get a razor to his crotch in a bad way.

"Stand up!" I ordered.

He quickly released my cock from his mouth and stood on the cot, his cock and balls hanging right in front of my face.

"Spread your legs as wide as you can and place your hands against the ceiling."

"Yes, SIR!"

His cock was angled straight out from his body, and his balls hung low from its base. Around them was a ring of hair that covered his balls and grew several inches down the length of his cock.

"Now remember, boy, I have a sharp razor on your balls. You'd better hold very still."

He leaned his head back against the wall and looked up at the ceiling.

I took the head of his cock in my hand and pulled down, applying the razor to the hairline. I scraped the razor down the last few inches of his abdomen and along the top of his cock. As the blade began to remove the hair from his cock, I felt it pulse in my hand. A low, long moan rose in his throat. For a moment I thought he would shoot his load; but it subsided, and I went back to work.

Pulling the cock to one side and then the other, I repeated the process, first taking the hair on the abdomen and then drawing the blade along the shaft of the cock. Each time he reacted in the same way. And each time it was a little more intense.

Then, lifting his cock, I held it flat against his belly. Though the hair didn't grow that far along, I started the blade right under the head and worked down the whole length of his cock until it reached the top of his ballsac. His cock had begun to ooze a nice amount of precome that seeped down the shaft and lubricated the blade. He rolled his head from side to side as if fighting off the inevitable. I stopped, and his breathing eased.

"Use one of your hands and hold your cock against your belly, boy."

I put my hand under his balls and lifted them, exposing the underside and stretching the skin. The blade sliced away the hair and I felt the balls moving in the sac as it passed over them. Then, putting the back of my hand under the sac and catching the bottom with my thumb, I rolled my hand and stretched the top surface so that the two orbs resembled nuts caught under a white-chocolate coating. Again the blade did its work, scraping around the balls and across the sac until the last hair fell to the sheets below.

"You're done, boy," I said.

"Oh, no, SIR, not yet. Please, SIR, fuck my naked butt."

Now it was *my* cock that throbbed.

"On your back, boy, and lift those legs. Open that ass for Daddy."

He assumed the position that had first revealed his ass to me. I slapped my cock against his smooth balls and watched his reaction. A smile crept across his face.

I took the condom from the back pocket of my 501s and opened the package. He began to stroke his cock. I laid it on his ballsac and placed the head of my cock against it. He reached down, put the condom over the head of my cock, and unrolled it, squeezing tightly when he reached the base.

His cock had been leaking large amounts of precome, which he now used to lube the outside of the condom, running the head of his cock up and down the underside of my cock and spreading the liquid over the latex surface. When he was done, he placed the head of my cock against his sphincter and said one word:

"Push!"

I did. One long, slow push until I felt the head of my cock pop into that warm cavern and then continued until the whole shaft was buried in his ass. His moan started when the pressure began and built until he felt my balls squashed against his asscheeks. His breathing intensified, and he began to stroke his cock with regular and deliberate rhythm.

"Open your eyes and look at me!" I commanded.

He did so. I took the razor, opened it and placed the back side of it against his lips. His tongue came out to greet it, and he began licking the dull side of the blade as if it were a cock. His eyes never left me as I increased the speed and force of my thrusts into his ass.

He took the blade between his teeth and held it there as I let go.

"Don't drop that," I said. "Remember, it's sharp."

My pumping had now reached a level that was driving his body against the wall. His hand was frantically trying to pump his cock to climax and hold off at the same time. He could feel the pulsing of my cock as I neared the point of no return.

When it happened, he was right with me. He felt the juices from my cock explode into the latex sheath and at that moment released streams of hot creamy fluid across his shaved chest. A scream issued from between his clenched teeth, and he went limp as I collapsed across him.

I took the razor from his mouth and replaced it with my tongue. For a long time we lay there, drifting. I eased my hips back and pulled out of him. His muscles tightened as if to try and hold me in longer, but he released them and we lay still, replete.

For a long time, there was silence. When he stirred, I stood and was about to speak. But he stopped me. He looked into my eyes and said: "Exactly six months from tonight, here, midnight. I'll be ready for a trim."

I nodded, dressed as I watched him rub the now-smooth flesh of his chest and thighs. He was still at it when I opened the door to his room and left.

The sun was rising as I left the baths and headed home. First thing on my agenda for the day was to mark an appointment in my calendar for six months from now.

* Internet address: captain.midnight@midilink.org

TITLE: Cigar Initiation
BY: Beartrap
FROM: The Vault—London, U.K.

Last night I went out with Leatherbear and his friend
Steve from Blue Haze. Like Leatherbear, Steve is heavily into sex involving cigars. Little by little, Leatherbear
has been letting me in on the sort of things he and Steve
get up to.

Interesting...

We had a good evening in the bar. Quite early on,
Leatherbear said that he thought I was ready to be initiated into cigar sex, something Steve agreed with very
promptly. From then on, the two of them made constant
references to this, lightly veiled threats and warnings
about what would happen when they got me back home.

I didn't know whether or not I was going to have a
good time, but I reckon the only way to know if you

don't like something is to try it at least twice. If you didn't like it the first time, there could be all sorts of reasons why you weren't in the right frame of mind to enjoy it. You should do it at least once more to be able to give concrete reasons why it's not for you.

Back at Leatherbear's flat, we talked for a while and then went to bed. So it's not going to happen tonight, I thought. We were all three lying facing in the same direction with Steve in the middle, his dick against my ass. This, of course, is one of those things that makes my ass start acting for itself. Very soon Leatherbear's hand was on Steve's dick, guiding it to my asshole.

Suddenly Leatherbear stood up and ordered me to suck Steve's dick while LB disappeared into the playroom. As I sucked on Steve's dick (nice heavy foreskin and just that little bit too long for my gag reflex—a sure sign that my ass would love it), I was dimly aware of the noise of Leatherbear collecting various bits of equipment in the playroom.

To my surprise I wasn't ordered into the playroom: instead, when Leatherbear reappeared, he told me to lie on my belly with my legs spread while Steve rubbered up. Leatherbear gave me the poppers and then Steve was up my ass while Leatherbear moved round and shoved his dick in my mouth. I realised that Leatherbear was lighting a cigar. As they passed the cigar between the two of them, they were getting rougher with me. By this time, I was on all fours rather than lying flat and was getting to the point when I *needed* to play with my dick. I couldn't because both hands were necessary to keep my balance.

Leatherbear pushed me away and Steve pulled out. As I turned over, Leatherbear pulled a gas mask over my face. I recognised the gas mask as one he'd talked about but hadn't tried with me. He'd rigged it so that he had control over how much air, poppers and cigar smoke the wearer got.

And now I was wearing it.

He started with poppers. "Tell me when you've had enough." I lay there breathing in the poppers while Steve pulled on my tits harder than they've been worked since I had them pierced. Then Leatherbear decided that I'd had enough, and suddenly I was breathing cigar smoke. Immediately I was as good as blind: there was too much smoke inside the mask for me to see anything clearly. I continued to breathe deeply, sucking in the smoke as the two of them pulled on my tits and slapped my dick around.

There was a sudden pressure at my asshole, and one of them started pushing a buttplug up my ass. It was the bigger of the two, the one I have to work for. I pulled in the cigar smoke as though it was poppers as I struggled to take in the buttplug.

If we'd been in the playroom, I expect I'd've been tied in the sling. On the bed, there was no helpful bondage. I hadn't been given permission to move my arms, so they lay at my sides. When I would have pushed against restraints for help against the pain in my tits and in my ass, I could only tense my arms. One of those times when no bondage is the heaviest bondage...

Finally the buttplug hovered at its widest point. Suddenly I was breathing poppers in with the smoke. As the poppers hit, my ass sucked in the buttplug the rest of the way and clenched around it. My supply of smoke ceased. As far as I could tell, Steve and Leatherbear were kneeling on either side of me.

There was a pause in which my ass started caressing the buttplug and Leatherbear and Steve passed the cigar between them. More poppers. As one of them began playing with the buttplug, the other placed fingers on either side of my left nipple and pulled the skin taut.

Leatherbear has used his cigar on me before occasionally, but I've never been forced to smoke, so it seemed reasonable to think that I was going to get burned more than I have before. I felt the heat of the cigar approaching and quickly realised I was right. I forgot about the buttplug fucking my ass as my attention was split between the fire on my tit and my straining dick.

Leatherbear ordered me to play with my dick while he and Steve passed the cigar between them. One would inhale deeply on it before burning my tits with it and then passing it to the other. I was wanking myself more slowly now: I didn't want to come without permission, and I wanted to make this *last*....

There was a break in their rhythm as one of them

gave me more poppers. Then I could feel the now-familiar heat near my ass. The slightest brush of a hand over my nipples now hurt like hell. My hand came to a stop and fell away from my dick as my asscheeks received their cigar's attentions.

"I think he's ready now...."

A hand gripped my dick and, as I'd feared, I felt the cigar approach the end of my dick. Right up to the point I screamed, I didn't believe they'd do it.

I felt them both shift their weight slightly on the bed and realised they were both wanking themselves. Or perhaps each other: I was too deep in the pain/pleasure they were giving me to be precisely aware of what else was happening.

"Now you're going to come." As Leatherbear spoke, I felt the cigar come down on one nipple. It stayed there longer than before and moved more quickly to the other. I grabbed my dick and started working it, briefly surprised that the pain of the burn was only serving to make it harder. As they kept burning my tits, I worked my dick faster, wanting both to come as soon as possible and to keep the whole scene going longer.

The abrupt withdrawal of the cigar from my tits and the splashing of their come onto me decided the matter. One of them was holding the buttplug so that my ass was gripping its widest point. I could feel every single burn on my body, but most especially on my tits and dick. My whole body went into spasm as I came.

After I'd stopped thrashing around the bed, Leather-bear said that there was one more thing I must do. I sat up as he told me to and he handed me the cigar.

I inhaled on it as deeply as I could, thinking: "Must? Shit, I was just about to *beg* to be allowed this!"

* Internet address: beartrap@vault.posnet.co.uk

TITLE: The Boy on the Bike
BY: davis trell
FROM: STUDSnet Central—San Francisco, CA

The boy on the bicycle followed the man in the car, pedaling hard, keeping up, till they stopped at the downtown light. He was breathing heavily as he slouched on the handlebars and stared through the window at the driver. He was about eighteen, I guess, but looked younger: his hair short, with blond bangs, a Ren and Stimpy T-shirt, short cutoffs, and high-tops. He had slim hips, strong legs.

The driver looked at the cyclist. This was the third time in the last ten days this had happened. Who was this kid? He was sure he didn't know him. He had a good memory for faces and his wasn't one he recognized. And that look—a frown, animated, turning hot and cold, a tongue that poked out almost imperceptibly. The lights changed. He moved forward on the green, and saw the youth ride away, taking a left on Morrisey. Next time, I'm going to take that left, he thought. Next time.

He was in his early thirties and worked for the EDD, finding jobs when he could for those who couldn't do it themselves. He parked, went in, down the corridor, into his cubicle, caught up on paperwork, drank the first coffee of the day. But he was clearly distracted. He usually didn't take sugar and cream, but the boy had awakened his sweet tooth. Why was he following him day after day? Coincidence? Same route, same schedule? But why did he stare in that way? Why wasn't he brave enough to roll down the window and simply ask? Tomorrow he'd ask.

Tomorrow.

He looked at the desk photo of him and Ben on that fishing trip they'd taken. They had become lovers on that trip. By the lake, they'd shared a tent, a sleeping bag, and each other. That beautiful night, that first night. They'd hiked in the day, swum in the river, caught fish, cooked them as night fell. The big tench sizzled on the campfire and fed their greedy appetites, washed down with white wine while the boom box played saucy melodies from the fifties when romance was innocent, but potent. Maybe the lyrics used words that men don't share with men—well, don't say out loud. They looked at each other lit by the fire, and sat close, both aroused.

Ben's mother never forgave him, wouldn't even speak to him at the funeral, just glared as the priest said those saddest words of all. It hadn't been his fault. He was a good driver, but couldn't avoid that sedan and took it broadside.

The photograph is the only memento, but not the only memory.

It's been a year since Ben died. He's been lonely since then. At first because of grief, then because of indifference. He eats alone, sleeps alone, tries not to masturbate, thinks of Ben, comes, and then he's racked with guilt. He tries to work hard, but it's not that kind of job. He's happy if he places those laid-off workers, puts them back in the workplace, even if it means a downturn for them careerwise. At least he was useful to others. He'll talk to the young man on the bicycle tomorrow, he promises himself.

The day's work is done. He packs his briefcase, goes to his car. On the steps of the building, he's surprised to see the biker, waiting. He sees him staring again. The kid gets up, walks over, pushing his bike, and stops by the car. He looks nervous. He's breathing awkwardly, his eyes downcast.

"What do you want? Why are you following me?"

"I don't know...."

"Why are you here? What do you want?"

"I don't know...." He says the same thing, the words barely rising above a mumble.

They just stand there, the key still in the lock, the car door half open, but he doesn't get in. They just stand there, the only sound, audible breathing.

Minutes pass.

"What do you want?...and don't say you don't know again."

He says nothing.

"Look, I've got to go home. This is plain ridiculous."

"Let me come with you."

"What for?"

"I don't know...." He looks so sad, like a puppy. He holds onto his bike.

"Do you know me? Have we met? I don't remember you."

"No, I just saw you at a traffic light a couple of weeks ago. I followed you."

"I noticed. But what do you want from me?"

"I don't know...."

"Oh, Jesus, not that again! I'm leaving!"

"Don't go. Please, let me come with you."

He began to notice the other office workers leaving, some from his department. Tongues would wag if they stayed frozen like that.

"All right. Follow me. I'll drive slowly."

He drove off and the bike tried to keep up with the car. At one point, he thought he'd lost him, but as he pulled up at the light, the boy caught up, stopped, stared in at the driver, and smiled. They moved on. Twenty minutes later, he reached the apartment complex and put the car in the garage. As he emerged he saw the boy again, panting faintly, staring at him. He decided to take the back stairs. The boy followed, carrying his bicycle up the three flights. He opened the door to his apartment, let the boy in, checked his messages. Nothing of importance.

"Would you like a drink? I've got apple juice, I think."

"That would be nice."

As he filled the glass, he asked the boy's name.

"Bryan."

He gives him the drink and the boy swallows it all, slowly, and his eyes keeps staring.

"Now, what do you want? Why have you been following me?"

"Don't you know?"

The apartment's not big, just a partitioned room, a kitchen, a TV and a neatly made bed, a sofa, a table by the window, the only decor a poster that Ben had bought. He takes off his jacket, unloosens his tie, sits back on the sofa, looks up at the boy.

"You've been following me for days, but won't say why. I'm supposed to guess. Have I got that right?"

Bryan shuffles his feet uneasily. "I saw you.... I just want to be with you."

"But why?"

"I don't know...."

105

"Oh, no. Not that again."

"I'm sorry...." He notices the photo of Ben. "Who's this?"

"Friend of mine. He died."

"I'm sorry...."

"It's OK."

"Was he your best friend?"

"Yes."

"Can I be your friend?"

"Why? Shouldn't you be hanging out with friends of your own age?"

"You're the one I want to be friends with." He sat down beside him and stroked his thigh. "Tell me your name...please...I want to be friends."

"Anthony, but my friends call me Tony."

"Tony? Don't you know what I want?"

"I'm beginning to get the idea, but it's all a little strange."

"I don't feel strange with you."

"Well, what do you want to do? Just sit on my sofa and say 'I don't know' all night?"

"I don't know— I'm sorry. I just don't know what to do. Will you show me?"

He stroked Tony's thigh, moved his hand up, to the crotch, and felt the growing hardness. He leaned forward and kissed Tony's lips.

Tony put his arm around the boy's shoulder, pulled him close, and kissed back. He lifted the T-shirt and felt the young man's back, and his hand glided and pressed tightly around the boy's waist.

Bryan pulled his T-shirt over his head, opened a few buttons of Tony's shirt, felt the strong chest. His fingers touched a nipple and he stroked and continued to kiss. Tony removed his shirt, lay back slightly, let the boy run his tongue over his torso and belly. Bryan put his hand on Tony's pants and explored.

"Show me what to do."

"Let me close the curtains."

He returned to the sofa, unzipped and pulled down his pants, and the boy just stared at the bulge in the underpants. He reached forward and pulled them down, too. His penis was hard, and the boy looked at it intently, not sure of it at first. He put his hand to it, felt the shaft, felt the balls beneath, stroked and rubbed. Tony stood close, brushing his hand over the boy's fair hair.

"It's beautiful. I knew it would be."

Tony brought the boy's head closer. Bryan's lips came into contact. His tongue wet, touched.

"Open!" whispered Tony, and Bryan took the man into his mouth. His eyes were closed, and Tony looked down as he filled the boy's cheeks.

Bryan started to move his mouth up and down, taking in more and more.

It was clear the boy didn't know what he wanted, or at least couldn't articulate his feelings or desires. He felt he was a target, a gun, both at once. He knew he had a fierce urge to be naked with a man, a teacher, a hero, a big brother, a stranger, someone who could set him on fire. He'd fixated and found such a one.

Tony was gentle and felt unleashed emotions that had been hidden by grief. He cradled Bryan close, led him onto the bed.

"I just wanted to be with you like this. To put my arms around you. I just want to crawl inside you. Let me hide."

Tony looked down on the mess of confusion lying beside him.

This man—this boy—was his. His to have just for the taking. His to have, his to hold; his to do with as he pleased.

He laid his hand tenderly on Bryan's belly, over the navel, pressing gently, making the abdomen sink and the chest rise, release that audible sigh. His hand moved forward, downward, underneath the band of Bryan's shorts, fingers spreading, burrowing into the pubic fur, surrounding, then fondling the boy-man's erection, flat-lying, pointing upward, stretching, bending in a strong columnar arc.

"Is this what you wanted?"

"I don't know… Yes! This is what I want."

"I want this, too. Hold your breath while I suck on your cock."

If Bryan was shocked by the vulgar word, he didn't show it. He'd learn more words that night, in the warmth of that bed.

For the first time in months, Tony remembered how good a man felt, smelled, and tasted. He turned his legs around, put them closer to Bryan's head. He wanted to be tasted, too. And as he sucked that sweet cock, he showed Bryan how to do the same for him.

It was gentle, no hurry to come, no fast head movements, just a languorous licking. Tony moved his tongue's attention to the nutty brown sac, to the seam that joins the two halves of the body, found the separation of buttcheeks, fingers pulling the two sides open, and let his hot tongue lick the skin-darkened hole of Bryan's warm ass.

Inarticulate, Brian didn't use words, but showed with moans and sighs the pleasure he was feeling. No longer sucking cock, but squirming gracefully as Tony pressed a fingertip against and opened up that warm, wet crater. The fingertip moved in, the fleshy part pushing into flesh.

Bryan arched his back, lifted his butt a little higher, and the fingertip slipped in farther, till it was joined by another fingertip, wrapped together as in a wish, and slipped in farther, slipped farther inside.

"Is this what you wanted? Don't say you don't know."

"More… I want more. I want all of you inside me."

Tony rolled over on top of Bryan, his legs between the boy's thighs.

Their cocks met together, rubbed each other. Tony took his hand to guide his dick into Bryan's waiting ass.

The pain was mainly mental, exaggerated by inexperience, magnified by the mind. But when the head was in, really in, going in farther, more of the shaft buried deeper, a pleasure center was triggered. Pain slipped away.

The thighs wide open, the legs turning in, taking as much cock as he could, Bryan became even more excited as the man lying on top of him started to pull and push. He started using his own legs, catching up with the rhythm of Tony's butt thrusts. This was being fucked. Yes! This is what he'd wanted!

Tony was having feelings he'd suppressed for so long, emotions he'd thought long forgotten. He ejaculated forcefully, filling the insides of the young stranger below him, spending, shooting, coming, delivering, overcome with passion, with romantic meaning.

Later he let Bryan feel the same, and when it was over, they lay in each other's arms, exhausted, crying and smiling. He thought of tomorrow, thought about the days that would follow, thought of the future. They'd work it out.

* Internet address: davistrell@aol.com or davist@dsp.com

TITLE: The Abduction
BY: Cubbie D. Cub
FROM: Genie—WRITERS.INK
—Cat. 9 (private)

I awake to the total blackness of a leather hood and a splitting pain moving up the back of my neck. My ears are pounding, completely cutting me off from hearing anything going on. From the cool breeze over my skin, I can tell that my captor has stripped me naked after knocking me out.

I guess I should explain.

A few months ago, I answered a local ad in one of the national leather magazines. The man who posted it was looking for boys wanting further training, and he was willing to work with novices. I wrote him a letter and enclosed a photograph of me wearing nothing but a hood, my hands bound together over my chest. He wrote back telling me how interested he was in getting to know me, to see if I was the kind of boy he liked to work with.

After a month, we had exchanged phone numbers and were talking all of the time. He would mail me instructions that would arrive the day before a call. I had to keep the envelope closed until 15 minutes before he called, at which time I was to open it and follow the typed directions. He had me in various self-bondage positions, wearing my ball spreader, a gates of hell, and other toys from my collection, plus a few which I had to find.

A month later, we decided to meet face to face. Our first meeting was very calm and casual, on neutral ground, a nice Italian restaurant in the next town. During the meal, he gave me various orders—nothing too wild to draw attention to ourselves but enough to remind me he was in charge. About halfway through dinner, he handed me a small package and told me to go to the bathroom and use what was inside and then return.

With my hands shaking, I took the box and disappeared into the bathroom. I entered one of the stalls farthest from the door. I unwrapped the box carefully. Inside I found a 3" ball stretcher and buttplug and some small packets of lube. Feeling myself start to grow hard, I put on the ball stretcher, knowing it would hurt enough to help my erection subside. Snapping the last button, I looked down at my balls in their tight skin prison. They looked all squished and purple. Very nice, I thought, as I worked the lube onto the buttplug. I fed the buttplug slowly into my ass. It was a perfect fit and I wondered why he had given me such an easy and enjoyable task...till I felt my fingers growing warmer. I sniffed. The lube had actually been mostly Ben-Gay!

I knew I had to get back to the table, so I gritted my teeth, washed my hands off and went back to him. Before I reached the table, the burning had begun in my ass, and I was doing my best not to squirm in my seat. He calmly watched the sweat pour down my brow as I tried to remain in control of the burning in my guts.

He sat there looking at me as he sipped coffee. The waiter came by and asked if we would like any dessert. He ordered some sherbet and a small slice of cheesecake. I told the waiter through gritted teeth, "No, thank you." He gave me an odd look and walked away. What seemed to be a lifetime later, he returned with Randy's dessert. Randy sat there calmly, eating slowly, as my body was telling me to yell and get up and go get this burning out of my ass!

Twenty minutes later, he finished the last of his third refill of coffee. The burning had subsided, so I was much calmer. We parted after paying the check, and he told me to expect a call from him soon.

In the course of the month, we went out many times to different public places. Every time I was presented with a box and told to go put on its contents. The wildest one I remember was when we went to work out at the gym and he had me wearing a seven-ring gates of hell on my cock under my jock and bits of Velcro inside my shirt right over my nipples!

Now for my current predicament.

He had asked me what one of my wildest fantasies was.

Without having to think long, I told him it was an abduction scene, where the Master would take me away and teach me new things and explain some of my limits. We talked more about what I had done and what I was curious to try. This past Monday he called and told me to cancel any plans I had for Thursday through Sunday. He said we were going to try my fantasy.

For the rest of the week, I had a roaring hard-on. Randy told me that I wouldn't know what day or time he was coming and to go about my business as usual. I called and told my boss I was taking Thursday and Friday as personal days to deal with some business. The rest of the week went smoothly until Wednesday night.

I had left work and had just parked in the garage and closed the door. I was heading to the door that connected the house to the garage, when my world became darkness and stars.

I guess he had found a way into my garage and been waiting for me. He must have carried me out to a waiting van, and now that's where I lie—naked and bound. At first I was worried, but when he saw me stirring, he leaned back and told me that avocados were in season. "Avocado" is my safe word, so I am able to relax a little bit, but not much.

This is all so exciting and new to me. Every fiber of my body is alive and tingling, trying to figure out where we are and what's going on. I feel myself being tossed around the floor. I guess we are somewhere out in the country on a dirt or gravel road. It feels much cooler now, so I am guessing it is late in the evening.

Okay, I feel the van stopping and Randy getting out. I hear a gate opening. Hmmm... He must have pulled just inside and relocked it. After about another five minutes, he stops the van, yanks me out and tosses me over his shoulder. He carries me inside. I feel myself being tied into place on some sort of wooden frame. I can hear him moving around and strain to hear what implements he might be preparing to use on me. I hear a door open and close. Except for the pounding of my heart and my ragged breathing, the room is silent. I don't know whether or not he is in the room. Fear begins to well up inside of me. What if he is some psycho who is just going to keep me tied here and leave me all alone in the middle of nowhere to die? As scared as I am, my hard-on never goes down and I stay at attention. After what seems to be an eternity, I hear a whip cut the air and it lands soundly across my chest.

He was with me the entire time watching me sweat and worry, building the tension. I hear music. Type O

Negative, Dark Gothic Metal. Randy sure knows how to set a scene. I feel the hood being loosened from behind. The air feels cool as it touches my sweaty face. The room is black except for a few candles here and there spilling pools of light into the inky shadows. The whip sings out once more. I can't make out where the swing is coming from before it makes contact with my chest again, leaving a large welt in its wake.

"Thank you, Sir, may I have another?"

I know my place well and respond as quickly as possible. By the twenty-fifth lash, I finish with "Thank you, Sir." This warns him that I am reaching the limit of my pain.

Randy steps out of the shadows wearing a full body harness and holding a nasty-looking whip. It looks as if it could tear me to shreds if he wanted it to. Randy grabs me by the back of the head and yanks back hard.

"You said you wanted to expand your limits."

"Yessir!"

"Good. Ride the pain, boy, and use your first safe word only when you are sure you can take no more!" He vanishes into the shadows, and the whip sings out again.

I grit my teeth. "Thank you, Sir, may I have another?"

After 10 more strokes, I begin to feel detached from the pain. "Thank you, Sir, may I have another?" I see the whip make contact with my flesh over and over again. My body reaches out as far as it can to prolong contact with the whip.

As suddenly as it started, the whipping stops.

Out of nowhere, I feel cold water hit my body, snapping me back to reality. My chest is sore and there are a few small trickles of blood here and there. Randy dabs them up carefully. He pulls a pin, and the bondage frame slips back into a horizontal position. Randy puts a pair of nipple clamps onto my nipples and slowly starts adding weight to them. I grit my teeth, but soon the pain is too intense. He watches me squirm, then start to scream and buck as much as the restraints will allow.

Randy moves down between my legs. I don't know what he is doing until I feel the razor begin to remove all of my pubic hair quickly and deftly. He uses hot and cold water at random. My cock is throbbing and bobbing as he finishes by removing the last bit of hair from behind my balls, leaving my entire crotch naked. I feel chills move up my body and, as I shiver, the weights begin to swing, and now a whole new set of pain moves through my nipples. It feels as if the alligator clips are going to rip my nipples free of my body as they move. I barely feel Randy pull my balls down and snap the 3.5" stretcher onto them.

A low moan escapes my lips.

Randy goes off into the blackness of the room. He must be admiring his handiwork as the weights swing, bringing fresh waves of pain to me. He returns, carrying a candle. I feel the searing heat as he begins covering my cock and balls in the hot molten wax. As he moves on to the seventh candle, I can feel the weight of the wax pushing down on me. Randy moves to the top of the frame and tugs away the codpiece and releases his cock. I gasp as I see the 5" stretcher on his balls, making his 10" look that much more impressive. He rolls a condom down the shaft. "Open up, you worthless piece of crap, and suck on my cock NOW!"

I comply, opening my mouth as far as possible as he brutally shoves his cock down my throat. I gag a few times, but soon I am able to take him all the way in me. He caresses my hair with one hand, when I suddenly feel the other slap my thigh with a vampire glove. The pinpricks make me close my mouth a little. Randy slaps my face and tells me to keep sucking, and if I scrape or bite him, I will pay. I stay in position as I receive four more swats from the vampire gloves. On the last swat, Randy drives his cock as deep as it will go. I can feel the condom filling with his load.

Randy flips me back upright and then begins to pull the wax off my cock and balls. It is painful, but I imagine it could be worse had he not shaved me first. Randy unties me and holds me steady in his arms until I regain my balance. He holds me close and nuzzles my ear. I feel completely safe in his care.

He tells me it's time for bed. He puts a different hood on me and leads me to his bedroom. There seems to be a sleeping bag on the bed, but as we get closer I recognize it to be a leather bondage sleep sack. He helps me get arranged in it and ties me in for the night. He strips out of my line of sight, and I can feel him climb into the bed next to me. I can feel the heat of him through the sack as he holds me close to his naked body. As I settle in for the night, I know I will never want this weekend to end.

* Internet address: cubbie@concentric.net

TITLE: The Squire's Story
BY: Stan Farwig
FROM: The Gift Shop BBS—Concord, CA

Gwyllym ap Gwynedd, a comely youth and virile stripling at the margin of his manhood, is the substance of our story, which sets forth the incidents by which he realized his deepest and most covert desires and attained his full estate.

It was in August when, the Dog Star in ascendancy, sensual humors and lethargy in equal measure are shed upon men, rendering them lecherous satyrs too indolent to pursue their yearnings and content to be undone by vagrant daydreams and extravagant fantasies never to be realized in this mortal world.

On such a languorous afternoon, Gwyllym ap Gwynedd drowsed and dreamed in the shade of a venerable oak behind his father's cottage. He was tattered by his father's railings, berating him for being no knight's squire. After all, he was not to be faulted that the first knight who had him to squire was elderly and died but four months after his employ; and he was blameless that other knights hereabout had no need of a squire for now.

So, beneath that oak, Gwyllym, his eyes dazzled by the far hills of Cymru shimmering in the glazing heat and his ears lulled by the incessant whirring drone of cicadas, yielded to his favorite fancy, of bold knights and their faithful squires setting forth on dangerous journeys to find adventures even more fabulous than those chronicled in *The Mabinogion* or *The Black Book of Carmarthen*.

Today, during the course of this drowsy reverie there came, as always, a moment when a favorite knight and his faithful squire leave off chivalrous exploits for rejuvenation at a secluded pool. In a bower among overarching ferns, they shed their clothes and, resplendent in their nakedness, wander together to the water's edge and... Here the epic would falter as a swift fervor flared in Gwyllym's britches and the knight and his squire would remain transfixed at water's edge until they evaporated in the violent paroxysm by which Gwyllym quelled such favors.

He would sometimes ponder the strangeness of this sequence and its outcome without determining its meaning, but not today. In the soporific heat of the afternoon, his hand drifted between his thighs without his bidding and, as the imagined knight and his squire remained poised on the cool moss, he clutched…

These pleasantries were broken by such a clamoring of voice and metal that even the cicadas were hushed for a moment. Dazed, Gwyllym started up. For an instant, he thought to be still enraptured by daydreams, for advancing on his haven was a knight all in armor, save the helmet he bore in the crook of an arm.

But that illusion was fast shattered when he recognized his father's voice and saw that he struggled to stay abreast of the knight. As they neared the oak, Gwyllym was struck with wonder, for this knight was as knights were recorded to be in the old fables and chronicles. Tall he was and broad in his shoulders; his face, now streaming with his sweat, was handsome with wide and clear eyes of golden amber, a strong and firm jaw and a finely molded mouth; his hair was thick and russet colored with glints of copper and gold along its curly course to his shoulders.

"Gwyllym, this is Sir Llyr," his father said, making a little bow in the direction of the knight. "He has lost his squire and heard you—"

"I did not misplace my late squire," Sir Llyr interjected. "I sent the clod packing with a kick to his arse." His voice was resonant and rich and just as Gwyllym had thought Lancelot must have sounded.

His father executed another bow and began: "To be sure, good sir—" and again was interrupted.

The knight had been inspecting Gwyllym head to

foot and all between, and now he smiled gently and said: "I'm told you wish to be a squire. Would you care to enlist for a trial to be this knight's squire?"

His father stood behind, hands wringing as though they held a goose by the neck and his head threatened unhinging in a fit of nods.

But Gwyllym needed no prompting. "I should he honored and happy if I were deemed worthy for your service, my lord."

The knight's smile widened. "Good. We leave forthwith."

"Oh, you bring a great boon, Sir Llyr," Gwyllym's father exulted. "It will take but a twinkling to have his clothing packed."

"The knight frowned and said: "Do not trouble. He will be wearing my livery and will not need for anything we cannot claim tomorrow."

"Oh, no trouble, no trouble at all. I'll hasten now—"

"Let me speak more plainly and risk being a churl," the knight said in a voice of commanding calm. "I dispatched my squire today because the buffoon managed to mislay my clothes. Had he otherwise I would not be here in full armor learning what a pig on a spit endures. So I am eager to be home and rid of this journeying oven."

"Oh, to be sure, to be sure, my lord. I'll bring Gwyllym's horse and your own quickly," said Gwyllym's father, all undone as he scurried away.

The knight wandered over into the shade of the oak and turned to Gwyllym. "I'm told you were in the service of Sir Grap before he died."

"Yes, but it was a short term, my lord."

"You need not address me so formally when we're alone," Llyr told him affably. "And did you enjoy the employ?"

"Truth to tell, as a squire is bound to do, it was not as I had expected."

"And what was it you expected?"

"Well, with due respect to Sir Grap, it was a very dull service."

The knight threw back his head and laughed merrily. "That I can certainly believe. Well, lad, you may find squiring for me not quite what you expected either, but I'll do my utmost to keep your service from being dull."

Just then Gwyllym's father approached, a horse reined in each hand, an apprehensive expression on his face. So the knight, in kindly tones, said: "I thank you for your courtesy and for producing so fine a son who will, I'm sure, do you much credit." Then he mounted his steed swiftly.

Gwyllym, in turn, mounted his horse. His father, greatly cheered, cried out: "God be with you, gallant knight, for the privilege you have brought us and may He speed you on in your good deeds for country, king, and family."

As they set upon the dusty road, his father called out

once more: "Be a good and faithful squire, Gwyllym, and meet all your liege's expectations." This behest was Gwyllym ap Gwynedd fated to fulfill.

When they had ridden awhile, the squire inquired: "We ride now to your castle, my lord?"

"Alas, I have no such castle myself," the knight replied regretfully. "We must rejoice that the kingdom has known peace for so long, but there is little chance in these times for a young knight to win such recompense. For my fealty, the king grants me an apartment in his own castle." He turned to Gwyllym with a melancholy smile and added: "It is comfortable enough."

The squire brimmed with admiration at the manner with which this knight sat to saddle, his back all straight and his head proudly erect, though the sweat ran in a torrent from his brow and the sun beat upon the armor with a cruel, blinding brilliance. This knight was every inch the stalwart champion celebrated in ages past by scribes in histories and bards in verse.

After they had passed some distance in silence, the new squire, his imagination filled with heroes and prodigious exploits, asked: "Do you come from some recent foray, sir?"

"No. Worse. From a tournament never mounted. And do have done with the 'my lords' and 'sirs' when we are in private company. You make me feel a decrepit relic."

In much confusion, Gwyllym stammered: "Oh, I will

cease, my lo—I will cease." After a pause to collect himself, he continued. "A tournament in this season? Never have I known such a thing."

"And may you never know of it again."

"But why ever would a tournament be decreed in such a heat?"

"Because the queen dotes upon a charlatan who boasts he is a second Merlin and because the king advances in his own dotage. This charlatan bade a tournament be held to avert Hecate from rising with the full moon and wreaking havoc throughout the realm. He gave assurances he would conjure this day to be as mild as a morn in May. So the queen urged it upon the king, but when at the first joust the heat caused both knights to slide off their horses in a faint as profound as any maiden's, the king had sense to cancel the rest."

"But if this charlatan fails so badly in his tasks, why is he not laughed at and routed?"

"Oh, all laugh well behind the queen's back, but she is told by the charlatan that Morgan le Fay still lives, sustained by magic, in her green chapel or Merlin's cave and vexes Merlin's descendants with her powerful spells. And hearing such twaddle, the queen shivers with fright and feeds the charlatan sweetmeats, as to a lapdog rewarded for tricks." The knight sniggered and added: "Though I'll wager this lapdog's trick is to bury his bone deep in the queen's lap whenever the king dozes."

Gwyllym was scandalized, for never had he heard

such talk of the monarchy, nor did knights speak so in the chronicles he had studied. He hastened to restore a courtly guise to their discourse. "Have you, sir, been to Tintagel to see Merlin's cave or his burial site at Carmarthen?"

Llyr accorded his new squire a wry glance. "Well versed in the old romances and medieval mysteries, are you? Let me warn you, lad, not to confine too much of your head to those, lest you never discover the romance and mystery that abounds all 'round you today."

That said, they entered the castle courtyard where not a soul was to be seen and over all a stillness lay like a dust. The knight dismounted and hurried to the stable door to give it a lively pounding. When that brought no response, he swore still livelier oaths and delivered it resounding kicks with his girded heel. Whereupon the door swung back and the stable boy emerged with a slow, sauntering step.

"Quick, you worthless chit, see to our horses and tend them well, or your backside will know my battering."

The stable boy, a rotund and rustic dullard, rolled his eyes and spread his mouth into a coy leer. Sir Llyr paid him no heed but strode to the castle stairs. As he took the reins from Gwyllym, the stable boy, with open insolence, appraised him fully and winked slyly. Gwyllym thought him addle witted and followed Sir Llyr.

Up three flights of stairs they went, and Gwyllym,

ever smitten with romantic fancies, wondered what famous feet had worn the stone of these steps he climbed, while his knight's endurance flagged with the effort after the day's folly.

Down a short hall they went. Llyr opened a great door and Gwyllym entered after him, into the knight's apartment.

The chamber was large and airy with windows of leaded glass on two sides. Through these, the afternoon's fleeting light made the wooden paneling gleam with burnished warmth. The room was sparsely but finely fitted in a manner becoming the fellowship of knights.

A wide bed with a coverlet of blue and embossed with the royal emblem in gold stood center of one wall, a cupboard at its side, a chest at its foot. On each side was hung a tapestry with scenes of royal hunts wrought cunningly with leafy trees and flowery meadows and in their midst, leaping stags and darting hares and fleeing geese flapping above them all, while huntsmen on horses and hounds on hind legs crowded the edges, destined to endless pursuit and never permitted a capture. A prie-dieu stood in one corner; in another, a table with scattered books upon it and a big-bellied lute, tightly strung, as well. There were plain chairs with ornate cushions of blue and gold and a table near the eastern window.

And there was a hearth which, strangely on such a

day, had a small fire kindled and a cauldron suspended over it. Near it was a tub larger and of finer wood, both better mitered and calked, than the squire had ever seen.

When he observed the cauldron, the knight said with satisfaction: "The serving wench obeyed for once and set things as I charged her." He sank down upon a stool not far from the great tub and said: "Oh, I am bone weary and ready for my bath. Come, lad, help me sally forth from this oppressive apparel."

Gwyllym hurried to where the knight sat and first drew off the sollerets and greaves and was much struck with the girth and graceful curve of the calves they covered, but this was nothing to the trembling admiration that stirred within him when he removed the cuisses and the massive thighs were revealed, with that between shielded by heavy mail that still girded the knight's body.

Llyr stood then that Gwyllym might detach the tasse and the mail fell forth in a shower of silver reaching just below his loins. The knight sprawled back again onto the stool and stayed impassive as Gwyllym eased the breastplate and paultrons off from him. Next he drew away the gorget and prayed the knight would not notice the shaking in his hands. He shook both because of the sturdy, broad neck the gorget had concealed and because now the knight stood once more and raised his arms that the mantle of mail might be withdrawn.

Gwyllym's knees liquefied as he raised the mail up

over the knight's head and Llyr stood before him naked but for a light loin cloth that hid the particulars, but not the máss of that which Gwyllym was most ardent and fearful to behold.

The knight sat once more and Gwyllym gaped at the beauty of his body glistening with sweat in the early twilight glow that streamed through the casements. The shoulders and arms were graced by muscle in swelling curves that coursed over his chest to raise hard mounds capped by nipples, deeply hued and circled by silken auburn hair that dipped into the cleft between and dwindled down to the breasts' boundary. In this downy recess, a small medallion was suspended on a metal chain. Three ranks of muscle tapered below until poised above the navel's rim. The belly lay level and smooth until embraced by dark and coarse-curling hair overtopping the veiling cloth.

Llyr smiled into his face and said: "That was most deftly and pleasingly done. I believe you have the makings of an excellent squire. Now if you will add water from the fireplace to the cool water in the tub until it is tepid, so I may bathe."

Gwyllym crossed to the fireplace where the cauldron hung and found there was a pail nearby. It took four trips before the water tested tepid to his touch and he could say: "I think the bath is ready now."

"Good, and I thank you," the knight replied. "In the cupboard by the bed you will find some flasks that hold precious oils brought back from the last crusade. Bring…let's see…the one marked sandalwood and the one marked musk and, yes, the one of attar of roses."

Gwyllym opened the cupboard and found it crowded with flasks and jars and boxes and many other unknown things. He, rummaging, found the three oils when the knight called out: "Oh, bring, too, the tall jar with cupids on its side."

Once back at the tub, Llyr instructed him: "Put the jar beside the tub just there, and pour six drops of each oil into the water."

The squire eased the stoppers out and counted each drop carefully until six was reached. The oils swirled over the water dispersing an iridescent sheen to its surface as a sweet aroma arose, hinting of shadowy domains afar and secret, irregular pleasures.

Llyr rose and strolled over to the great tub and smiled again upon Gwyllym before turning and saying: "Untie the knot on my breech."

The knot rested just where the cleavage between the knight's buttocks began and the sight of those stout and solid spheres caused such a trembling in the squire's fingers as to nearly undo the undoing of the knot.

As soon as the knot was loosened and the cloth came off into Gwyllym's hands, Llyr turned to face him. Gwyllym was near overthrown by the bold contours of the stout penis and slack scrotum.

The knight steadied himself on Gwyllym's shoulder

as he stepped into the water, carefully lifting his scrotum and penis to clear the walls of the tub. The gesture caused a wrenching twist in the squire's stomach and his own penis, which had been alert since the knight's undressing, now stirred restlessly in its close confinement.

The knight's head disappeared beneath the water and reemerged with a look of deep contentment. "Blessed Mother, this is near heaven. Lad, go behind and knead my neck and shoulders with good strong hands."

Again Gwyllym's gut was wrenched at the thought of touching this peerless knight's flesh, but he did as he was bidden. With even strokes, his hands wandered over the firm, smooth flesh and his palms were permeated with its animal warmth as his nostrils were by exotic scents rising now from the knight's drenched hair and lustrous skin.

Llyr murmured: "Oh, lad, your touch hovers me even closer to the brink of heaven. Did you do such duty for Sir Grap?"

"Oh, no. I never saw him bathe at all."

The knight snorted. "No, probably you wouldn't. Knights of his age held bathing a degenerate practice that would rob a man of his strength. And, in truth, such knights remained strong...strong in the stench they bore."

Suddenly Llyr sat up and exclaimed: "I forget myself. This has been a hot and dusty day for you as well. Come, share the bath with me."

Gwyllym was filled with much alarm, for while the prospect was tantalizing and caused a flutter in his stomach, he feared the knight's reaction when he spied his new squire's cock now fully engorged. The innocent squire was much confused by the turmoil he felt in mind and body that his cock without his prompting should behave in such an impudent manner.

Llyr pressed further: "See: there is room aplenty in the other half of the tub."

"Oh, my lord, it is a great honor to be invited to share your bath," the squire stammered, unsure how to continue.

"Oh, 'tis no great honor, lad," said the knight. "Any worthy knight not only presses tasks upon his squires, but shares his pleasures as well."

Still Gwyllym hesitated, whereupon Llyr spoke sharply: "I was not so soiled as to cause the water to be polluted, but suit yourself." And he rested his head back and closed his eyes.

Abashed that he gave offense and anxious to share this handsome knight's tub, though he knew not why, Gwyllym turned his back and quickly doffed his clothes, all the while entreating his cock to retreat. For once it obeyed, more from distress than its owner's will, and as the squire turned back and approached the tub, his cock had almost rested its head upon the pillow of his balls.

Strange to tell, as Gwyllym neared the tub and made to step over its wall, he was distracted by a fleeting image: at their pool his knight and squire stepped from the cool moss on its bank and, as their hands joined, entered the water for the first time. The vision was vanished in a blink and the squire stepped into the tub. Llyr's head still rested back with eyes still shut, but at the water's disturbance, he looked up, and his glance roved the full length of Gwyllym's naked flesh.

"Well, Gwyllym you have a splendid and lithe form that would do credit to any knight you serve."

The knight's frank stare and evident admiration caused the squire to shiver with pleasure and feel a lurch in his cock. He sat down in the bath swiftly to conceal his response and murmured: "Thank you, my lo—my thanks."

He pressed against the bathtub wall behind so not to crowd the knight, but both their legs touched at the calf, and though he moved his own gently to free the other pair, still they seemed to meet, and he felt another lurching in his cock. And when the knight shifted his body but a bit and his buttocks came to rest on Gwyllym's feet, then his cock began to rise again in earnest.

"How does the water feel, Gwyllym?" the knight asked pleasantly, his eyes ever examining the squire's face.

"Oh, it feels most fine, my lo—most fine," he answered, ever aware of the pressure of the knight's legs against his, the hard and sleek weight upon his feet.

With a wicked grin, Llyr asked: "When I came out with your father, what were you commencing there beneath the oak?"

Gwyllym felt panic. Another lurching in his cock caused it to stand fully erect. "I was but seeking respite from the terrible heat of the day," he answered meekly, not daring to look down to learn if his sturdy erection could be discovered beneath the water's concealment.

"From your hand's position and its caressing movements, it seemed you might be seeking respite from a more terrible heat within by way of some licentious pleasure."

Gwyllym felt the flesh of his face flush with guilty shame. He lowered his eyes and said: "Oh, my lord, no youth who aspires to serve a virtuous knight would indulge in such a vile act."

Llyr threw back his head and laughed heartily. When he had recollected himself, he said: "Don't blush so, lad, though you do it prettily. Nor does a squire ever utter a falsehood to his virtuous knight, as you have said. Every man, even unto the pope himself, I'll wager, avails himself of that respite when nothing better is about to tend lascivious need."

Gwyllym felt a rush of relief that turned him bold and he asked: "Every man, my lord?"

The knight grinned rakishly and answered: "Yes, every man, including 'my lord,'" and rested his head back and closed his eyelids once again.

They sat in silence for long moments and the squire's gaze drifted down from the Knight's face to fix upon the rutilant nipples that rode their firm crests just above the water's reach. The bold nipples still held him transfixed when the knight again opened his eyes.

"You stare at the medallion on my chest? It was bestowed upon an ancestor by Arthur himself, or so it is imputed in my family." He reached up and lifted it over his head, holding it out to Gwyllym. "Here, look at it more closely if you like. It's a fine piece of work."

But as Gwyllym reached for it, it slipped from the knight's fingers and plummeted into the murky waters below. "Oh, what a dolt your master is! See if you can find it, lad." And he leaned back in the tub and rested his arms along the wall, a thin smile spreading over his lips.

The squire began to feel along the length of the tub's bottom, straying forward until at last his hand grazed a metal strand. But at the instant the knight shifted his body again ever so subtle and Gwyllym felt a strained, expectant shaft pressed against his forearm. His hand turned as unruly as his cock, and the fingers curled themselves deftly about the thick stalk. And while he was terrified by his audacity, his fist was enthralled by the sensation a strange cock brought and would not surrender it.

Great was his amazement and great his relief when Llyr sighed deeply and said: "Ah, lad, you learn quickly what pleases a knight most and eases his distress." And great the commotion in his mind and his loins at the knight's broad smile of delight.

"Jostle and jerk it as though it were your own hot

piece; make it ache with glee and strain to burst with its desire," the knight enjoined, and Gwyllym tightened his grip. His fist began to journey back and forth as it had so often on his own demanding cock, from base to where he felt the thin covering of skin flow over the tender head and recede with the downward stroke.

The knight trembled, groaned, cried out: "Ah, you do shock my prick to an ecstasy," and he grasped the tub firmly to heave his pelvis up so the rigid shaft and lolling balls broke the water's surface as might some creature of the deep—no!…rather as an opulent Venus rising from the sea.

Gwyllym, who had never before viewed a stiffened cock save his own, and that not nearly so near, was enthralled by the great trunk springing from its hairy thicket, encircled by veins as vines clasped to trees, by the turgid head florid from thrashing in its filmy sheath, and by the hefty balls sprawling at the root in their furrowed pouch. Gwyllym's free hand strayed forth to fondle this pouch and feel the globes pitch to and fro.

"How it entices my vision to watch my cock made plaything in your fingers," said the enamored knight, his eyes as firmly fixed as Gwyllym's on the turbulent encounter between his legs.

The squire answered: "Never have I known so searing or savage a frolic when I have toyed with my own plaything. I thank you for allowance to sport so with this lavish cock of yours."

"No thanks is due for such game as this where virile playmates share their manly toys," replied the knight, now gasping with the strain to arch his cock aloft from the water and with the stress applied to it. "But is there not something about it that arouses a lust and longing to know its shape, its fiery span, its unrelenting force along your tongue and the roof of your mouth, to feel the vigorous thrust of it between your lips? It has so inspired many a man before you. And it is hot impatient to learn the contours and textures of your mouth."

The knight's proposal astounded the squire, for never had he heard the like; but once the notion was conceived, then he was consumed by a ravenous urge to swallow whole the largess he held. He bent over and enveloped the cockhead greedily, his tongue roving over and around its brawny perimeter and lapping at the summit's cleft. With gentle force, Llyr gradually goaded the shaft to pass entire between the yielding lips and the squire, his nose tickled by pubic hair aromatic with savory fragrance, felt the rigid stake planted between tongue and palate, the head lodged at his throat. Fierce was the power that flowed in his mouth, to hold so brawny and beautiful a knight prisoner in such a feeble dungeon.

To this confinement the knight consented willingly: "Ah, Gwyllym, hold fast my cock, suck on it till it clamors for release."

Gwyllym, his one hand freed, freed the bally pouch from the other hand to grip the buttocks below that he might support the squirming knight, so great was his rolling and roiling, ramming and writhing as his cock would flee its bondage and then rush back into deep captivity. And, though the squire's own piece pleaded for deliverance, his hands were wholly infatuated by the sturdy, undulating buttocks they held.

At length the knight shuddered and withdrew and, sinking back in the tub, said: "Time now to trade the sides and for me claim my turn at play."

And with the knight's turn, Gwyllym learned the force of another man's touch upon his cock, which arousal surpassed all he had ever experienced before.

"By the saints!" the knight exclaimed. "You conceal a truncheon to bring men readily to their knees, if they have the sense to know that in such a bawdy skirmish the vanquished are assured the trophy. Stand and let me see this prize."

The squire struggled upright on wavering legs and earned the knight's admiring grin. "Truly, this is as fine a trophy as I have had to hand. I'd best busy myself earning the decorations you will bestow upon me."

With that the knight lifted the cock he held so that he could bury his face beneath it and his tongue flickered and curled itself under and over and around the squire's ballsac before his mouth enveloped it, turning the lad giddy with its teasing probe. But that giddiness was as naught to the pandemonium that followed when the knight, with practiced tongue, began to slowly lick the shaft from base to flaring head and then, pulling back the shielding skin the better to swivel the sensitive underhead before he plunged it between his lips.

All the world dwindled until it was confined within the snug, moist lodging and all Gwyllym's awareness was of the duress that rippled from the cockhead into his loins. He grasped the knight's head between his hands and sank the shaft deeper until all the length was ensnared in the caressing mouth and he was teeming with delighted torment.

Llyr left off the frenzied cock to seize the squire by his waist and pivot him about and then the knight's tongue began to journey from just below the dangling ballsac in an ever-lengthening track until it parted the buttocks to lap and nuzzle the opening as the squire was overwhelmed by a desire never before known, never suspected. And then the teasing tongue was done.

Gwyllym looked back over his shoulder and saw the knight holding the jar with cupids and spreading a thick unguent from it over all his rigid cock. When finished, the knight pressed close behind, an arm reaching around the squire's waist to grasp the waiting cock. Putting his mouth close to the squire's ear, the knight said in an urgent and ardent voice: "Listen, sweet Gwyllym, I wish to pierce you with my lance, and the ointment on it will greatly ease the prick it gives you. There will be a brief pain followed by great delight. Do you trust me in this and give your assent to be fucked?"

With the knight's fingers jostling his cockhead and the remainder of his body beset by a lechery surpassing any he had known, he murmured: "Oh, yes, fuck me, gallant knight."

With that consent, Llyr parted the buttocks and slowly eased the cockhead between, gradually extending the opening. Gwyllym was much aroused at the touch of the thick shaft on his buttocks and the first prodding of the entrance, but there followed the searing pain the knight had foretold and Gwyllym gasped loudly and with a thrust backward, he claimed the knight's cock entire. Both then bellowed, the knight with the pleasure he felt throughout his cock at this rapid entry, and the squire with the wonder of feeling the full, hot length deep within him.

The knight began his long, rhythmic thrusts, matching them to the strokes he applied to Gwyllym's straining shaft, both moaning and mewling with the effort and the exultation it produced. Gwyllym's cock swelled with a force as never it had before and his come spewed forth into the knight's deft palm to be rubbed over the tormenting cockhead, doubling and redoubling the squire's agonized pleasure almost beyond his endurance.

At last, the knight cried out: "Ah, you aching bastard cock!" and plunged it in to the base. Along the length of his back, the squire felt the knight go rigid and quivering just before his ass was flooded by the hot juice that coaxed a final salvo from his own balls.

The knight held him close, his face pressed into the squire's neck as their ruttiness was quelled and they both, uncoupling, sank back into the bath.

With a boyish grin, the knight asked: "Well, Gwyllym, is service to me as you expected?"

The squire stammered: "Oh, no. Never did I dream that squiring would be so...so..."

"So *un*dull, perhaps?"

Gwyllym nodded vigorously.

"You would not object to more rounds such as this?"

"As often as you desire."

The knight frowned slightly and said: "As often as we *both* desire, Gwyllym. This would be no delight to me, unless it is equally a delight to you."

"Please know," said the squire solemnly, "I have never known a delight nearly so perfect. I realize now that my past bawdy play was halved, and you have completed it." He hesitated and then added: "May I say, you are the most beautiful and splendid knight I have seen?"

The knight's voice showed how deeply moved he was in answering: "I am pleased that you find me so. And you are as fine and fair a lad as any knight could have to squire. But now that we are both well refreshed, we should quit this bath."

They climbed out of the tub, and the knight fetched cloths to dry themselves, each peering at the other all the while to admire the grace of motion in the action and the beauty of each body part as it received its attention.

When they had dried, Gwyllym picked up his discarded britches. "No, no," said the knight, "forget your clothes for now." He crossed over to throw back the lid of the chest at the foot of the bed. He drew out two white robes of fine-spun linen. "Here, wear this for the night, but don't fasten it that I may to gaze freely on your seductive nakedness."

But the knight fastened the robe about himself. " 'Tis time we had our supper, and I doubt that after the day's disaster many will be feasting with the king, who has, himself, no doubt, taken to his bed. I'll steal down to the kitchen and cajole our victuals. And you make free to take your ease."

While the knight was gone, Gwyllym sat at the table and watched the early moon rise within the lingering sunset. He was much amazed at these past events, for never was such recounted in the histories and romances he had read. There had always been damsels of ineffable beauty whom knights were forever saving, or pledging their unsullied love, with an occasional mention of tryst somewhat less than chaste, but never a hint that wayward sport had transpired between heroes. He was much taken with the notion and began to envision Sir Lancelot and Sir Gawain stripped bare and facing each other in an enchanted forest, where leaves and moss spread a soft and green bed between them, and they both took the measure of each other's...

And now Llyr returned bearing a great tray spread

with platters of delicacies and flagons of wine. "I was right; all are supping in their chambers tonight, but none are so blest in their company as I," Sir Llyr said gallantly as he placed the tray on the table. "Come, let us feast, lad."

He undid the tie so his robe fell open before he sat and Gwyllym fell awestruck once more with the grace and power of the body he had just learned. He was about to eat when a whim struck him, and he ran to the tub while the knight watched in surprise.

The squire drew up the sleeve on his robe and plunged his arm into the water. After but a moment, his arm emerged with his hand holding the medallion on high. "I never completed the commission you gave me."

The knight howled with laughter. "It'll not be charged against you, for I provided further tasks for you."

The squire came to him to place the medallion about his neck, and thereby touch the knight again. And as the knight bent his head to receive the pendant, he took the opportunity to circle a nipple on the squire's chest with his tongue and delighted to see the squire shiver so.

Then they dined, and when they had finished their meal, the knight reclined and asked: "Do you sing, lad?"

"No, not at all well, I fear," Gwyllym answered, anxious lest this disqualify him to be squire.

"It's not a thing to fear, Gwyllym. It is something I will teach you as well," said the knight affectionately.

145

"I should very much like to hear you sing, if you would," said the squire, much comforted.

"Would you?" said the knight, and he sprang up to retrieve the lute.

"I'll sing you a verse or two of 'The Truthful Knight's Confession,'" Llyr announced as he returned, testing the strings' tuning. When he was satisfied they sounded true, he struck some gay chords, and in a sweet and lilting tenor, sang:

> Randy knights may sing a maiden's praise
> On my honor, they lie, they lie
> No jiggling tit nor luring cunt can raise
> Passion so quick or prick so high
> As handsome squires with bouncing balls ablaze.
> Randy knights may sing a maid enslaves
> Sprouting cocks with spreading thighs
> On my honor, they're knaves, they're knaves
> No lusty man, but a lout denies
> Sucking, fucking squires a knight most craves.

His song finished, Llyr put the lute aside as Gwyllym exclaimed: "Oh, you sing with a fine and lovely voice, Llyr."

"I'm happy you find it so, and happy that you call me by my given name," said the pleased knight. "Now's the time for dessert, and it's sweetmeats, I fancy. Serve me, please, Sir Squire."

Gwyllym searched the tray and said with consternation: "There's nothing left. The cook forgot your dessert."

The knight sighed and said: "Sweet lad, come 'round and let me teach you how to serve dessert."

The squire came around the table as the knight pushed aside the supper dishes and then reached up to pull the robe from the squire's shoulders so it fell to the floor. "Now place your delectable bottom just there where my plate lately stood, and I'll have my savory served."

Though he felt quite silly, Gwyllym did as the knight had told him. No sooner was he seated than the feel of the table against his buttocks and balls and the closeness of the knight turned silliness to lechery, and his cock turned stout again.

"No cook in kitchen ever fashioned sweetmeat as sweet as this meat spread before me now," the knight said and once again the squire's ready cock knew his close, moist mouth and the teasing tongue that lashed it.

Below he spied the knight's fist busy buffeting his own soaring piece and, though he found it a lewd and entrancing sight, the pleasure surging up from his loins caused him to give himself over to it and he sank back on the table among the supper things and yielded himself entirely to the knight's diversion and his own. His legs drew up of their own accord and came to rest on the knight's broad shoulders as the knight's agile tongue roamed over his cock and balls and below.

By the time the knight's mouth enveloped the shaft again, the squire felt the swelling flux commence. Its burst brought him erect in a raging, ranting rapture. The knight held fast to the rioting, erupting cock, flogging it with his tongue to coax its utmost yield until the squire was on the verge of begging his mercy.

Just as Gwyllym had shot his last bolt, the knight reared back, his face contorted by a look of fierce concentration and his hand around his cock flailing wildly. The squire shoved off the table and dropped to a knee and the knight willingly surrendered his heaving cock for Gwyllym to swallow entire. It was but a few thrusts, and the knight rose staggering halfway to his feet, one hand braced on the chair arm, the other cupped fast behind the squire's head to press his face close. And, as the knight quaked and yelped, Gwyllym felt the cock swell and jerk in his mouth and the hot flood filled his throat and he knew again the joy of fulfilling the carnal needs of another man.

The knight fell back spent into his chair, but still Gwyllym held the shaft close in his mouth until it waned and fell flaccid.

"Ah, lad," gasped the knight at length, "you suck well. I am well drained."

Gwyllym grinned and said: "I, too, enjoyed my dessert."

"And I am more than willing to supply it whenever you crave a sweet," replied the knight. "Now the hour is late, and this has been a day filled with many a wearying event. Are you ready for sleep?"

Gwyllym nodded and the knight rose and led him to the bed. The squire had wondered where he would sleep, but never did he entertain the notion that he would share the knight's bed.

Yet he did.

And quartered in the knight's sturdy arm, Gwyllym felt such a tumult of elation and wonder that he was certain he would not sleep at all that night.

But of course he did.

Dawn's glistering edge had just begun to peel the dark skin of night from heaven when Gwyllym, nested close to his knight, was enfolded by a dream. Behind sleep-blind eyes, his contrived knight and squire took form, now fully immersed in their pool, and busy at water frolic. Freed of waking will, the scene was endowed with a preternatural radiance that etched every detail with a clarity never glimpsed in Gwyllym's summoned fancies.

The water swirled 'round the couple, green with the green world bounding it, and against it their flesh was luminous with the myriad tints of mother-of-pearl. Suddenly the knight climbed onto a rock ledge and stood proud and erect in all his parts. He held out his arms to the squire below; but as Gwyllym, who now found himself the squire, began to hasten to his lover's arms, he was halted by a ticklish nuzzling at his scrotum. Much amazed, he halted and stared down into the shadowy depths, thinking he was set upon by an affectionate fish.

He looked up to where his knight stood, beckoning with one hand while the other proffered forth a great inducement. Again he made to hasten, but with his next step, his penis was plucked entire into the furtive mouth below and he was filled with both terror and bliss. "Ah," he thought, "whether this be a monster fish or other watery brute creature, it knows well what gladdens a cock."

And Gwyllym awoke, sitting up startled, to see Llyr's head bobbing in his lap. The knight uncoupled his mouth to say: "I did not mean to unnerve you with my morning's greeting."

The squire, still sleep-filled, said: "I dreamed I was in a pond and a great fish was nibbling my cock."

The knight laughed. "With bait such as this, you should be able to pull in many a catch," he said and resumed his leisurely sucking.

"Ah, Llyr, you do pleasure me beyond the telling," said his squire, "but draw closer that we may close the gap in a capering circle."

So Llyr, without leaving off the treat he held, swept around and kneeled so he arched above the squire, a canopy of fleshy delights. Gwyllym pulled down the swaying penis and eagerly secured it with his mouth as he toyed, first with the floundering testicles, then the hardened nipples.

But when a wandering finger explored the buttocks' crevice, the knight broke off his sucking to stare below at the work performed on his cock and his ass. All flushed, he hastily withdrew from the squire's carousal to leap from the bed and hasten to the tub.

When Gwyllym saw the knight returned with the cupid jar, he rolled over to present his buttocks, but the knight laughed and said: "No, you misread my intent. Turn back, sweet Gwyllym." And when the squire turned back, he was amazed that it was his own penis the knight began to overlay with the ointment as he continued: "There are knights who ever demand to be topplers and never to be toppled and topped, but my taste ranges wider, and I am pleased at times to be unknighted and made liege man to my squire. So kneel to your task, lad."

When the squire had knelt, the knight slipped deftly under him and encircled his waist tightly with his legs. "So, Sir Gwyllym, with your broad blade held on high, I pray you with its blows…not to shoulders, but betwixt cheeks…reknight me."

With that, the knight reached low to seize the squire's well-lathered shaft and, gripping him ever closer with his legs, directed it so his buttocks were parted. Gwyl-lym needed no further guidance, but thrust his rigid cock, gleaming with salve, into the waiting gap.

He felt as though the cock were consumed by a scorching fever as the passageway closed around it. The knight's eyes stared wide and wild with amazement. Gwyllym's hips began to ram his piece in and out of the staunch buttocks, and the knight matched his efforts with mighty thrusts of his pelvis. Each stroke increased their mutual fury and rapture. The knight jerked his cock with one hand while the other teased the squire's nipples. Gwyllym reached under to fondle the knight's balls, and the knight, his head thrown back and his body taut with abandon, groaned and called out: "By all the spurting cocks of the kingdom, you are the greatest fucker to be had…impale me harder, you fucking lad…my ass thirsts for your hot juices to enamel it."

But a few strokes more, and the squire was compelled to leave off his exertions, rigid and racked throughout his body by his violent cock's antics as it spurted forth its heavy load.

The knight's face was transfigured by ecstasy as his own mighty piece responded with its barrage and his belly glistened with the deluge.

When the tumult subsided at last, they rolled apart and laid still for calm to overtake them. And after a while, the knight looked over to his bedfellow and, concerned over the expression he found, asked: "Gwyllym, you seem very pensive. Are you troubled?"

"It's just, well, I'm not sure that I have proved myself deserving to be your squire, and have had no assurance that is to be my future."

A smile of melting tenderness overcame the knight's lips and he reached out to muss his bedfellow's hair. "You foolish child, to entertain such doubts after our fine encounters."

The knight rolled onto his stomach close to the squire and, leaning still closer, he said solemnly:

"Hear me, Gwyllym ap Gwynedd: a worthy knight loves and cherishes his squire above all else and, as I do strive to be worthy of my rank, I now declare my life, my fortune, and my love to be shared with you as I pray you share those with me. May this, my kiss, be a seal and surety upon this pledge to you, my lovely squire." Having said, the knight leaned down his face, grave and tender, that he might press his lips upon his squire's.

And with that kiss, Gwyllym ap Gwynedd, a comely youth, realized his deepest and most covert desires, attained his full estate as a well-loved squire, and crossed over the margin into his manhood with his stripling years concluded, as is now our story.

* Internet address: stanfar@pacbell.net

TITLE: Close Shave
BY: Ray Cornett, aka Writer@seattle.com
FROM: Rendezvous—Seattle, WA

James told me the last time we were together that he was interested in shaving. Both shaving others and being shaved. Though I've had limited experience with it, I always aim to please with the people I love.

Let's start with the setting. There's a lot of candlelight; the blankets have been stripped off the bed; the ropes are laid out for easy access. There's a stack of pillows in the center of the bed. A washbasin, shave cream, and a woman's razor are laid out on the floor within reach.

Cast of characters: Myself: 6'1", brown hair, hazel/green eyes, medium build, 8" cut cock, very little body hair.

James: 5'6", brown hair, dreamy brown eyes, nice build, 6" cut cock, and very fuzzy. (Something I like!)

As I'm rushing around, making these preparations for

my date with James, the doorbell rings. He's early. I run down to greet him wearing only my shorty nightshirt. (The one he likes so much.) After a quick hug, he follows me up the stairs. I'm assuming he follows me to watch my butt, but I never ask. When we get into the apartment, I pull him close and give him a long, deep kiss.

"Howdy, Handsome. Wanna play?" I say. (I never have been shy.) "I've got something special planned. Hope you're up to it. Let's get naked and into the shower."

Without comment, he starts getting undressed. I set the shower water and we both get in. After putting some soap on my hands, I start washing his body; making sure to get everything clean, but more to tease him than anything else. James has a nice body, it's a joy to work on. I let my soapy hands roam around his body, gently touching the back of his neck, lingering at his nipples, working down to his groin. Once I get there, I gently wash his crotch and ass at the same time. When his balls pull up close to his body, I move my hands down onto his legs, soaping them lightly to a nice lather. When I reach his toes, I stop and rub them for a while, driving up his sexual tension.

Standing up, I give James another long kiss. "Ready for an evening you won't soon forget?"

"I guess," he says a little apprehensively. "What are we going to do?"

"I'm sure you'll enjoy it, and you'll find out what we're doing here soon."

With that, I shut off the water and grab a towel. I rub all of his body dry. He's still hard when I get to his groin, so I go down on him. He moans and grabs my hair, pushing me all the way down on his hard cock. I manage to extract my mouth from his body with effort and stand back up to lead him into the bedroom.

As soon as the bed comes into his view, I hear him gasp.

"Just what do you have planned for me?" he asks.

I grin. "Guess you'll just have to find out," I say as I lead him over to the bed.

"Lie down, please. If anything happens that you can't handle, just snap your fingers. We'll make that our signal for when to stop." I lay him gently onto the stack of pillows, making him comfortable, then tie his hands carefully to the headboard, telling him about the easy-release on the rope in case there's an emergency. Then I go down to the foot of the bed, tying the ropes around his ankles, taking time to nibble/suck on his instep and toes. His moans say all I need to hear about what I'm doing.

After putting some hot water in the basin, I ask him how he's doing. He responds with another nice moan, and I proceed. Setting the basin on a table by the bed, I grab the rag and wring it out. I start drawing it playfully across his lower back and butt. After rewetting it, I lay the rag down on the area I'm planning on shaving and start kissing the back of his knees to give his skin time to absorb the water and make it easier for the shave.

James squirms a little as I kiss the back of his legs. I

enjoy the feel of his body as I caress and kiss him. When his moans reach a fever pitch, I stop. Pulling off the rag, I lie down on him. Because of the difference in height, our bodies mesh nicely. My hardening cock lies in the crack of his muscular ass. He tightens the muscles in his cheeks, and my cock throbs from the attention.

I pull myself up off his body and reach for the rag again. Once I've washed his back and butt one more time, I go for the shaving cream. As I spread it softly across his lower back, he arches it, moving himself up to my touch. I reach over for the razor and shake the water out of it. Very gently, I draw the razor over the highest area of hair on his back. He groans as the razor gently shaves him smooth. As I move the razor lower on his back, he arches again.

"Careful now, Hon. You don't want to be squirming when I'm working on you with a razor."

"Sorry," James says. "Couldn't help that."

I continue to work the razor over his lower back, removing all the baby-soft hair there.

When that's done and washed off, I kiss him gently and rub my hands over the small of his back. The feel is quite different; it definitely meets with his approval.

"Hmmm. That feels wonderful!" he coos.

"It's going to get better. Just wait."

Once I return from the bathroom with fresh water, I again run the rag over his butt. I've shaved a person's butt only once before, and it makes me a little nervous to do so.

But I'm determined to try this both for him and for me.

I gently apply shave cream to James's butt. When my hand runs down the crack of his ass, he squeezes, holding it in place for a second.

"Just be sure you don't do that when I'm shaving. That could hurt," I say as I finish applying the cream to his peach fuzz.

James assures me that he won't and says he has wonderful "muscle control" down there. I'm getting anxious to find out, but I keep my cool about it. I reach over for the razor, still a little worried about shaving him, but enjoying the hell out of this scene we've created.

James groans as I run the razor over the top edge of his butt. As I pull the razor down the outer edge of one cheek, he tenses the muscles and I wince. "Did I cut you? Or are you just enjoying this?"

After assurances that he's enjoying this a *lot*, I continue. With each pass, I get closer to his hole. Electricity seems to fill the air as I run the razor carefully over his bottom. James groans and pulls gently at his arm restraints, creating a very interesting visual effect.

"Hurry, please. I want you."

"Be patient now," I say, patting his butt. "We don't have to rush through this. We've got plenty of time." I continue my slow, gentle shaving of him.

Reaching under him, I grope for the head of his cock. It's soaking the pillow with precome. I try to stroke him a little, but the pillows interfere, so I pull my hand back out and suck the precome off my fingers before I continue. All of his butt is shaved now, except the area right around his hole.

"Now, you need to be very still here. This could be dangerous, and I don't want to hurt you." (I always overassure people in situations that I'm not very secure about.) I wash around his hole thoroughly and gently apply some fresh shaving cream. I start carefully right at his asshole, working out to where I'd already shaved. James lies completely still as I do this, but his moans tell me he's enjoying what I'm doing a great deal.

With a sigh of relief, I finish his shave. I wash off the excess shaving cream and sit back on my haunches to admire what I've done. James has a *fantastic* ass, and I enjoy looking at it, whether or not it's shaved!

Without saying anything, I lean down and kiss the top of his crack. James moans again in response. I let my tongue move down his crack a little, almost to his glory hole. James tightens his ass muscles around my tongue. I have to chuckle at the fact that he's trapped my tongue in his cheeks.

Once he relaxes his grip, I pull his cheeks apart and go down hard on his asshole. This time *I* groan at the wonderful combination of tastes and scents that greet me.

I continue to let my mouth and tongue rove across his clean-shaven ass, trying to concentrate on his hole. At one point, while my tongue is working his hole feverishly, James's ass muscles start contracting in rhythmic motion as he screams, "I'm coming!" He's straining against the bindings by now.

When he relaxes, I sit back up. "Well that was nice. Wonder if I can do it again." And my tongue goes to work on his ass once more, more gently this time.

Reaching for the lube, I pour a small amount at the top of his crack, and let it run down to his hole. Once it reaches there, I put a finger against his asshole, stroking at the opening, trying to loosen the sphincter. Applying more lube to my finger, I press gently into his ass. He yields to my touch and lets me loosen him up.

Reaching farther into his ass with my finger, I find his prostate, massaging it a little. James groans and pushes his ass back against my finger. The desire is finally getting the better of me. My cock is throbbing and wanting to be inside him.

I apply a generous amount of lube to myself, and press it to his ass opening. He relaxes his ass to let me inside. Slowly, I push into him until our bodies meet. A shiver runs through my body as I lie down on top of this beautiful little man.

I raise my hips off James slowly, pulling my cock out almost all the way. Then push all the way back in. I can feel my balls tightening. I'm getting real close to coming. After taking a couple of deep breaths, I continue, knowing I'm not going to be able to last long, but wanting to bring him pleasure. It takes just a few short minutes before I reach the point of no return.

James grips my cock hard with his ass, screaming "Push!" That's all it takes. I can feel the come gushing out of my body. I am totally spent.

After a few minutes of recovery, I raise off him. James winces slightly as I pull out, and I try to reassure him that when I have been fucked, that seems to be the most painful part for me as well. James releases his hands as I untie his feet, and he rolls over. His cock is wet and hard.

"Apparently, I didn't satisfy you completely tonight—not yet, anyway."

James assures me that I've done quite well and pulls me down on him to kiss me.

I move my kisses down his body, stopping at his nipples, then belly button, working down to his hard cock. When I finally reach it, the flavor of his shaft is wonderful! Working my mouth up and down on him quickly, I'm rewarded with a nice load of come and once again we are left breathless.

Without bothering to put away our equipment for the night, I grab a blanket, and we snuggle down for the evening.

* Internet address: Writer@seattle.com

It had always been my fantasy to be part of a biker gang. Ever since I first saw Hell's Angels riding around with their greasy leathers and body decorations, the idea of being apprenticed to such a biker had turned me on something rotten. When I saw the film *Mad Max III*, the idea got stronger, for there were these guys in the film who were clearly the slaves of the other bikers, chained to the bikes, doing what they were told and nothing else. And then I saw a TV documentary about a bikers' gathering in small-town America.

One scene really struck me hard and has never gone. There was a prospect, an apprentice, basically a guy who wanted to be a full member of the gang and who had to serve his time doing just that—serving. Of course, the full details of his servitude and initiation weren't shown on the programme so I'll have to fill in the details by telling you what happened to me.

Though I had a bike of my own, as a rookie I wasn't going to be allowed to use it. This was one of the first conditions of my acceptance into the gang. During the months I was to live with the gang, I had to learn to respect and trust the other members and that meant that, when the gang moved from one site to another, I had to count on them to take me with them. If I failed in my duties, I could be left behind.

I was to be assigned to one biker, the one who had first spotted me as a potential member, and was to do whatever he said. He was free to use me or lend me out or even discard me completely if I failed. I was told to bring nothing with me but the clothes I stood up in: an old pair of Levi's, a T-shirt, some thick socks, and my sturdy army boots. I had to leave my leather jacket behind as well, and was told to wear an old denim jacket. I had to earn the right to wear my leather jacket, just as I had to earn the right to ride my own bike. Anything else I might need would be provided.

I remember exactly when I first came across a member of the chapter. Chapter One it was called, and unlike most other biker gangs, was exclusively male. I never did find out if they were all gay, but certainly few of them seemed to have any sexual energy to spare after they'd been fooling around with me and the other trainees and each other.

I came across Ted down at Box Hill, one Sunday afternoon around 4:00. Box Hill was a famous meeting place for motorbikers, though most of the guys were just kids with massive HP repayments and insurance premiums that would never get paid 'cos they were bound to smash up their bikes or themselves in a short space of time.

Real bikers, with working bikes like messengers or practical bikes like mine with a decent seat and petrol tank, were rare. Most kids rode racing replicas with dreadful riding positions which meant that the short range of their tiny petrol tanks was a blessing. After 60 miles or so, they needed to get off and let the blood flow back into their arms and legs.

This particular afternoon I'd arrived late when most of these "pretty" bikers had gone home and some of the regulars were still around comparing piston rings and other bits of hardware. To me the men were far more interesting than the bikes, but the bikes were nonetheless an essential accessory. I'd walked a couple of circuits of the bike park and was sitting on my bike wondering what to do next as the place was, by now, getting pretty deserted.

Just as it looked like it was time to go this guy rides in. Low-slung Harley, greasy boots, leather jeans and jacket with scrappy denims under and over the jacket, black crash helmet, mirror sunglasses and a camouflage-green scarf over his face.

I leaned casually against my bike, pretending to be

looking elsewhere, but I couldn't keep my eyes off him. He got off the bike and removed the scarf, which he tucked into the back pocket of his jeans, then tipped off the helmet and hung it over the bike's handlebars. Under his helmet was a black woolen cap which he kept on. Bits of ginger hair stuck out all round the cap, matching his scrubby ginger beard. The sunglasses made it difficult for me to tell what he was looking at. He lay back on the bike and looked as if he was going to sleep, but I couldn't be sure.

I realised that I couldn't stand frozen in one position by my bike forever and decided to walk around the parking area, deliberately looking away from the biker in case my interest was too obvious. But every now and then I glanced over at him. He was still laid out on his bike, eyes hidden behind the sunglasses.

It was time to make a decision. If I continued walking in this direction, I'd have to walk right by him. And if I turned and walked back the other way, I might lose sight of him. I decided to brazen it out and continue walking toward him, casually scanning the remaining bikes in the bike park. My heart beat harder as I got closer to him. I was walking in one direction—directly toward him, 'cos that's the way the path went, and looking anywhere but ahead of me.

I stumbled as my foot landed directly on top of an empty Coke can, which flew out from beneath my foot, and I watched it roll away under his bike.

"Careful, boy," the soft, firm voice said.

I looked up and saw the biker turning his head away from me, to rest his gaze once more firmly on the horizon.

"Sorry, Sir," I said without thinking. And I stopped dead still.

The problem with a vivid imagination is that your fantasies sometimes leak out at times of tension without your realising it. Why had I said anything at all? Why had I called him "Sir"? It was obvious why I had thought it. But how had this guy snared me so easily with his voice and his attitude that I had dropped my guard and allowed my inner feelings to spill out?

Without turning his head, the biker spoke again. "That's OK, boy. You won't do it again."

My heart raced faster and I snapped my jaw tight to stop the natural response of "No, Sir!" escaping my lips. Was this man toying with me? Was I imagining him speaking? My head spun. A strong coffee was what I needed. I dashed on past the biker, not daring to look at him, and headed for the café. I dared not turn around until I was through the trees and inside the café. Back across the park area, the biker seemed not to have moved. Maybe he'd fallen asleep. At this distance I certainly couldn't tell.

I reached the head of the queue and ordered a strong coffee and a doughnut. I consumed them both quickly, the searing coffee reminding me that I was not dreaming.

I felt somewhat calmer and decided that I'd had enough excitement for one day. As I headed off out of the café toward the bike park, I saw the biker standing by his bike, getting ready to ride off. He was tying the camouflage scarf over his face and replacing his helmet. He started the bike and rode out of the park, not even glancing in my direction despite passing only a few yards in front of me.

I felt a swell of disappointment. Maybe I had imagined it. Maybe he was talking in his sleep. Maybe he turned and spoke without seeing me. Maybe he had his eyes closed and it was a reflex action on his part. As much of a reflex as my response. I sighed to myself and returned to my bike.

I pulled my bandanna mask out from inside my open-face helmet, which I'd left slung over the handlebars of my bike. People at Box Hill are honest; you can leave things like helmets without any worry. I tied the mask over my face and reached for my helmet. My hand stopped. There was a piece of paper tucked under the elastic of my goggles. I pulled it out and unfolded it.

It read:

Boy—
>   *Meet me here at midnight. You get only one chance.*
>   *Ted*

I realised I didn't have any choice.

It was midnight. I'd arrived early and left my bike in the now-deserted car park. I was wearing some old denim jeans and jacket, and a leather jacket over that. On my feet were some old, muddy steel-toe-capped Wellingtons into which I'd tucked my jeans. I had an old T-shirt on under the jacket, but nothing on under the jeans. I liked my cock and balls to hang free. The bandanna mask I wore over my face on the bike hung around my neck over another one I always wore around my neck. I wasn't sure what I was expected to wear, but I made sure that I didn't look too unlike the man I was waiting for, and that I didn't get too cold, either.

I stood with my back against a tree trunk, hiding in the tree's shadow from the bright full moonlight. My open-face helmet and goggles lay on the ground by my side. From where I stood, I had a good view of the car park and the road into it, and I expected to be able to hear or see the visiting biker before he saw me. It was about ten minutes before midnight and I relaxed, not expecting Ted to arrive yet. I was sure he'd want to raise my anxiety by keeping me waiting.

Suddenly I heard movement behind me. Before I could move away from the tree, firm hands gripped my wrists and pulled my arms around behind the tree, securing my wrists with what felt like the cold steel of handcuffs. I started to panic, not knowing whether this was Ted or some unwanted intruders on my scene.

A figure walked around from the back of the tree. It

was the biker I was expecting. The greasy leathers and masked face were unmistakable; apart from the substitution of goggles for sunglasses, he looked the same as earlier.

The biker didn't say a word, but ran his gloved fingers over my face and head. When he reached my mouth, he prised my lips apart and thrust a gloved hand inside, playing with my tongue and pushing his fingers farther back until I choked on them. As he withdrew them, he brought up his other hand. In it was a large wadded bandanna which he forced into my mouth and held there with his gloved palm. His other hand went on to explore the rest of my body, unfastening my jackets and exploring my chest. His hand rubbed over my tits and he squeezed each of them hard, my groans stifled by the gag.

His hand moved down to my crotch, and he soon discovered my cock and balls hanging down the leg of my jeans. He gripped my balls and squeezed until tears emerged from my tightly squeezed eyes. He was exploring how far he could take me in an efficient and skilled way. I feared how much further he would want to go.

The biker placed his body flat against me, pinning me to the tree, one knee raised to press hard against my balls. He unfastened one of the bandannas from around my neck and tied it tightly across my mouth to keep the gag in place. His face was less than an inch from mine and he stared hard into my eyes through the goggles, keeping all of his body pressed tightly against mine and pressing farther with his knee into my balls. His knee couldn't have failed to notice that, despite being positioned down my leg, my cock had grown quite hard.

After some minutes, he moved back and removed some tit clamps from his jacket pocket. They were no ordinary tit clamps; they had a large black weight hanging from each side. The biker ripped my T-shirt up the middle and squeezed my tits into life with his hands before applying the clamps. The weights were heavier than any I'd experienced and the strain spread through my chest.

The biker stood back to admire his captive.

Suddenly he spoke. "So you turned up. I knew you would. I can spot guys like you a mile off. They stand staring most of the time. What they see is someone like me, a total biker. And they want to be like me. They want to be owned by me. Yet they are usually pathetic. They're usually too scared to go all the way and live the biker's life. Sometimes, though, I see a guy who could really make it, given the right training."

He stopped speaking for a moment and walked slowly toward me. He gripped my now-rockhard cock firmly with his hand and squeezed very hard. He kept on squeezing harder and harder so that my erection in fact started subsiding just when I thought I would come in my jeans.

He stepped back.

"That's good. I like someone who's turned on. It keeps them interested and helps them tolerate what I have in store for them. Not that you're going to touch that cock of yours while you're in my hands. I'm in control of your body now. That's what you want, isn't it?"

I grunted and nodded.

"But you're still a fair-weather biker. A weekender who jumps out of his gear and into his smart clothes once Sunday night is over."

I shook my head, but he wasn't really looking at me. He was looking past me behind the tree.

"If you want to be like me, you need to make a total commitment. I wonder if you're prepared for that."

The biker clicked his fingers in the air, gesturing past me at someone or something.

A second figure appeared, and my heart beat fast at what I saw. The figure was totally encased. His head was covered in a tight-fitting rubber hood with just the eyes visible. A large metal ring hung from his nostrils. The mouth area seemed distended, and I realised that behind the flat round flange of rubber, similar to a buttplug's, was a large gag filling this figure's mouth. Around his neck was a wide collar secured by a large padlock. Most noticeable was the word "prospect" written on the hood in rough white letters across the figure's forehead. The rest of the prospect's body was covered in tattered denims and leather garments. His cock and balls hung out of the jeans, and wide leather bands were padlocked around his balls and cock so that his balls hung low and his cock was constricted in its size. Chains ran from the ball strap to straps locked around his ankles so that when he was standing straight up, his balls were pulled down tight. The prospect held his arms behind his back so I couldn't see whether there were any restraints on his wrists.

The biker clicked his fingers and the prospect dropped to his knees and placed his head between the biker's boots, his arse facing away from the biker, toward me. I saw that his hands were covered with heavy rubber gloves with wide straps locked over the wrists which were pulled high up his back and chained to the back of the collar. To my surprise, the back of his jeans was wide open, exposing his bare arsecheeks. The biker pulled a wide leather strap out of his jeans and started laying into the prospect's arse. Even in the moonlight, I could see the skin reddening as blow after blow struck home. The prospect started groaning and crying out as much as the gag would allow.

The strapping stopped. The biker stood to one side of the prospect, who was quivering visibly. He looked straight at me.

"Obedience isn't about allowing oneself to be trussed up like a chicken," he said in his soft, seductive voice. "It's about accepting what you're given even when you can avoid it."

He laid into the prospect's arse again with the belt. Adding further to what I expected was already a searing pain. The prospect remained still, though he continued to groan and squeal.

After what must have been around 30 strokes, the biker stopped his beating and clicked his fingers. The prospect stood upright at attention, his eyes staring straight ahead into the distance.

"Now it's your turn to show your resolve," the biker said in my direction.

He walked toward me and fingered the chain linking my now very sore tits. As he played with the chain, the weights moved up and down and the numbness in my tits disappeared as fresh blood tried to flow into them. The pain was intense, but not as intense as when he removed each clamp in turn and massaged my flattened nipples until the pain had changed into a dull ache.

The two men released me from the tree trunk and turned me around quickly, securing me once again around it, but now with my chest against the trunk. My arms were secured around the other side high up so I could not slip down.

The biker unfastened my jeans and pulled them down around my ankles, exposing my arse to the night air. The prospect stood beside the tree to be within my sight, but I could no longer see the biker. I soon heard and felt his presence as the whistling of his belt through the air was followed by a cracking as the strap hit home.

I jolted upright against the tree. Stroke after stroke followed until my arse felt on fire and tears again trickled down my face.

I, too, was groaning and crying, but louder than the prospect had. My sobs were intermingled with muffled cries of "No!" and "Stop!"

When the biker sensed he was reaching the limit of my tolerance he stopped and had obviously signaled to the prospect. I could see the prospect pull a small bottle and another bandanna out of his pocket. He fastened the bandanna over my nose and mouth and dabbed some poppers onto the mask. The poppers were strong. As I inhaled them, I became a little dizzy.

The strapping started again. Every few strokes, the prospect administered some more poppers until my head was swimming and the fire in my arse felt as if it was spreading throughout my whole body.

Finally the beating stopped and the two figures walked away from me. I could not move. My cock started to harden, rubbing against the tree trunk. The poppers mask was still potent, and I struggled to retain some alertness through its soporific effects.

After some time, I became more alert and tried to loosen my bonds, but to no avail. My arse was now a little less sore, though I was sure that it would hurt even more once I had to sit or lie on it. I tried again to loosen my restraints. While my concentration was on my bonds, a blindfold was suddenly fastened across my eyes. My arms were untied. I was forced down onto my knees, my back against the tree trunk, my arms fastened once again behind it and my feet pulled to either side of it. I sensed a figure standing close in front of me and could feel what felt like a finger running over my face.

Suddenly the gag and mask were removed, and a large cock covered in what felt and tasted like heavy rubber forced its way into my mouth and down toward my throat. The tree trunk prevented my moving my head, and I was forced to gag on it. The figure in front of me started a rhythmic fucking in and out. A voice close to my ear told me to be careful with my teeth because if I ripped the rubber, I'd be whipped again.

I carefully kept my teeth away and sucked as hard as I could with my lips and tongue on the metallic-tasting rubber. As the rhythm of the fucking increased, a popper-soaked rag was fastened across my nostrils. My mouth being filled, I was forced to breathe it in, and as my head swam once again, the fucking speeded up until I felt totally controlled by the figure in front of me. I assumed I was being face-fucked by the biker until I heard the now-familiar sound of leather on skin as the biker started beating the prospect's arse. As the beating speeded up, so did the fucking, until I could sense, from the prospect's tensing muscles, that he had come inside the rubber.

My own cock was now rockhard as well, and I longed to come. I felt a boot being placed on my cock and my cock being squeezed against the tree trunk.

"You'll not come tonight, boy," the seductive voice told me.

"No, Sir," I said, my mouth now being my own for the first time in ages.

The blindfold was removed, and I saw the biker's crotch right in front of my eyes. His cock was hard, his large balls hung low out of the fly of his jeans. I leaned forward to try to suck it, but he pushed my head back against the tree with his firm hands.

"Being a prospect is about doing what you're told and nothing more," the biker said, his seductive voice taking on a firmer, harder edge.

"No, Sir," I said.

The prospect was now moving around behind me. He released my arms.

"Stand up," the biker ordered.

I stood up.

"Hands behind your back at all times unless told otherwise!" he snapped when I started to move toward my own cock.

The prospect returned within my view and knelt with his forehead on the ground.

"Look at this creature by my side," the biker said. "He's been mine for three months now. He's always hooded and gagged, always chained and restrained. Always, except when it suits me to feed or water him or make him work or exercise. And if you think he's allowed any sexual pleasure, well, in those three months, he's rarely been allowed to come. And when he does, it's under my control, never by his own hand, and always inside that rubber sheath so that his prospect cock never gets touched. He even has to eat, sleep, and piss wearing those rubber gloves."

The biker paused. I looked him straight in the face, which was still covered with the mask and goggles. "Is this the commitment you want to make?" The voice emerging from behind the mask was once again soft and seductive.

I looked hard at the biker and at the prospect. My mind was confused. I was frightened as much by the pain and discomfort of the treatment I had experienced and had seen being administered to the prospect as by my own longing for the captivity to continue.

I nodded and whispered, "Yes, Sir."

The biker looked at me hard, his eyes piercing through the goggles.

Silence. I wondered whether I'd said the wrong thing. I said nothing more, fearing that whatever I said might further diminish my chances of seeing more of this powerful man.

After a few minutes, he reached down and encircled my balls with his gloved hand, squeezing and pulling them while keeping his eyes set firmly on my own.

"I think you need to think about this," he said. "But I'll give you something to help remind you what losing control is about."

He snapped his fingers once again. The prospect hurried over and knelt down beside my crotch. I looked down and just glimpsed the biker hand the prospect a shiny metal object before he grabbed my chin and pulled my head upright again. I felt the prospect slide a wide, cold metal object around my balls and then snap it shut. I flinched as I expected the skin to get trapped; but it didn't, and I relaxed.

"You're going to remember this night for a while," the biker said menacingly. "We're leaving in a minute, and we're taking your helmet and bike keys with us. You'll find them in the bushes behind the phone box up at the next roundabout. It's only about a mile or so. I don't want you slouching on your way up there, so I'm going to lock a hood on you. If you run there and back, not many cars will come by and see you. We'll leave the lock combination on your bike somewhere once we've seen you reach the phone box. Of course, all that running will be a strain on your weighted balls. And as for that hard cock of yours, well, we can't have you wanking away out here."

The biker grabbed my hands and thrust them into some industrial gloves whose outside was covered in a rust-coloured plastic paint over what looked like a surface of gravel. The gloves were locked on with combination locks, so that any attempt to wank would be extremely damaging to my cock.

From his pocket, the biker produced a leather hood.

Without thinking, I dropped to my knees in readiness. The hood was shabby and obviously well used and had just two eyeholes through which I had to both see and breathe. Before zipping it on over my head and securing the zipper to the collar with a padlock, the biker once again rammed a bandanna gag in my mouth.

While this was happening, the prospect had wheeled round his Master's bike and sat on it, waiting. The biker gave my balls a final squeeze and left me, on my knees, with a red arse, balls shackled, with a locked metal collar and unremovable hood, in a public car park in the middle of the night. I was shell-shocked. And randy as hell.

The biker and his slave rode off out of the bike park leaving me to start my speedy journey up the road to the roundabout. Few cars passed me, and when I heard them coming, I lay low in the ground, as there were no bushes to hide in.

The helmet and bike keys were where the biker had said. I raced back to the bike, breathing as hard as the tight hood and gag would let me.

Back at the bike, I found the combination number written in wax crayon on the tank of my bike and I unlocked the gloves. Then I realised that I couldn't see the lock on the hood and so had no way of releasing myself. I also discovered that the combination didn't unlock the ball weight.

Then I saw a note tucked under the bike seat.

Boy—

Hope you have a good ride home. I'm sure that, once there, with the use of a mirror and a strong light, you'll have no difficulty removing the hood.

Be here at midday next week if you want to enter the life of a prospect.

You are to wear a T-shirt, denim jacket, old jeans, thick socks, and strong boots. Bring the hood and gloves and padlocks. Nothing more.

If you join us, everything will be provided for you.

You are to leave your old life and be ready to make a new one.

Don't come on your bike, but take the bus. If you pass through being a prospect and enter the Chapter as a full member, you will be allowed to return to collect your bike and any other belongings.

You are to bring no money beyond the bus fare here, and nothing valuable. Leave your watch at home because time will not be under your control.

If you do not turn up I will assume you have decided not to submit yourself to me. In which case you had better find your own way out of the ball weight because I won't let you out.

And if you don't turn up, don't expect another chance. I won't visit this bike park again. We are moving on.

Ted

I fingered my ball weight and toyed with the lock, breathing deeply through the hood which I would have to wear all the way home. I pulled a bandanna out of my pocket and tied it over my nose and mouth, covering the rest of my hooded head with the helmet and goggles. I set off home, hooded, gagged and ball shackled. Was I going to return?

Once again, I knew I had no choice....

* Internet address: bandanas@dircon.co.uk

TITLE: The Prince and the Pauper
BY: davis trell
FROM: STUDSnet—San Francisco, CA

"You'll have to be bathed, young man. A little too much of London's grimy streets."

Prince Hal can't be punished for being bad. This is the boy king to be, as they say, even though he has just reached his eighteenth year. But I can be punished in his place. So now I have this great job inside the palace. I am the whipping boy.

If Hal forgoes a royal prerogative and breaks etiquette, like farting and giggling in front of the Spanish ambassador, I'll be in for it. Short, hard swats with the royal slapstick, across my bare buttocks. If Hal were to, say, flash his joint in front of Lady Wellesley, I'd have to be spanked right royally, by the Master of the Bedchamber, one Miles Houghton, so fuckin' good-looking, usually I sperm off as soon as my jerkin is removed. I encourage the prince with suggestions for activities that guarantee me a thrashing.

I look so much like him that naked in front of the mirror you can't tell prince from pauper, except his butt is white, and mine flecked with pink imprints of hand, whip, and teeth marks. And he still has the royal foreskin, while I'd been docked as a child. Often we lie under the quilted sheets in the humongous large four-poster bed, where we can draw the curtains and I tell him of my life down in Pudding Lane.

Like the time the parish priest asked for a volunteer, to help him fill the censer, arrange the altarpiece, practice the catechism, and tell my parents I'd be late home tonight.

My blue-blooded friend enjoys my red-blooded stories. Like going down to the docks, going down on the sailors, earning pennies, which I would give to my mum, and hide from my stepfather, who'd only waste it on ale.

I tell my stories of Cheapside life, in bed, having my bottom cleaned out by the regal princely tongue. He's getting better at it. I'm a good teacher. But usually when it comes time to put in the royal scepter, he makes a keflummox of it. Still, he does his best, and my buns get sticky. He licks it off himself. Extending the royal prerogative, he said one time he wanted to fuck me. He couldn't do it right, said he needed to be shown. But when I clambered on top of him, Prince Hal told me to stop. No way he was gonna let a peasant fuck the royal butt. So we went back to the stories.

"You have such an interesting life! It sounds such fun, not like here, in the boring palaces of Westminster. I wish I could go where you live and play."

He's from another world. He thinks grit and grime are cute. He has no concept. But I don't tell him the truth, I sugarcoat the reality of what it's like out there. Big mistake, as it turns out.

He gets this idea that we should switch clothes. He rubs some soot from the chimney on his face and demands that I put on his white tights, periwinkle-and-ermine robe. He climbs out the window, down the trellis, and slips out the gate, headed for London's poor quarters, where I used to live.

I could get used to the life of luxury. I eat a few of the peeled grapes, but get bored quickly.

Prince Hal follows the river, like I told him: "All the way to Whitechapel, past Blackfriars bridge, turn left and your nose will show you the way from there." For the first time, he feels free of responsibility and the court, that was so stifling. No one marks him. He feels wonderfully ignored. From the Embankment he looks down at the mighty Thames, boats passing by, laden with goods to feed the populace, his subjects. He's lost in a reverie when the stranger approaches.

From behind.

I'm fed up with grapes, so I ring the little tinkly bell, and a footman comes in and I ask for a chicken banquet and the booby thinks I'm the prince and scutters off to the kitchen to go fetch. But when he comes back, with him comes Lord Burleigh, the king's top minister, the lord chamberlain. He's come to check on my welfare. I must've said the wrong thing and he realizes I'm not the real McCoy. He goes under the bed, pulls out the royal bedpan and checks out the royal urine.

"My prince, art thou well? You know that chicken upsets the royal stomach. The doctors have said it doesn't agree with you."

"Fuck it, I'm the prince! I get what I want!" I'm emboldened. I'm gonna brazen it out.

"Sirrah, lookest thou at the ships, dreaming of adventure upon the high seas?"

The prince looks up, sees a soldier, and is mildly annoyed at the invasion of his privacy. "Thou art impertinent to address me thus. You have not my permission to speak. I gave you no leave."

The man roars with laughter.

"Cheeky young tyke! Thinkest thou art the bees knees?" He slaps Hal hard on the rump so that it smarts, and laughs again. "Don't worry, I'll pay. Three pennies is the going rate, methinks."

He grabs Hal by the arm, pulls him up as he climbs his horse, and places England's heir in his lap. He spurs

his horse on and they ride off, to a darker part of town.
There he dismounts, ties up his steed, pulls Hal down,
enters a grim alley, and expects the prince to perform.

"Suckest thou cock, boy? Show thy stuff!"

He exposes a broadsword-size penis, pulls Hal down to
it, stuffs his engorged member in between the princely lips.

Things are not going too well at the palace. I've not
been acting princely enough. The royal bedroom's full
of people who think I've gone mad.

"Leavest me alone! Get thee the fuck out, except
Miles Houghton. 'Tis my wish he should stay."

They leave, scattering like rabbits, till only Miles, my
chastiser from my whipping-boy days, remains.

"Come close. The prince wishes you to partake of a
royal request."

"What is Your Highness's wish? I'm yours to
command." He's so subservient, and I want him so.

"Ever wanted a poke up this royal ass?"

Miles looked shocked at what he takes as lèse-majesté.
But his codpiece grows forward, so I know that he might.

Meanwhile, the real prince, dressed in my hand-me-
down rags, was gobbling the cock of the soldier that had
fresh picked him up. Much bigger than Tom's, the
current whipping boy, he thought. Until then, that was
the biggest penis he'd e'er seen. But this was mancock,
and had seen many a battle, breached many a wall. It

sure tasted good as Prince Hal sucked all the taste out of this piss-stained cock.

"Prithee, boy, thou'rt good. Keep up like this and I will be delivered and feed thee a gollop of spermiage, and thou'll quaff of my dick."

Oozing and spurting like tapioca (that had to be exported from the East), the prince swallows the unfermented whey like cream, after the soldier ejaculates into the boy's brimming mouth.

Edmund de Quincey, home from the wars, is delighted with his luck. He has taken a fancy to the young stripling and decides to have sixpence more fun with the lad.

"Make we anon to the charming hostelry, The Bucket of Bones. They've a room upstairs for the likes of you and me. Sally we forth, and you'll be mine till daybreak."

The prince is overcome with the big man's charm. He thinks this is like the adventures Tom Canty, the whipping boy, has told him about. They ride off into the fast-encroaching night, and Edmund spurs hard into his steed's flanks, urging him on, causing the prince, now seated aback, to hump fortune's soldier like a puppy in heat.

The Bucket of Bones, a threadbare alehouse-slash-hostelry, a den of thieves, vagabonds, and cutpurses, is a rickety wooden shack, sawdusted to soak up bodily fluids. It smells of unmentionable odors, the air rent with musky smoke and cusswords. Everything I had told

Hal about, that had sounded romantic to the future king, he can now sample for himself. A royal turn-on.

Edmund strides to the bar, clutching his prize close, and throws down four groats on the counter, the price of that upstairs room.

Back at the royal bedchamber, I'd commanded Miles to take off the codpiece, take off the brocaded doublet, the hose, the shirt, and lie with the prince.

"Miles, thou'rt hung like a horse. Big helmet. Looking good."

"Sire, art though well? What you're proposing, if good King Henry were to discover me thus, the executioner's ax would sing its sweet song." He kneels on the expensive blankets, the disheveled satin sheets, me pushing close with my butt, my legs wrapped around his hips, his balls hanging down, the weight resting on my urchin dick, pressing up against his gorgeous erection.

"Be not afraid, Master Houghton, and serve. Take firm hold of the royal bone, taste the flesh, suck deep, finger the butt, get me ready so I can take all of you in my princely hole. The prince needs a good shagging."

"Thou speakest like a costermonger, sire, but I will do my duty. Thy princely cock thus will I take into my mouth."

"Suck softly, but hard. Use the spouting when it comes to oil up the prince's ass, so he can receive your staff, so I can contain its admirable size."

He is cautious at first, flitting glances at the oaken door, but soon gets into what he's doing and does it really well.

The one-eyed alekeeper accepts the fee for the room and pours out a measure of malmsey wine. Edmund imbibes deeply and offers the dregs to the prince, who drinks coyly, flirtatiously. Not a cock in the place remains soft.

"That youth is verily a sodomite's dream! Where'd you find him?"

"By the Embankment leaning over a balustrade. The breeze wafted and I got a glimpse of his lily-white ass, eminently fuckable."

Edmund started to boast of his conquest, but his face goes silly as he crumples, the blow on the head unexpected, but effective.

Three men, filthy, teeth black, surround the prince.

"A marketable boy," crows one.

"Ay, a sellable boy," croons another, "to the swashbucklers out on the Spanish Main, where a cabin boy's the only entertainment on the lonely high seas."

I lie on my belly, gripping the lacy pillows to stifle my moans, tearing the fabric with my teeth, as Miles rides atop me slamming all ten inches of pleasure into my three-inch-deep hole. He had penetrated, got his rosy-red tip to force its way in, rammed the shaft as far as it would go. He drives it in farther. I want that rod so bad!

He pushes hard, keeps thrusting, each blow entering me farther, deeper.

"Jesu, Jesu...harder...harder...more...more..."

When he comes, it is magnificent. He hugs me hard till all is spent, till I am filled, till it splashes out and the hot come cools in the air, but not before warming me thoroughly throughout.

He lies on top, releasing me gently as he pulls out his mighty weapon. He kisses the nape of my neck, my shoulders, back, slips down to my butt and starts to lick off the sticky sperm and my sore-tired asshole. His ministrations are tender. He strokes my trembling, quivering buttcheeks and then notices the prince's butt is marked with pink welts, and remembers who put them there. Him. A lack of foreskin is the final clue.

"Tom Canty! The whipping boy! Thou'rt not the prince!" He puts a silver dagger against my throat.

I tell him what happened.

"The prince! He's out there in Cheapside?!? You let him go to the worst—the dirtiest part of town?"

"Hey, he's the prince. How'm I supposed to stop him?"

He dresses rapidly, tells me to do the same, and jumps out the window onto his horse, waiting below, shouting back at me to follow. We gallop off to my birthplace.

"How the fuck do you expect to find him?" I yell, but my words fall on deaf ears.

Miles's thought process runs thus-wise: the real

prince has run off to go to the vilest part of town. From what that idiot Canty tells me, he's romanticized the shittiest region of the city. The prince is eager to get laid. I know something of the sodomite underworld. Where would I go?

The prince shows no fear, though surrounded on all sides. "Unhand me, varlets. Obey me, your prince! Touch me not!" Not only do they touch him, they grab him roughly, bind him with rope. They know a ship due to sail at midnight, so they bundle him, squirming, in a baggage cart, normally used for horse meat. The wagon rumbles ominously toward the dockside over cobblestone streets.

The prince works hard to free himself, the skin tearing round his wrists and ankles, as he is bumped and joggled in the back of the cart. One finger free, then another, then a hand. He undoes the knots around his ankles. He sits up, seeing the backs of his captors who are urging the horses on.

"Help, help!" he screams loudly. "Save your prince!"

Is it luck? Coincidence? Lack of authorial skill? Just at that moment, Miles Houghton and Tom Canty hear the prince's cry. Miles stops the stampeding wagon, slaughters the ruffians, and rescues the boy who was born to be king.

"Thou'rt my savior! I will shower you with gold, give you an earldom, knight thee—But first, could we rest awhile at a charming hostelry I know? I left a friend there. We have unfinished business…but we'll need four groats. Do you have any cash?"

All is well come the morning, after the wildest night….

Miles got his earldom. Edmund's employed as royal bodyguard, and I got the worst whipping of my entire life.

So, dear readers, you've heard my story. It's time to bid adieu to the pauper who was known formerly as Prince.

* Internet address: davistrell@aol.com or davist@dsp.com

TITLE: Nights
BY: Ajay Vanden
FROM: big tedd's—Melbourne, OZ

Reading about all these guys getting it on here made me think about last night. You see, I spent the weekend over at a friend's place. He's straight and he doesn't know I'm gay, so it does complicate things a little. Anyway, we slept in his room with me in a rollaway and him in his own bed, in opposite corners of the room, which meant that we could look over at each other's sleeping form. I had a restless sleep 'cause the house had duct heating which came on occasionally. I wasn't used to the noise, so it kept waking me up. Once during the night, I heard a faint sound of blankets rustling. As I listened, I realised it was rhythmic and coming from Matthew's end of the room. My straight-arrow mate was jerking off with me in the room!

To make sure that it wasn't my imagination, I pulled the covers off quietly and snuck out of bed. The roll-away squeaked as I did so. I froze on the spot. The sound from the other side stopped, and then resumed. Quietly I crawled, commando style, across the room, till I knelt beside Matt's bed. The noise was louder here, but still not enough to convince me I wasn't hearing things. I could see his form sprawled out in the bed, but could not make out if there was a bulge in the area of my desire. My heart was pounding in my head so loudly, I was sure it was a bass drum that would wake Matt up.

My hand snuck out cautiously to where I thought his groin should be, and hovered a centimeter above his blankets. Suddenly the blankets rose up high, taking my hand with it before descending again. A mere second or two passed before the blankets rose once more. A sob of joy escaped my throat as I realised I had just felt the boy of my dreams jerking off right before me. What should I do? I wanted to put my hands underneath the blankets and feel the steel hardness of the flesh they concealed. I wanted to pull back the covers and take that pole of granite and lovingly jerk it up and down for him. I wanted to take that mountain of manhood and slide my lips over it, sucking the essence of his life out through the cockslit. I was sure Matt felt my hand over his groin, but he gave no indication of having done so nor showed any sign of being aware of my presence. I saw this as a negative sign and against my desire. I returned to my bed and popped my nut thinking blissful thoughts of what could have been.

The dawning of another day streamed through the curtain slit to fall upon my slumbering body, stirring me to wakefulness. Across the room, my dream god slept, with no sign of having come anywhere to be seen. My morning hard-on craved for release, so I pulled back the covers enough so that my pole could be seen straining through my briefs. I laid my hand beside it to make things even more obvious, and lovingly stroked that throbbing flesh with a lazy finger, all the while sending thoughts across to Matthew, imploring him to wake and see my monkey.

In answer to my thoughts, he woke. I saw him sit up and look across the room to where my covers rested just beneath my hips and the horny hardness lurked. I closed my eyes, willing him to come over and touch me. My cock jerked at the thought. I heard him take a step or two, but I did not know in which direction. The suspense was killing me, but I dared not open my eyes. Moments passed like eons. Indecision hung in the air like a spectre. Then—in the blink of an eye—he was gone. I was left with my throbbing flesh untouched. The boy had gone to relieve himself, but would return soon enough. When he returns, I thought, he will sense my desire and act upon that which had built up over the night within these walls.

What did we do? Well, since I'm almost out of time, it will have to wait, like I did.

Can you keep it hard till then? <grin>

* Internet address: mindmeld@geocities.com

Another dull evening in the bar. On the one hand, I was
regretting that I'd gone there on my bike, which meant I
couldn't have the beer or three that would have made
the evening at least bearable; but at the same time, I was
glad that I hadn't wasted money on beer and a taxi. The
bar had just closed, and rather than hang around in the
bright closing-time lights, I left.

I was squatting, removing the disk lock from my
bike's front brake disk, when I noticed that a bike had
pulled up near me. I glanced up: a Kawasaki GT750.
Nice…I'd nearly bought one myself. As I stood up, I
checked out the guys on the bike. Both were wearing
full bike leathers, both were well-built, with the pillion
perhaps a little bigger than the rider. The pillion was

wearing a helmet with a shaded visor, so I got no real idea of him, but the rider... You can't see that much of a guy's face when he's wearing a full face helmet, but I knew I was interested in what I could see—a thick dark 'stache that made my asshole itch and eyes that knew what the 'stache was doing.

They sat there alongside the parked cars as I pocketed the disk lock, got on my bike, and started him up (all my bikes have been boys). I'd been in the bar for a couple of hours, so he took a couple of minutes to warm up. They waited. When I moved off, they followed.

"So," I thought, "I might be in luck after all."

As I approached the first major junction, I slowed, letting them overtake me, hoping for an indication of where they were going. They pulled up on my left but weren't indicating a left turn. We were at the front of the queue, so they had no real need to indicate. Did they intend going left or straight ahead?

I took a chance and took off straight ahead as soon as the lights changed. A glance in the mirror told me they were following, as they did through several more sets of traffic lights. I was doing fifty down the dual carriageway (you're not really speeding until you're doing twice the legal limit) when they overtook me, the pillion indicating that I should take the next right. I followed them through increasingly narrow side streets until they stopped and parked. I waited in the road, ready to ride on. There seemed to be a brief snatch of conversation between the two of them, and then the pillion approached me. He raised his visor slightly and spoke.

"He says you should park your bike and follow me." He stood at the kerb while I parked and locked my bike.

Although the rider had entered the house through the front door, the pillion led me around the house to the back. As I walked up the path, I removed my crash helmet, but the pillion left his on. I still had no idea what he looked like. At the back door, the pillion turned to me and told me to take off my jacket. As he unlocked the door he glanced over his shoulder and, almost as an afterthought, added, "and the T-shirt."

"Okay," I thought, "none of the let's-get-to-know-each-other shit first. Sounds good." As I raised my T-shirt over my head, his fist jabbed into my belly, winding me. I doubled over trying to get my breath, more surprised than hurt by the unexpected attack. I felt his hands at my neck, and then a collar being fitted. He dragged the T-shirt off my arms, pulled me upright again and pushed me face first against the wall.

"Don't speak. Put your arms behind you."

The handcuffs weren't a surprise, nor was the blindfold. Taking hold of the collar from behind, he guided me into the house. Judging by the smell and the hard flooring, we seemed to have entered the house by a door into the kitchen. There were a few paces over carpet; then it was back to a hard floor. He let go of the collar and I remained standing where I was. I heard a door close.

A new voice: "Get his boots and jeans off."

A slight rattle. I felt a chain being fastened to the collar. Then my right foot was pulled away from me and the boot and sock removed. I lost my balance and started to choke as my neck took my full weight. I was helped up quickly, and then my left foot was pulled forward. "You'll be more careful this time, won't you?" This time I kept my balance, and soon he was undoing my belt and zipper. As he pulled my leather jeans down, he ran his hand over my ass.

"I'll give you a chance to play with that later. Get the fucking jeans off."

Having removed my jeans, the one guy backed away and I sensed the other move behind me. "I'm going to be very generous to you, boy."

"Sir?"

"I'm going to let you have a look at him." Standing directly behind me, he removed the blindfold and held my head in both hands, controlling my line of vision. "You. Naked. Now."

The pillion undressed quickly, yet made it appear unhurried. He was well muscled without being an anatomy chart, with a thick pelt of dark fur across his chest and arms. Suddenly I realised that he was wearing a collar. When he removed his boots, I could see the same dark hair along the tops of his feet. He dropped his jeans, and I only barely registered the hair on his legs as my attention fixed on his dick. The top guy obviously knew what was going on in my mind: he pressed his crotch against my ass.

"Getting a little hungry down there? You'll have to wait for that."

The pillion folded his leathers and turned to place them neatly on top of mine. As he turned, I saw that his back was almost as hairy as his chest. Still, I could see the fading bruises and marks of previous scenes.

"Show's over."

The blindfold was back and the top guy moved away from me. "Tie his balls up."

While the pillion tightly wrapped a length of leather thong around my dick and balls, the top guy unlocked the handcuffs and lifted my arms above my head. Then he fitted leather restraints around my wrists and fastened the restraints to a metal bar above my head. As the pillion knotted the thong, I could feel the pressure in my dick building.

"Tit clamps. Two pairs."

A brief pause—and the pillion was standing in front of me. He was being tied to the same bar as I was. Then there was the sudden pressure/pain of tit clamps. Moving a little and hearing the pillion's sudden intake of breath made me realise that we were sharing the two pairs: our nipples chained together. There was a pull on my balls as the spare ends of thong were tied to the pillion's cockring. Our dicks were pressed against each other's bellies, each of us leaking precome onto the other. He pulled his chest away from me slightly and I leaned my head back and groaned as the clamps bit into me. His mouth came down over mine, the hair of our 'stashes mingling as our tongues searched each other's mouths. He leaned more and more heavily onto me and I pushed against him.

I heard the belt land on my ass before I felt it. The first rush of pain ran down my legs and up my torso. By now I was leaning so far backward that I could only jump forward: the pillion had been protecting me (and himself) from what he knew was coming. I moaned as the secondary pain started, the blood rushing back to the site of the pain. He held my mouth. I heard the crack of the belt again and this time felt him stiffen against me as he dealt with the pain. Still, he held my mouth. My turn again. This time I cried out when the belt landed, though we quickly found each other's mouths again. I kept pushing against him, relishing the feel of his fur against me, of his dick pressing into my belly, of my dick sliding against his belly. He tensed again as another blow landed. The next blow on my ass was harder again. I cried out and jerked, pulling on the tit clamps. It was rapidly followed by another blow on his ass. He must have twisted as he jumped at the pain: it felt as though my left nipple was being torn off. The beating continued with the pillion getting the worst of it, to judge from the noise of the belt.

We had lost each other's mouths: no comfort there.

Instead, there was the constant jerky pull on my tits and the occasional surge of deep, low pain as one or other of us pulled on the other's balls by moving the wrong way.

Silence. I was panting heavily, my breath catching occasionally, though I was determined not to cry with the pain. My ass was on fire. I could feel the immediate pain of the damaged skin and the deeper pain of the bruised muscles. My tits were almost numb, but my balls were already beginning to forget. The pillion moved slightly, and I was surprised to realise that I still had a hard-on. Not that I was very concerned about that at that moment: I was more concerned with resting after the beating. I felt the top guy untie the knot in the thong that held my balls to the pillion's. He took the two loose ends and tied them in an extra knot about my balls. Then I felt him release the pillion's wrists. There was a brief pull on each nipple as he took the clamps off the pillion and let the two chains fall against me. The pillion stood close against me and kissed me before backing away slightly. I screamed as he removed the clamps from my nipples and then gripped them tightly to prevent the blood rushing in too quickly.

As the pain subsided, I relaxed against him, using him for support. A stray thought crossed my mind: I had no idea what the top guy looked like, other than in full bike gear. The pillion released the restraints from the bar and pushed down on my shoulders. Gratefully, I sank to my knees. Although very turned on by what was happening,

I needed time to recover from the beating I—no, we—had just taken. I sagged on the floor, trying to bring my breathing back to normal. A hand on my collar pulled me upright. I could feel the hair on the pillion's legs against my back, and then I felt the stream of piss on my chest. I leaned forward, hoping at least to get the piss into my face. It stopped. Then there was a hand on my forehead. I could feel the leather of the top guy's boots against my legs and the tip of his dick on my lips. I tried to lunge forward, but the hand held me back. At the same time, the pillion squatted behind me and held my arms. Helpless, I waited. My attention was divided between the two men's dicks. I could feel the pillion's pressing against my back. The top guy's was right in front of me, but out of reach.

I felt a dribble of precome slide down the length of my own dick and moaned. That seemed to give the top guy the cue he wanted: he pushed his dick into my mouth and continued pissing. I soon established a rhythm of swallowing the piss, then letting it fill my mouth again as I worked on his dick for a few seconds before being forced to swallow again. The stream slowed as he got harder and I found myself being allowed a little more movement. I leaned forward to take as much of his dick in my mouth as I could. I felt the pillion moving behind me, and then his dick was pressing against my asshole. The top guy pulled away from me and I heard leather meeting flesh. I counted six strokes, starting, it seemed, with heavy and ending with vicious.

"You play with his ass when I tell you to, not before." The top guy kicked me over and with his boot moved me around until I was lying on my back. "Sit on his face and get your hole wet. And better make sure it's properly wet: it's the only lube you're getting."

The pillion squatted over my face and lowered himself very slowly. For some seconds, all I could feel of him was the heat from his flesh and the hairs on his ass brushing my skin. And, of course, there was that smell of old and fresh sweat with a hint of shit. I strained upward with my mouth to find his asshole. Once I found it, he continued to lower himself until my head was resting on the floor. I worked all around the hole, sometimes licking, sometimes biting, before probing the hole with my tongue.

As my tongue entered his asshole, I could feel the top guy's boot on my balls. The pillion leaned forward and took my dick in his mouth. I spread his asshole with my fingers and, remembering what the top guy had said, spat into it. Then back to licking and biting around the hole before spreading and spitting again. At the same time, the pillion was still sucking on my dick and the top guy was working on my balls with his boot. At a word from the top guy, the pillion stood up. Then I felt something heavy and made of rubber placed on my face.

After a moment or two, I realised it must be a

buttplug. The pillion squatted down again: I could feel his weight as he spread his ass over the buttplug. I pushed upward to help get it into his ass. He worked slowly and methodically, shifting from side to side, working the plug into his guts. I could taste the occasional dribble of my own saliva flavoured with his shit as it dribbled out. His breathing became faster as he approached the widest point of the plug, and then, with a gasp, it slid home. He stood up and lifted me into a sitting position before indicating that I should be on all fours.

"Now you can play with his ass."

I was half-expecting him simply to thrust into me, so the heat and wetness of his tongue and the scraping of his beard came as a surprise. I pushed back into his face, keeping my legs spread as far as I could, as he took his turn to spit into my ass. I didn't know which I wanted more: for him to continue rimming me or for him to get his dick into me. But the choice wasn't mine to make. Abruptly, his mouth was gone from my ass and in its place was the head of his dick. He pushed in firmly and his dick slid home without any of the usual problems I have about having to take it slowly. He put his arms around my chest and pulled me into a more upright position.

I felt the warm flow in my guts as he pissed inside me. Just as I became aware of the smell of cigar smoke, the top guy pushed his dick into my mouth and started pissing. It wouldn't be the first time I've had a dick in my mouth and another in my ass, but it was the first time I've had both of them pissing into me. The top guy's flow soon stopped: he'd already emptied his bladder over and into me once, but the pillion kept on pissing.

I started to work on the top guy's dick, but he pulled away from me. It was a relief when the pillion stopped pissing: any more, and I'd be in danger of cramping. The top guy clipped the wrist restraints together behind my back while the pillion held me 'round my belly with one hand and 'round my throat with the other. My guts were full; I clenched my sphincter in an effort to retain the piss and was rewarded by the pillion thrusting a few times inside my ass. Abruptly, the top guy pulled the blindfold off me. I blinked at the sudden light, despite its dimness, and at the stinging sweat which suddenly ran into my eyes. As my vision cleared, I had my first real look at him: boots, chaps, Muir cap, hair every-where.... He pulled on his cigar and blew the smoke into my face.

"I want you to see what happens next."

A few more pulls on the cigar, and he squatted down in front of me. He knocked the ash off the end of the cigar and held it in front of my face. The pillion gripped me more tightly. I looked from the burning tip of the cigar to his eyes and back again. He stroked the right side of my chest with his left hand, and then moved closer with the cigar in his right hand. My eyes flickered from the cigar to his eyes to the cigar.... He stroked the air half an inch from my skin: I could feel the heat and flinched. The pillion squeezed me briefly. Another pull on the cigar and another, closer, air-stroke. My breath was coming short and shallow. He reached down with his left hand and held my hard-on for a few seconds, smearing the precome around the head. He raised one eyebrow. Then the cigar again. This time it touched.

I cried out and tried to jerk away, but the pillion had me held fast. The pain made me clench my ass around his dick, and he responded by thrusting into me. The top guy reached down to my dick again, but slapped it this time. My dick was so hard, it ached. Then he returned to my chest. I tried to keep quiet, but the pain made me first cry out again, and soon I was screaming as he traced lines in my flesh. The pillion held me immobile as I tried to struggle. I was on the verge of crying when the top guy stood up, took a deep pull on his cigar, and leaned over me. His mouth fastened over mine. He exhaled the smoke into my lungs. He broke away, took another pull, and again filled my lungs with his smoke. After the third time he did this, I was beginning to feel dizzy from the smoke, but found that I had recovered myself from being burned sufficiently (not that I hadn't got off on it: it just took a lot out of me) that I was enjoying the close contact, the tobacco taste of his spit, the gift of his secondhand smoke.

He stood up and pulled over a chair which he sat on with his legs spread. He beckoned, and the two of us crawled over so my face was directly in front of his dick. He leaned back in the chair, pulling on the cigar. Permission had unmistakably been granted, so I started licking at his balls before moving up the shaft to take his dick in my mouth. At the same time, the pillion started fucking my ass in earnest. The top guy's breathing changed as I worked on his dick, getting faster, almost panting. I glanced up briefly to see him clenching the cigar between his teeth as his hands came down to grip my head. It changed from me sucking him off to him fucking my mouth. I reached down and grabbed my hard, wet dick. My ass was beginning to leak: I could feel trickles of piss running down my legs as the pillion fucked me. The top guy pushed my head down farther on his dick and held it there as he came in my throat. He pulled back slowly to allow me to breathe, though he allowed me to keep his dick in my mouth. He nodded at the pillion, who obviously was close to coming himself. He thrust harder and faster into me, each stroke hitting my prostate. I needed both hands on the floor just to keep my balance. All too soon, he was coming....

The top guy pushed me away from his dick and the pillion pulled me into a more upright position. "When you look in the mirror now"—I winced as his fingers traced the pattern of the cigar burns on my chest—

"you'll see my initials." He nodded at the pillion and left the room.

His dick still inside my ass, the pillion took hold of my aching dick and, with a few strokes, brought me to the point of coming.

"Let go of my piss!"

A few more strokes and I came, at the same time letting his piss flow over the both of us. The pillion pushed me away from him and unfastened the restraints around my wrists. He stood up and walked over to the door. As he opened it, he said, "Clean yourself up and get out. He wants you naked at the back door at eight o'clock tomorrow night." A brief smile—and he left.

* Internet address: beartrap@vault.posnet.co.uk

TITLE: Blond Bear
BY: Ray Cornett, aka Writer@seattle.com
FROM: Rendezvous—Seattle, WA

Blond bear. That was the only way to describe him.
Though he didn't fit all the "bear" requirements either....

He was about 5'7" tall, blond hair *(everywhere!)*, icy
blue eyes. Very butch young man. It surprised me a little
that he was in this bar. In a bar at all, for that matter. He
didn't look old enough.

But there he was nonetheless, playing pinball and
sipping beer. I walked over and asked if he minded if I
watched. I didn't bother to tell him I wanted to watch
him, not the game he was playing. He played well, too.
Watching his muscles move in quick reflex was very
nice. Made me wonder what else he did well. After a
little small talk and a very good score on his game, he
walked over to the bar and sat down. I wanted him, but

couldn't tell if he was interested (something I'm usually very good at).

I picked a table where I could watch him some more, and waited to see if he *was* interested, or if springtime in the Northwest was making me too horny to be sensible. After watching him move around the bar, or just sitting there, I figured he wasn't. (Damn it.) I'd had enough to drink, and didn't want to get frustrated over this little cutie, so I grabbed my belongings and left the bar.

As I was leaving, I noticed him standing out front at the bus stop looking around. I figured, what the heck, the very least I'll get is a little nice chatting.

I stopped at the bus stop. "Could I offer you a ride somewhere?"

"Sure. I hate waiting around for the bus." He got in, and off we went.

Turned out he lived in the north end, a miserable bus ride from where we were. So I was feeling very much the Good Samaritan as we drove along. Now that I was really close to him, I noticed that he looked a little closer to my age. Still very handsome, though. As we drove and talked about the happenings of the day and other small talk, I felt a hand brush briefly against my thigh. Not being the shy type, I decided to change the topic of conversation.

"You know, when I saw you in the bar, I found you very attractive. I hope you don't mind me saying that. I know you must hear it a lot."

He was blushing badly at this point and just said, "Not really." He drifted off into mumbling.

"I know a nice place out here we can just sit and chat for a while, if you're interested."

He replied that he was, and I took a little detour. I parked the car on one of the more secluded streets in the north end, and shut it off.

"So, tell me about yourself," I said.

He told me about his work, hobbies, stuff like that. About that time, I noticed his wedding band.

"Are you married?" I asked.

"Yes, I am. But I find there are things that my wife can't or won't do for me that I need."

"Oh?" I replied. "Like what?" Leading question, I know.

"Well, I like being fucked." He said it so softly, I had to ask him to repeat it.

"Really. That can be a bit of a problem," I said, putting my hand on his thigh. He didn't jump or react badly, so I slid my hand to the inner part of his thigh. Still no bad reaction.

We continued talking, trying to keep the silence from getting deafening. I kept making little massaging motions with my hand. After a few moments, he undid his seat belt and slid down a little in the seat. I took this as a go-ahead and started massaging the main muscle that runs up the inside of the legs. He seemed to like it. He was definitely getting more relaxed about me touching him. I moved my hand up a little bit, to the seam at his crotch, just barely touching his scrotum through the material as I continued to massage his leg.

He closed his eyes and sighed a little, so I got more aggressive. I moved my hand up far enough that I could rub against the sack holding his balls, and the part of his ass that was accessible. He started shifting a little as I got closer to his asshole. Moving into it as I stroked him. He was really getting into this.

I leaned over and gave him a little kiss on the cheek. He turned to face me and started kissing me back. Nice kisser, too! I asked if he would like to move to the back-seat where we would have a little more room to maneuver. He complied readily.

Now, trying to do anything in a Pinto Pony with a manual transmission is not an easy feat, let alone when both guys are pretty fair sized. We DO manage when we have to though.<g>

Without the brake and stick shift between us, I was freer to let my hands roam about his body. (And he had a very nice body, too!) We took off our shirts and I started sucking on his ample nipples. I thought he was going to jump through the roof!

"What are you doing!?"

"Don't you like it?" I said. "It's something I enjoy a great deal."

"No, don't stop. It feels wonderful! It's just that nobody's done that before."

I couldn't believe it. He had perfect sucking nipples. I let a hand move down onto his hardening cock. He moaned lightly as I did. When I slipped my hand into his pants, the head of his cock was dripping with precome. It was great, made things slippery enough to jack on him a little.

Eventually I persuaded him to take off his pants. That way I could get at what I really wanted. His ass.

We kept kissing and groping for a long time. When he felt my hard cock, he gave a little gasp.

"You're good sized aren't you?"

I couldn't deny it, and it was ACHING to fuck him. Even if we had to do it parked out here in the boonies! "Yes, I am. And I want to use it on you, soon."

He shied away a little. Guess he was afraid of getting hurt. It was easy enough to calm him. (It wasn't the first time I had to calm someone before doing that.)

I just kept stroking him. I knew that if he relaxed, it wouldn't hurt at all. (Wish I could convince myself of that at times.) But it was lots of fun just playing with him. I grabbed some lube out of my work bag (never leave home without it!), applied a little to my fingers, and started playing with his ass, sticking a finger and then two up his ass to try to loosen things up. In time, it paid off. Even if I hadn't gotten him horny enough to succeed at fucking him, I got him aroused enough to try it.

(Now comes the tricky part.)

I put the passenger seat all the way forward and tilted

the seat back forward as well. Then, when I put my knees on the floor of the car, I had something to support my legs. (Not terribly comfortable, but it does work.) Grabbing a condom out of my bag, I applied it and a good amount of lube. I positioned the head of my cock at the opening to his anus, just teasing him a little, starting to push in and backing right out again. He started whimpering....

I couldn't wait much longer. I VERY slowly and carefully pushed my cock into him, just an inch or so. He winced, and I pulled back out. (That was not working.) I relubed my fingers and tried a little more massage. This time he relaxed more quickly. I was able to add the second finger almost immediately. I decided to try for something a little bigger....

Slowly, once again, I pushed just the head of my cock inside him. He didn't wince this time. He even seemed to be relaxed enough to want more. I complied gladly. Very slowly, I pushed farther and farther into him. He really seemed to enjoy it. He reached the point that he could give his ass muscles an occasional squeeze. It was a very good feeling.

When I got about an inch from the hilt, his eyes widened dramatically. I started pulling out. Sometimes getting everything in can be a little painful. But he grabbed my butt, and started pulling me back in. (Granted, he didn't have to pull *too* hard. He had a *wonderful* ass!) I resumed pushing, and managed to get all the way in this time. A wonderful feeling, being completely buried in another person. Feeling his balls rubbing into the hair in my crotch. I started moving in and out of him, slowly. The feeling was great!

Sometimes a slow fuck is the best in the world. I applied a little lube to his cock and balls, rubbing them as I moved slowly in and out of him. We were both really getting into it. The car rocked gently as we did. As I fucked him, I leaned over and started sucking one of his nipples. Before I knew it, I felt a warm rush between our bellies. He didn't even get the chance to scream. He looked up at me rather sheepishly, like he was going to try to explain what just happened. Obviously, he didn't need to.

"Boy!" I said. "You must like having your nipples sucked more than you realized."

He replied something about the combination of feelings being more than he could handle. It all caught him by surprise. I didn't feel the need to explain. It felt great to me; at least, I knew I was satisfying him.

I increased my speed slightly. He enjoyed that feeling almost as much as I did. He started moaning. I leaned back over him, sucking on him again, and rubbing my belly against his cock and balls, trying to see if I could make him come again.

I could tell I was getting close to coming; the head of my cock started getting that familiar blood rush.... I had to try to get him off again. Being in the rather confined space of my car, I knew I couldn't get down low enough to actually suck on his cock. Had to try something... I arched my back slightly, giving me a little more room to get a hand in at his cock, and sucked on his nipple some more. (For someone who had never tried it, he was really getting off on it.) He was starting to get good and hard again. I raised myself off him, taking him firmly in hand. I applied some fresh lube and started pumping like mad, pumping faster on his ass as I did.

A few more good pumps, and he started shooting all over himself. What a scene! It made me *too* hot. I was *so* close. I thrust deep and hard. He screamed a little and suddenly I was shooting inside him. "YES!" was about all I could manage to say. Just about all other brain function had ceased.

I extracted myself from him. I cleaned things a little and asked if he was all right, wanting to make sure I hadn't hurt him with that final thrust.

"No, I'm great. It's just that your cock got so big. I was glad you came when you did. I probably couldn't take too much of that size."

He did just fine, and I assured him of this.

We sat there for a little while, talking about things—his situation at home, and mine. I dropped him off near his house. He asked me for my phone number as he got out of my car. I gave it to him, of course. Don't know if he'll ever use it, but sure hope he does.

* Internet address: Writer@seattle.com

TITLE: Guarding Adam
BY: Robin Man
FROM: STUDSnet—San Francisco, CA

The parking garage stank of human offal and vomit, the
accumulated refuse of two hundred years of neglect and
squatters. It was cool here, though, and dark. Since the
sun went funny, we didn't get to see a whole lot of dark
anymore since even the fucking moon was lit up like a
neon sign at night. You could get burned by it now, if
you were not careful, but most people were. That is, the
ones who had not died in the first series of flares over a
century ago.

I waited for my contact, idly fingering the butt of my
gun. I wanted to pace. I did some of my best thinking
while pacing, but too many people thought you were
nervous when you did that. If this guy was as Corp as
my people said he was, it would not do to look nervous.

Soon there was the hum of an engine, and a small black car pulled up near the brace where we were supposed to meet. I watched from the shadows, switching my left eye to imaging IR. The car was well insulated to prevent IR spying, but I watched their air-conditioning exhaust. The macrocomp in my hindbrain analyzed the outgassing and estimated two humans, approximately adult male. I was satisfied and stepped out around the pillar. The form of the car irised open, and I saw a black-suited driver, his eyes wrapped in a VR web. He turned to me, and I felt the sweep of ultrasonics across my chest. Slowly I walked forward, hands visible and the longcoat swept back to reveal my bare chest and jeans. I tried to keep it casual, accepted the datachip from the driver and watched as the car closed up again and silently hummed off back to the surface.

I retreated to a quiet corner and slid the chip into the universal port on my wrist.

A man appeared to rez up in front of me. He was dressed immaculately, his creases so sharp they probably cut flesh. He appeared in his late 40s, a touch of frost at his temples, and a middle-Euro cast to his features. It wasn't him, of course, if my employer really was a "him." Just another VR construct. At least he didn't skimp. This was not "standard business executive 45."

The image turned and drew a cigar out of its pocket. It flared to life and he began to speak in a sonorous voice. "Mr. Mason. Your services come highly recommended by a very interesting array of people. This chip contains the first half of your fee as well as all the personal information you should require. A simple bit of bodyguarding."

With that, he turned. Behind him was a young man my age, hair short and black, with a nicely lean muscled body. My cock gave an involuntary twitch as the image walked forward and waved slightly. He seemed a little shy and not a bit conscious of his beauty. "Hi, I'm Adam," he said and then faded away. Mr. Euro was back, wreathed in a cloud of smoke. "Adam is my nephew, and your charge for the next two weeks. He is a programmer, working on the latest series of data-transformation algorithms for my company. He is coming to the SanFranMetro area tonight on the nine-o-five suborbital from Bonn. Meet him there. To him, you are Daniel Conner, his guide and driver. Keep him safe for the two weeks, and the rest of this is yours."

He pulled a small black chipcase from his vest and "handed" it to me. I "accepted" and felt the snap of the money transfer. Its primary job done, the image faded away. I could still "feel" the data about Adam in there, and dumped it to my onboard processors and then erased the chip. I checked my balance and whistled.

I had about two hours before I had to be at Trans-Central, so I had to scoot.

Traffic on the Thirty-third wasn't all that bad, and certainly not for me. My bike weaved through the lines of creeping vehicles and beetlelike buses. The moon was at exactly half tonight, so I didn't bother with the glasses or UV screen. The searing air felt good to me, and the wind whipped under my coat to caress my bare chest. I put the cycle on autopilot, pulled a shirt from the back cargo compartment, and laced it up. Got to look good for the kid, at least. I gunned the cycle again and whipped through a barricade, jumping into the airport parking lot and coming to rest by the main doors. "Guard," I said to the cycle, and it folded up into its rest mode. I pushed through the doors and went in search of Adam.

He wasn't hard to find, and that was bad. Two other men had him between them when I found him, and were quickly making their way down to the subways on the escalator. I got on the escalator and in a few seconds of judicious pushing and shoving I was right behind them. I reached around and japped one guy hard in the ribs with a short punch. I felt the rib give way like a twig and helped it up and into his lung in one smooth motion. My other hand found the pressure point in the other guy's armpit and crushed it in a single wet snap. Mr. Left rolled into the railing, driving the razor-sharp rib into contact with a whole host of other parts. He slumped, stunned and gurgling. Mr. Right simply went unconscious, and I maneuvered him into the crowd. They would keep him upright until they parted at the bottom. Likewise for his partner. I snaked one arm around Adam's chest and pushed him forward, doing more shoving until we got to the bottom long before the other guys would. I wanted to be out of the terminal before they closed it down. Adam turned to me, shocked. His eyes were wide with fear, and rightly so. Kidnappings of this sort rarely turn out well for the victim, and he had probably been briefed on that since he was a kid. Some of his friends had probably not made it out of grade school.

"It's OK, I'm your guide, Mr. Laker. This way, please." I had one hand on his arm and hustled him out of the terminal. He relaxed a bit and let me guide him, which relaxed ME a bit. A smooth operation—one, two, three. We were out in the lot, the mechabike already unfolding into a speed config at my command, inside of twenty seconds. I juiced it and we were on the road before the barricades snapped up behind us, sealing off the area. We were halfway to my place when the first news reports began to circulate.

Adam's arms were around my chest, and his left hand was spread out across one pec. His grip was sure and strong, and I could feel the lean suppleness of his body against my back as we weaved through traffic at better than a hundred miles per hour. He clung to me like a squirrel, and I juiced the bike some more, feeling his grip tighten. It was a good feeling, and I started hotdogging a bit to put the fear of God into him. His arms tightened some more, and he laid his head on my shoulder, his eyes shut tight against the wind and grit. I leaned forward, and we picked up more speed, Gs tugging at us both. I slung us off on a short exit, and then slowed dramatically. Adam's eyes eased open and he gasped for breath against me. Like I said, it was a good feeling, him pressing into me like that.

"You OK?"

He just nodded, eyes still narrowed against the whipping wind. I slowed some more, and turned down into the old garage where I made my home. Doors slid open and shut as I sent the right codes at the right time, and finally I stepped off the bike, pulling Adam with me. The cycle obediently folded into recharge configuration, and I was left alone with this trembling kid.

He was my age, 25, but I thought of him as a kid. He was some Corpboy, raised in a closed walled community where they still had lemonade stands and cookouts. I suppose no one had the heart to tell them the last lemon trees shriveled and died in the searing sun fifty years ago.

I put my hand on his shoulder and guided him into the living room. He slumped down on the couch and I sat beside him after shucking the coat. "You OK?" I asked again, touching his chin and bringing his eyes into line with mine. He had good eyes, soft and brown, and my cock pressed uncomfortably against my jeans. His lips were rosy and he had perfect even white teeth. His neck was strong though, and his arms had been tight against my body the whole trip. He had some muscle on him, and not vat-grown either. I knew the difference. I put my hand on his shoulder and massaged it, then slid it down Adam's arm. Hard sleek muscle met my inspection. I smiled, hoping to relax him. I squeezed his arm once more and got up to get us something to drink. "Beer?" I called out to him.

"Yeh," came the tentative reply a few seconds later.

"You're safe, Adam. I'm the guide you were supposed to meet." I called from the kitchen. I padded back to the living room to find him standing and staring into my aquarium. I made a noise so he wouldn't be spooked, and sat his beer down. He came over and upended it, his throat working until it was half-empty.

"Thirsty and scared, huh? Anyone ever grab you before?"

"Uh…no. No. I mean I had the defence classes and everything.…"

"And they didn't work, did they?" He flushed with embarrassment, and I smiled. "No need to feel bad. Those guys were pros. You never had a chance with them."

"So how—?"

"I'm a pro, too." I shot him a smile. I unlaced my shirt and shrugged out of it, throwing the neosilk into the hamper across the room.

"Oh." Adam finished his beer, and sat there, his eyes snapping around at every sound.

I shook my head and sat down beside him. I put my hand on his shoulder again, and gave him a friendly squeeze. "You seem pretty strong. Those classes didn't go totally to waste."

"Uh, yeh. I lift and stuff, and my uncle has a personal trainer for me. I try to keep in shape."

Interesting attitude for a Corpboy. "Care to use my sets? It'll get some of that tension out of you...." He smiled gratefully and I showed him my small gym. He surveyed the equipment, and picked what I would have picked for him. He was pretty good, then, and knew his limits as well as what he wanted to accomplish. I was starting to like him more and more. That intensified a lot when Adam stripped to his waist, and didn't stop there. He had a nice body, long muscled like a swimmer's and hard with strength. His skin was a smooth even brown, mixed heritage: a little white, a little black, a touch Oriental. Maybe a little Amerind to account for his straight raven-black hair. Typical executive-gene stock, something for everyone. A foot in the door to any place on earth or the colonies. His beauty was exotic to a streetboy like me, and I stared. He caught me eyeing him and smiled slightly, then turned to slide off his tight black underwear. He had a smooth rounded ass, and when he turned around, his cock swung around a second later. It was long and soft, veined and natural with a fleshy hood over his cockhead. Unusual for his class. I was natural as well, but that was from never having a doctor around.

He stretched and touched his toes. He looked right at me. "Do you mind the nude bit? It's something I picked up in New Canton." I shook my head and stripped as well, then walked over and kissed him on the neck, my hand sliding across Adam's smooth hairless chest. He stiffened, and I kissed him again, nuzzling his strong neck and pressing my stiffening cock against his warm brown body. He relaxed as I kissed higher, up into the stiff short hair at the back of his neck, my hand drifting lower to grasp his now-hard cock. "Can't think of a better way to guard your body, man," I said in his ear.

"Go to it," he whispered, his head back and eyes closed, his hips forward and pumping his cock slowly on my hand. God, he was beautiful. I knew he was a virgin at this or any other kind of sex play, and I was determined to make it good for him. He was mine for two weeks, and I wanted to make sure at least one of us enjoyed this assignment.

I played with his cock a little, feeling it fill out in my hand to a nice thick eight inches. I skinned back his foreskin and played with the sensitive spongy knob there, and he trembled in my grasp. I guided him to the floor slowly, his cock brushing barbells on the way down. Adam stiffened and whimpered as the cold metal caressed his cock, and a thick bead of precome honey oozed out onto my fingers. I rubbed the liquid onto his cockhead, the lube letting me squeeze him harder and feel his cock jerk in my tight fist. My other hand roamed over his sweet lean body, feeling his well-defined physique. He was perfectly proportioned, well built and damn strong. His arms were veined with his strength and his legs rippled with barely concealed power. I was more and more surprised by this supposedly soft Corp-baby. He was athletic as I was, and he could probably beat me in the pool with those long limbs of his. He kept his eyes closed, rocking back and forth slightly as my hand masturbated him as slowly as I could manage it. He was really turning me on now.

My own cock pressed against the firm smooth flesh of his café-au-lait buttocks, hard as rock. I stopped touching Adam's sweet body to skin myself back, and turned him around. I guided his strong hands to my cock, and he grasped the thick six inches as if it was something alien to him. I wrapped his fingers around it and showed him how to play with me, what I liked for him to do, and then I did them to him. He gasped and gripped my cock hard, then began to masturbate me clumsily.

I shook my head and smiled; he was a total newbie at this. He might have only played with HIMSELF by accident, let alone played with another guy on purpose. He literally didn't know what to do, how to react to the waves of blazing pleasure I was sending through him. I looked at him with IR, touched his hot spots, watched as his body temperature climb as he got excited. He groaned under my hands, and I moved forward, still holding his cock as he held mine, and kissed those beautiful lips. He opened his mouth and I filled him with my tongue. He let me kiss him deeply, and tried to follow me as we parted. A line of spit dripped down his chin to his broad chest and I followed, leaving a glistening trail across his pecs as I tended to his now-upright nipples. I bit one gently, rolling it between my teeth, and he gasped softly.

His cock started to jerk in my hand, and his eyes snapped open. I squeezed the base of his cock and touched a few pressure points I knew. He stopped on the edge of his first real orgasm, teetering on the brink. His wide brown eyes begged me. "Please," he formed on his lips. I shook my head and he slumped against me, shivering in his need to come. I denied it to him, drawing out his first pleasure as long as I could. I would keep him a virgin all night if I could. I was another matter.

His hands tried the same thing with my cock, and I pulled away from him, pressed forward, and bore him back to the floor. I straddled him, my balls against his balls, my cock pressed against the hard flat muscles of his washboard stomach. I fucked my cock against his broad stomach slowly, letting him feel the heat from my manhood. I felt my come rise and grunted as I splashed his brown flanks with rope after hot rope of my come, snapping out in long, hard spurts as I ground my meat into his smooth, hairless body. He bucked under me, my hand still on that nice hard rod of his, and he turned in my arms.

I rose from him, and let go of his cock. I bent down and ran my tongue over his strong muscles, and began to slowly kiss my come off his deep chest. He groaned as the kisses swept over his body, burning and cool at the same time, leaving his chest clean of my come. Then I bent over his handsome boyish face and kissed him again on those sensual lips. He opened his mouth and I filled it with a generous taste of my mancome. He gagged and coughed, then swept my mouth with his tongue, tasting the salty thick seed until he had it all. He loved my come.

I stood up, leaving him on his back, and he opened his eyes. Adam got unsteadily to his feet, as if he was unsure those strong legs would hold him, and followed me. I turned and watched him stumble down the hall in the dark; he had no night-vision enhancements, probably no enhancements besides a little gene twiddling to make him more athletically inclined. I turned and caught him under the arms. "Ah!" he exclaimed, and his body fell against mine. We wound up on the floor with him on top, and his hard cock pressed sweetly against my hip. I laughed out loud and turned a bit, and his cock met my hot hard meat full on. Adam gasped at the feel of our cocks together, and I took them both in one fist, pumping them together. He shivered again, and I felt his nuts contract. Again I kept him from it, slowing him down, letting him down easy from the edge of his first time. Finally he relaxed against me, and I took him in my arms. My biceps surged, and I swung the boy up easily. He was easy to hold, and I walked with him to the bed, and sat on the edge, cradling him in my arms. He moved slightly, and I hugged him to my chest, feeling close to my beautiful charge. I kissed him again, and then slid my hands across his muscles, feeling the hard, smooth curves of his perfect young body.

His hands began to explore me as I straddled him, stroking my back and sides, feeling my pecs and the hard nipples that seemed to beg for his touch. He was catching on, seeing what was good for him and trying it on me. I corrected him a few times, showing him what I liked, and finally we were both lying down, full against one another. His hands were as large as mine, and we had a comparable grip. We wrestled playfully, testing one another, and we were even as far as our raw strength.

I drew him to me and reached around, caressing the smooth brown globes of his ass until I came to his sweet tight virgin pucker. I tested him and he stiffened. I kissed him. "It's OK," I said, " I want to see how much of a virgin you are, guy...."

"Don't hurt me...please," came his soft plea, and I kissed him again.

"Never, Adam, never. You are a sweet, beautiful young guy—I could never hurt you. And I won't let anyone else hurt you. Ever."

I continued to explore his virgin hole, stroking it and

touching it with a lubed finger until it opened for me. I plunged into his hot guts, and felt his ring grip me hard, trying to push me out. I pressed on and found his prostate. Gripping his cock with the other hand, I started to massage his prostate.

Adam came off the pillow with a cry, and his cock surged. This time I let it come, I slid my lips over his sweet dong an instant before he started to blast. He groaned under me and twisted as I worked him over, my lips on his swollen cockhead drinking his thick virgin come, one hand pumping and working his cock, the other, buried in his tight ass, bringing him off with slow hard even strokes on his most private place of all.

Adam twisted in his ecstasy for what seemed like an eternity as he gave up his virginity to me. I sucked and stroked and poked him until he was finally spent, his hot young body covered in a thin sheen of sweat. Salty sweat dripped off his red face as he staggered to the bathroom. I helped him clean off, and sat him on the toilet. I sat at his feet.

"You OK, Adam?"

"Yeh…yeh…. God, that was incredible. I…never did anything like that before. I saw it once or twice, but never thought about doing it. That was marvelous. I mean, you save my life and practically fuck me later. I don't even know your name, man. Never gave me the time to ask."

"Cody. Cody Mason."

"I thought your name was Conner something!"

"Hmm? Oh, that's bullshit your uncle told you. You deserve to know my real name. Not too many people do."

"Cody. That's a nice name. Cody." He was tasting my name on his tongue. "Make love to me, Cody. I mean, all the way. I've got to know." His voice was suddenly low and soft. I looked up at him. He was totally serious.

I stood up and took his hands, and guided him back to the bed. He lay down and I followed, my hand caressing the curly pubic hair at the base of his cock. He had softened somewhat, but now he stiffened again. I continued to caress him there, running my fingers through the stiff hair until his cock was red and ready. Then I dropped my hand lower, feeling the soft flesh between his balls and his hole. I began to work his hole again. He twisted a bit at the sensation and I calmed him, my other hand stroking his chest and then his brown flanks. I spread his legs wide and fingered him, loosening him gradually until I finally slid a second and third finger into his body.

He was as willing a guy as I had ever had, and my cock followed my fingers, oiled and hopefully easy for him to take. I pressed into him as gently as I could, holding him still so he didn't hurt himself. His legs were on my shoulders, so I could see him and react. He relaxed and pushed back, letting me sink slowly into his strong body. I let him get used to my six-inch cock, then pushed another half-inch into him. He groaned but took me all the same, eager to have his tight virgin butt fucked by a man who knew what he was doing.

I am a professional, after all.

Soon it was more than I could stand: his beauty and strength, the heat and the tight hard friction on my cock was more than I could take, and I shot my come into him, fucking back and forth as Adam groaned at the sensation I shot through him, sliding against his prostate with my cock on every stroke. I made sure I hit it every time, working him as well as working me, and we came together. Adam shuddered in my arms when it was over for me, and I slid out of his tight ass. He would be sore and hurting for a little while, and I helped him with his burning ass. Then I straddled him and squatted on his hard cock, taking his eight inches up my ass easily. He was good and ready, too, a randy young hunk who could pump his cock in me without fear of hurting me in the least. I had taken worse than this Corpbaby, and under worse circumstances. Five years in a cell does that for you, especially when you're a juvie with my rugged good looks. I had been like fucking honey to every bear in the place.... That was why I usually liked to be in charge with another guy, but Adam was so innocent at this I trusted him utterly not to try anything to hurt me.

Adam pumped at me hard, and I gripped his cock until he cried out and shot his come, dumping a good load in me and staying around afterward. He liked having his cock in me, and I liked having him, I found. He was not thick enough to hurt me, just big enough to make me feel every delicious inch of him. I rode my pretty charge for a little longer, until he groaned and gripped me, stroking his cock hard and deep into my body as he came a second time.

I let Adam go and pulled away from him. I lay down beside him and held him tight in my arms, and he snuggled against me, secure in the knowledge I would keep him safe. I stroked his hair as he nodded off and hoped I could keep the promises I made to him in my heart right then. Then I tried to join him in sleep, his deep breathing taking me away at last.

* Internet address: robin.man@studs.com

TITLE: Touch Me
BY: Reedr
FROM: The Gay Blade—Toronto, CANADA

I watch him every day. He's always there about this time in the afternoon, stretched out in a hammock slung between two maple trees. His skimpy faded red shorts ride low on his narrow hips; his darkly tanned body oozes sweat and lazy lustful sex.

I lie on my bed, looking at the mirror propped up on my windowsill. I see him there, a cool reflection of the hot man in the next yard. I see my own naked leg, my arm moving as I grasp my quivering flesh in one hand.

"Touch me," I whisper.

I know he can't hear me, doesn't even know I'm here. I know that making the connection is all up to me. I watch him move his big hand over his chest, his fingers lingering on first one nipple, then the other. My own hand mirrors his actions. I imagine it is his sweat I feel, his skin slick under my touch. My ass wriggles against the knotted sheets. I hear my breath coming in short gasps.

"Touch me."

I flip over on my stomach, my chin just above the windowsill. He has bent one leg, his knee resting against the hammock. The wide leg of his running shorts falls back and I see the swollen stained cup of thin cotton that contains his cock. I swallow. My mouth is dry. I grind my own aching cock into the bed. The springs creak and strain. My heart pounds. My eyes are fastened on the man. I can almost smell him from here —precome oozing into the thin cotton, sweat gathered like honey in his armpits.... I grunt and gasp. Come spurts into the dirty sheets. I close my eyes and shout, no longer able to hold back.

"Touch me!"

My orgasm exhausts me.

When I raise my head and look again, he isn't there. My whole body shakes with sudden nervous spasms. I look from the open window to the mirror, seeking his reflection, at least. Nothing. I feel more alone than I have felt for some time, now. I look down at my naked flesh, smell my own come. I long for another's smells to mingle with my own. Now I have lost even the reflection of a desirable man.

A sound at the door startles me so much I can't open my mouth. Words are stuck in my throat. Clumsily, I try to wrap myself in the soiled sheets. I watch the door, mesmerized as it starts to open. I haven't had any visitors for some time. I thought everyone had forgotten me, moved on. I wonder what they will think when they see me, whether I will see the pity in their eyes.

I blink, clearing my vision. Sometimes the light plays tricks on me now. This time I seem to see the reflection of my man, but not in the mirror, not in the glass. He is standing in the doorway. I can smell the sun and the sweat and the sex. He is smiling, his eyes a hot summer blue. He comes in and closes the door behind him.

I relax my grip on the sheets gradually. They fall away. I feel his eyes on me, touching my dry skin, licking my parched lips. Now I'm afraid to speak, to break the spell.

He is standing beside me. He takes the mirror and adjusts the angle to reflect the bed. I see us both revealed there and what I see is his vibrant macho sexuality, my pale boyish aestheticism. I hadn't seen myself that way before. I know that he has no memories of my earlier, sturdier self, and I smile. He reaches down and lifts the sheet away. My cock swells, looking bigger than ever between my slender thighs.

Slowly, he pushes the waistband of his shorts down to his knees. His cock is short and fat, his balls heavy and covered with golden fuzz. I can smell the faint aroma of urine.

"Touch me," he says.

* Internet address: REEDR@blade.com

TITLE: The Foreman
BY: Wolf Pendleton
FROM: STUDSnet—San Francisco, CA

When I first moved into my house, it was in an extremely isolated, rural setting. That was a large part of its appeal after years of apartment living—privacy! There were a few neighboring houses visible at a considerable distance from the front, but the view from the back encompassed only the grass on my property, a large field beyond it, and a cluster of trees at the far end of the field. The novelty of lying out in the sun bareassed pretty much wore off by fall, but not the peacefulness of the isolation. I vowed that if the field in back of my plot ever started to develop, I'd sell the house and move.

It took almost a year before progress caught up with me. One spring day I came home from work to find the field behind my house full of concrete blocks and plywood, and the very next morning, a yellow earth-moving truck showed up to start digging the foundation of a new house...directly behind my property. Shit! Time to call the realtor!

I'm not sure why I delayed making that call. Maybe it was the lack of time to go shopping for another house, or the considerable expense involved, or just inertia. But in the meantime, the foundation of my dreaded new neighbor was scooped out seemingly overnight, and the house itself started to go up. I got in the habit of watching the construction crew in the late afternoons, and all day on Saturdays, when they also worked. The site of the new house was so close to my bedroom window that I could see virtually everything going on over there with almost no effort, and using binoculars brought them in so close they might as well have been in bed with me. I was a little surprised to discover that I was such a voyeur, but it wasn't all that surprising under the circumstances. I had happily given up my old fast-lane urban lifestyle when I moved out to the country, thankful to have escaped with my sanity and my health intact. For a long time I enjoyed just keeping to myself, working out with free weights to stay fit and using the extra time to read and listen to music, getting to know myself better as my stress levels dropped lower and lower. But those old urges never really went away, nor did I really want them to. After all, nobody had put a gun to my head to force me into my old lifestyle, and I gave it up only because the routine got tiresome and the dangers became too obvious to ignore. But the pleasures had been undeniable at the time, and I now realized as I watched the hunks on the construction crew that I missed that part of my life. I was pretty damned horny, in fact.

And there were a few guys on the crew I would have welcomed into my bedroom any time! They were a rough-looking bunch, actually, as construction workers tend to be, but all of them were also exceptionally well muscled and deeply tanned from the work they were doing. Lying on my bed and watching them through binoculars got to be something of a daily afternoon ritual after a while. All of those sweating, straining bodies presented an embarrassment of riches. If their personal grooming habits sometimes left something to be desired—dirty hair, bad teeth, protruding beer bellies —I was willing to concentrate on the good points.

One guy was very different from the others. The rest of the crew seemed to treat him like "one of the gang," and he acted much like the rest of them, alternately cursing and clowning around and periodically fondling himself in that absentminded way that a lot of really macho studs have. Like the rest of the men on the crew, he'd usually haul out his cock to piss whenever the need struck him, even in the middle of a conversation with one of the other guys. He appeared to have absolutely no inhibitions about it whatsoever; in fact, he seemed to actually enjoy pissing freely like that. In general, he struck me as being a really earthy, physical sort of man. But he walked around the construction site with an authority that the others seemed to lack, and although he was doing the same hard work that everybody else was doing, he often seemed to be telling the other workers what to do. I finally decided he must be the foreman, or whatever they called the head honcho at a construction site. This guy seemed to have all the answers, and he frequently stayed long after the rest of the crew had gone for the day, hammering this or sawing that until it was completely dark. I figured he was just trying to set a good example for his men, although I couldn't figure what he hoped to accomplish by staying so late; once his crew was gone, there wasn't anybody left to set an example for.

He stood out physically, too. For one thing, the guy must have been six-feet-six, with long and powerful arms and legs and massive hands and feet. He seemed to be built on a different scale from the rest of his crew. Yet from what I could tell by looking at his body through his T-shirt and skintight jeans, there wasn't an ounce of fat on his big frame. His stomach was absolutely flat, and his waist appeared to be quite narrow, although I guessed those dirty Levi's were probably at least thirty-eights. He was just so big, and his shoulders so broad, that a thirty-eight-inch waist looked small by comparison. Like most of the rest of his men, he sported a full beard and mustache. His dark brown hair was slightly curly and quite long, covering his ears and cascading down to his shoulders when it wasn't tied back in a ponytail, which was at least half the time. But it always appeared to be freshly washed, even at the end of a long day's work. Examining him more closely through my binoculars, I saw a man who was probably well past thirty, with the worn-but-affable expression of a guy who had seen it all. His eyes were blue, and twinkled when one of the men in his crew spoke to him; beneath his bushy mustache, his teeth gleamed white and perfect as his mouth screwed itself up into a boyish grin. One afternoon I watched him pause to light a cigarette and the afternoon sun bounced off a small gold ring inserted through his earlobe. And once the wind was right and portions of the workers' conversation carried right into my bedroom. The foreman's voice was a deep bass, articulated with a slow, comfortable drawl. Although I couldn't make out the content of the conversation, I heard enough to recognize the constant flow of obscenities, of which his favorite seemed to be "fuckin'." But the tone of his speech, whatever he was talking about, sounded to be one of consistent, almost-boyish good humor. And I heard one of his men call him by name. His name was Greg.

As the spring progressed, I kept finding excuses to put off calling my realtor, but I was a lot more conscientious about making my daily afternoon date with the bedroom window. As the weather warmed up, one guy after another started going shirtless and the sightseeing just got better and better. But I found myself paying more and more attention to Greg at the expense of the others. Stripped to the waist, the hunky foreman looked almost like a god, with the sort of solid muscular definition in his chest and back that only hard work can achieve. Although he had a fair amount of fine brown chest hair, the increasing darkness of his tan skin created the illusion that he was almost hairless. The wiry hair running down from his navel into his jeans was more noticeable, though, and when he'd lift an arm to position a beam and hammer it in, his armpit hair showed dark and furry. The large eagle tattooed on his left upper arm appeared to be an expensive, professional job; its wings outspread, it covered his biceps, even as it seemed poised to fly off at any moment. It seemed to suit him.

By the start of summer, the framing of the house was complete, and the crew split up into two groups—one working on the roof, the other doing construction on the hill sloping down from the back of the house. As time progressed, it became apparent that this was going to be a large concrete deck with an in-ground, house-level swimming pool sunk down to the level of the sloping hillside. Greg was assigned—or maybe he assigned himself—to the crew working on the deck, and was soon in the midst of what seemed, to my untrained eye, to be the most labor-intensive part of the whole project. The men were hoisting around enormous pieces of construction material that looked like they weighed a ton; their upper bodies were perpetually slick and shiny with sweat as the temperature climbed first to 90, then to 95, then to nearly 100. Watching them dripping in the heat, I could almost smell them.

Finally the workers started showing up for work wearing shorts of various types, mostly khaki or denim cutoffs. I got the feeling that if this wasn't Greg's decision as foreman, it was still a policy that he enthusiastically endorsed. Greg wore faded Levi's 501 cut offs that were shorter and tighter than anybody else's. He wore them slung low, a good four inches below his navel, and the top of his crotch hair often peeked out over the top. After watching him lean over a couple of times to expose his hairy asscrack, it was clear that he wasn't wearing a jockstrap or anything else underneath. Those cutoffs covered less than a skimpy pair of gym shorts, and Greg's hairy treelike legs were bared from his ankles to his hips. And he wore them so tight that when he had to piss, he couldn't just unbutton the fly to take out his pecker—he had to undo them completely and slide them a few inches down his torso, freeing his balls and exposing his thick pubic bush in the process. Those cutoffs, along with his construction boots and work socks, were the only things he wore from that point onward. If they undoubtedly made the work somewhat cooler, they didn't make it any less tiring. For the first time since the project started, I noticed that Greg no longer stayed after the rest of the crew had left for the day. He seemed as exhausted as the rest of them.

With the deck finally completed toward the end of July, the exterior of the house was essentially complete and the work turned to interior matters: wiring, plumbing fixtures, drywall, glazing. Consequently, I saw less and less of the workers, including Greg, except when somebody would arrive or leave. I'd occasionally spot Greg heading out to his pickup, consistently shirtless and in his cutoffs, but the vision didn't last very long before he was behind the wheel and pulling away. I did notice that the pickup was usually there long after the rest of the crew had left for the day; and after the wiring was completed, electric lights would occasionally burn inside the new house until well after dark. So apparently Greg was back to his old habits, now that the really heavy labor was behind him. But I hardly ever got to see him in the flesh. My afternoon routine slowly faded away, and I even spent a couple of hot afternoons driving around the area looking at other houses, although I didn't find anything I liked well enough to investigate seriously, and I still put off calling the realtor. I figured there'd be time enough for that. Like maybe when Greg's pickup was no longer parked down the street in the evening when I got back.

A couple of weeks later, I found myself drinking beer

out on my patio in the early evening, watching it get dark and enjoying the night air. The August heat had moderated somewhat and the humidity had dropped, and it felt good sitting outside in just my gym shorts after several weeks of being trapped inside my air-conditioned cocoon. Across the yard, I saw a light switch on inside the new house. A quick glance to the front of the lot confirmed the presence of Greg's truck, meaning he was working late again. I didn't expect to see him, though; I hardly ever saw him now, and the idea even passed through my mind that maybe I should go over there on the pretext of looking at the new house next door before it was too late, Greg and his workers were gone for good, and the house was inhabited by some pretentious yuppie couple with kids, cats, and BMWs. But the heat was lulling me into a stupor and I didn't feel like getting up and throwing on shoes and a shirt, so in the end I just sat there, gazing toward the light in the window.

My attention was abruptly refocused when I heard a slight stirring next door, followed by the appearance of a tall figure slowly loping out onto the deck. The sun had set behind me, so sitting there on my patio I was completely concealed in the darkness beneath the overhanging roof. But it was still light enough to clearly make out the long hair flowing freely and the eagle tattoo screaming proudly from his muscular upper arm—it was Greg, all right, still shirtless and wearing his tight cutoffs as usual, and barefoot as well. That house must be damned near complete if he's walking around the site barefooted, I thought to myself. Greg shuffled around the deck somewhat aimlessly, dragging on a cigarette and staring into space. Finally he came to a stop at the far end of the platform, which dropped off abruptly, without a safety railing, to the ground almost a full story below. He threw his cigarette butt off the edge, then reached down and unbuttoned the top of his cutoffs. Bladder-relief time again, I thought. But instead of lowering the shorts just enough to get his cock out to piss, as I'd seen him do numerous times before, he calmly unbuttoned them completely, dropped them to his ankles and stepped out of them, then walked back to the center of the deck, totally naked.

Suddenly he vanished with a loud splash. My God, the pool! They must have filled the pool!

I was halfway across the yard before I even realized what I was doing. Then I started having second thoughts —here I was, a complete stranger to this guy, intruding on his privacy with no idea how he'd take to the notion, especially since he was in the middle of skinny-dipping. Well, it wasn't like it was actually his house, I rationalized, and I knew he wasn't modest about his body—not after seeing how he handled himself around his crew. And the shorts I had on didn't leave a whole lot to the imagination, especially since I wasn't wearing anything underneath them; I was almost as naked as he was. Well, maybe that would put him at ease? I didn't give a fuck. I was driven, knowing that this could be my last, best chance to get to know the guy. I didn't realistically expect that anything more might come of it than our maybe ending up sharing a couple of beers, but I had to give it my best shot.

When I got to the deck, I scrambled up the rough wooden stairs that had only been recently built into the side, and found myself staring out over a vast rectangle of concrete, empty except for the dark square of the pool in the middle. I was surprised that I could even make out that much until I realized that the moon had come out; almost full, it illuminated the cloudless night enough to cast shadows. Greg was nowhere to be seen for a moment until I saw first one, then another hairy, beefy arm emerge from the water to slap down on the tiles ringing the pool. I half-expected the eagle tattooed on his biceps to start shaking its feathers dry. So positioned at the edge, he pulled his upper body out of the water, leaving himself submerged from the waist down, and looked upward. That's when our eyes met.

"Uh, hope I'm not interrupting anything," I said as quickly as I could get out. "I'm Wolf; I live next door," I continued, pointing toward my place a few yards away. "I've watched this house go up since last spring. I was outside just now and when I heard the water splash, I couldn't believe there was a pool here, so I figured I'd come over and take a look." Okay, it was a lie, but it was the best I could come up with on such short notice.

"Well, howdy, neighbor!" he replied, pushing himself completely out of the pool with his powerful arms and grappling onto the deck. He stood facing me, face to face—or actually, face to neck, since he towered over me —and offered a huge wet hand, which I shook eagerly. By the time I withdrew my hand, most of my front was wet, including my shorts, from where he'd dripped on me. His beard and long hair were completely soaked, of course, and water poured off every quarter of his power-ful body to form a thick puddle around his big feet, quickly spreading until I was standing in it, too. Close up, he was far hairier than he'd looked through the binoculars, especially with it all plastered to his wet skin. His chest hair was fine, silky, and abundant, and his belly and forearms and legs were all covered with dark, wet down. Below his navel, the hair grew thicker until it merged into his wet, furry pubic bush, and his balls hung suspended in a nest of damp hair that looked to be nearly as thick. I noticed the water pouring off the end of his prick and it reminded me of all those times I'd watched him piss. Not surprisingly, he seemed completely unaware of his nudity. When a stranger showed up, he did the courteous thing—he got out of the pool to shake hands. I didn't get the feeling that it made any difference to him that I was half-naked myself; it just wouldn't have occurred to him to give any thought to what he was or wasn't wearing at the time, even if he wasn't wearing anything at all. He seemed to possess no self-consciousness about it whatsoever.

"Hey, sorry, Wolf, I'm gettin' you all wet and I haven't even introduced myself," he continued, pulling my mind back to reality. "Name's Greg, I was foreman on this job. One hell of a house, hey? Puttin' in this deck was a fuckin' bitch with the heat and all, but it sure looks good now, huh?"

His pride was infectious, even though I had rued the day they started building this house. Now I found myself dreading the day they finished it. "Yeah, it's a nice one," I replied. "This deck is something else. All I've got is a little patio! Guess you couldn't resist checking out the pool once they filled it, huh?"

"Yeah, man," Greg grinned. "Hell, I helped build the fuckin' thing, I figure I'm entitled! Hey, you're gonna live right next to it, you've got some rights, too…why don't you check it out?"

I hesitated. "I dunno, Greg. You built it, you can do what you want; but you think it's okay for me?"

"C'mon, Wolf, I'm still makin' the fuckin' rules around here…and there ain't nobody around for miles, who'd even know? Anyway, I've already dripped all over you so much, you've got nothin' to lose now. Just get outta those wet shorts and jump in! Don't be shy. I'm not!" He laughed.

Greg stood there dripping, watching me like the eagle tattooed on his arm and waiting for me to strip. By this point I had more than half a hard-on poking through the wet crotch of my shorts, but he obviously either hadn't noticed it or didn't care, so I just slipped my shorts down and stepped out of them, then approached the edge of the pool next to him. My cock stuck out prominently. Greg just smiled.

"Hey, man, we're really gonna enjoy this," he said somewhat cryptically.

We jumped in together and swam around, eventually starting to splash each other like two unsupervised kids. The water was fairly warm; I achieved full erection quickly and stayed there, but with my cock underwater I figured it wouldn't matter. But then Greg started with some really rough horseplay, and his hand kept brushing against my hard prick. I started worrying about it, but then Greg pulled himself out of the water again, sitting on the edge of the pool with his legs spread wide, and damned if his cock wasn't even harder than mine.

"Hey, Wolf, c'mon up," he said quietly. Maybe this was going to be all right after all!

I had no sooner placed myself on the edge of the pool than Greg had me on my back, his wet body pressed against mine and his tongue stuck deep in my mouth. As I returned the favor, I felt our hard tools throbbing against each other's stomachs. And I thought *I* was horny!

Greg kissed me with a hunger that was all-consuming; I actually almost shot off just from the intensity of it. I was relieved when he disengaged himself just long enough to turn around and swallow my cock to the root without a moment's hesitation. I knew I couldn't hold off for long and I suspected he couldn't, either. I started sucking him off as well, the two of us sixty-nining right there at the edge of the pool. We dripped on each other continually—first water, then, soon enough, passionate sweat. With my mouth full of Greg's prick and my nose buried in his musky crotch, I soon lost it. Even as I felt myself starting to go, Greg took his mouth off my cock and bellowed like an ox as he filled my mouth with so much spunk I couldn't swallow fast enough to keep some of it from dripping down my chin. Then I shot off myself, splattering come all over Greg's face and his thick black beard and mustache before he managed to get my cock back in his mouth to gulp down the rest. I was scarcely done pumping my load down his throat before he was back up at my face, sticking his tongue in my mouth to share my own seed with me. We kissed for a long time, stopped long enough to lick our sperm off each other's faces, then kissed some more, wrapped in a tight hug.

It had gotten cool enough that I was immediately aware of the warmth spreading through my crotch when Greg started pissing on me. Our bodies remained entwined as he thoroughly soaked my cock and balls with his hot manwater. I started to pull away when I thought he was done, but at that point he grabbed his prick, aimed it at my chest, and started pissing again. I just lay back and enjoyed the incredible sensation of being hosed down by this incredibly hot stud. My cock grew hard again quickly as Greg moved his stream from my chest up to my face, and my lips opened as if they had a mind of their own. He finished emptying his bladder by pissing in my mouth, and I swallowed every golden drop hungrily.

Greg looked at me lying there in a huge pool of urine, my wet hard-on glistening in the moonlight, and started grinning. "Looks like you're ready for another round, Wolf," he laughed. "I'm ready for a good fuck, and I've already got ya all lubed up…wanna take advantage of it?"

I didn't have to be asked twice. I had Greg's legs up on my shoulders and my slick cock up his asshole in record time. His hole was tight, but his piss was a pretty effective lube, and he pulled me into his guts as if he really needed to be plugged. By me. And after all those months of doing without, and after watching this stud all summer long and getting hotter and hotter for him, I was ready to do some plugging. I'm amazed I even lasted as long as I did, which wasn't very long, before I was spraying his insides with my second load of the evening. And while I was still in there—I figured, what the fuck, I'd return the favor—I started pissing up his asshole. And since Greg just looked up at me with a smile and sighed contentedly, I kept pissing until I was empty.

Neither one of us seemed in any sort of hurry to jump in the pool and wash off each other's juices, so we just sat together in silence for what seemed like a long time, shoulder to shoulder with our feet in the water. The moonlight cast an eerie glow on our naked, sticky bodies as they dried slowly in the cooling night air. From time to time I looked over at Greg. I'd have sworn the eagle tattooed on his arm was looking back at me. But I didn't say anything. Greg was obviously a loner, not the type to make idle chatter just to keep a conversation going, and not the type I would have thought comfortable expressing affection to another man, either. But he'd surprised the hell out of me tonight, and he surprised me again when he reached over and started stroking my thigh gently. When he put his big arm around my shoulders and hugged me, something snapped. It had been building in my mind for weeks, anyway. Now, after having had some of the best sex in my life with a man who seemed to enjoy me as much as I enjoyed him, I had to spit it out and force the issue.

"How much longer till the house is done?" I asked quietly.

"Whatsa matter, Wolf, you wanna know how much longer you can come over here and swim bareassed?" He chuckled to himself. I didn't think it was funny.

"Just answer the question, Greg. Please."

He took the cue and turned serious. "Landscapers are comin' Monday," he replied, looking down at his big feet slowly splashing back and forth in the pool. "Maybe another coupla days on the fixtures, another week to tie up loose ends. Middle of next week at the outside."

"Then where'll you go?"

"Whaddya mean, where'll I go?"

"Where's your next gig, or whatever the fuck you guys call it?"

"Fifty miles up the interstate. We gotta take what we can get. Anyway, that one's easy money. The guys can handle it without me."

"Without you?"

"Yeah, I'm gonna be too busy gettin' moved in, at least for the first few weeks."

"Moved in?" I was totally lost.

Greg started grinning, finally chuckling so deeply he actually shook as he pulled me still closer to his rock-solid body.

"Wolf"—he turned toward the building—"this is *my* fuckin' house!"

I never did call my realtor!

* Internet address: wolf.pendleton@studs.com

MASQUERADE

ATAULLAH MARDAAN
KAMA HOURI/DEVA DASI
$7.95/512-3

Two legendary tales of the East in one spectacular volume. *Kama Houri* details the life of a sheltered Western woman who finds herself living within the confines of a harem—where she discovers herself thrilled with the extent of her servitude. *Deva Dasi* is a tale dedicated to the cult of the Dasis—the sacred women of India who devoted their lives to the fulfillment of the senses—while revealing the sexual rites of Shiva.

"...memorable for the author's ability to evoke India present and past.... Mardaan excels in crowding her pages with the sights and smells of India, and her erotic descriptions are convincingly realistic."

—Michael Perkins,
The Secret Record: Modern Erotic Literature

J. P. KANSAS
ANDREA AT THE CENTER
$6.50/498-4

Kidnapped! Lithe and lovely young Andrea is whisked away to a distant retreat. Gradually, she is introduced to the ways of the Center, and soon becomes quite friendly with its other inhabitants—all of whom are learning to abandon restraint in their pursuit of the deepest sexual satisfaction. This tale of the ultimate sexual training facility is a nationally bestselling title and a classic of modern erotica.

VISCOUNT LADYWOOD
GYNECOCRACY
$9.95/511-5

An infamous story of female domination returns to print. Julian, whose parents feel he shows just a bit too much spunk, is sent to a very special private school, in hopes that he will learn to discipline his wayward soul. Once there, Julian discovers that his program of study has been devised by the deliciously stern Mademoiselle de Chambonnard. In no time, Julian is learning the many ways of pleasure—under the firm hand of this demanding headmistress.

CHARLOTTE ROSE, EDITOR
THE 50 BEST PLAYGIRL FANTASIES
$6.50/460-7

A steamy selection of women's fantasies straight from the pages of *Playgirl*—the leading magazine of sexy entertainment for women. These tales of seduction—specially selected by no less an authority than Charlotte Rose, author of such bestselling women's erotica as *Women at Work* and *The Doctor is In*—are sure to set your pulse racing. From the innocent to the insatiable, these women let no fantasy go unexplored.

N. T. MORLEY
THE PARLOR
$6.50/496-8

Lovely Kathryn gives in to the ultimate temptation. The mysterious John and Sarah ask her to be their slave—an idea that turns Kathryn on so much that she can't refuse! But who are these two mysterious strangers? Little by little, Kathryn not only learns to serve, but comes to know the inner secrets of her stunning keepers.

J. A. GUERRA, EDITOR
**COME QUICKLY:
FOR COUPLES ON THE GO**
$6.50/461-5

The increasing pace of daily life is no reason to forgo a little carnal pleasure whenever the mood strikes. Here are over sixty of the hottest fantasies around—all designed to get you going in less time than it takes to dial 976. A super-hot volume especially for couples on a modern schedule.

ERICA BRONTE
LUST, INC.
$6.50/467-4

Lust, Inc. explores the extremes of passion that lurk beneath even the coldest, most business-like exteriors. Join in the sexy escapades of a group of high-powered professionals whose idea of office decorum is like nothing you've ever encountered! Business attire not required....

VANESSA DURIÉS
THE TIES THAT BIND
$6.50/510-7

The incredible confessions of a thrillingly unconventional woman. From the first page, this chronicle of dominance and submission will keep you gasping with its vivid depictions of sensual abandon. At the hand of Masters Georges, Patrick, Pierre and others, this submissive seductress experiences pleasures she never knew existed....

M. S. VALENTINE
THE CAPTIVITY OF CELIA
$6.50/453-4

Colin is mistakenly considered the prime suspect in a murder, forcing him to seek refuge with his cousin, Sir Jason Hardwicke. In exchange for Colin's safety, Jason demands Celia's unquestioning submission—knowing she will do anything to protect her lover. Sexual extortion!

AMANDA WARE
BOUND TO THE PAST
$6.50/452-6

Anne accepts a research assignment in a Tudor mansion. Upon arriving, she finds herself aroused by James, a descendant of the mansion's owners. Together they uncover the perverse desires of the mansion's long-dead master—desires that bind Anne inexorably to the past—not to mention the bedpost!

MASQUERADE BOOKS

SACHI MIZUNO

SHINJUKU NIGHTS
$6.50/493-3
Another tour through the lives and libidos of the seductive East, from the author of Passion in Tokyo. No one is better that Sachi Mizuno at weaving an intricate web of sensual desire, wherein many characters are ensnared and enraptured by the demands of their long-denied carnal natures. One by one, each surrenders social convention for the unashamed pleasures of the flesh.

PASSION IN TOKYO
$6.50/454-2
Tokyo—one of Asia's most historic and seductive cities. Come behind the closed doors of its citizens, witness the many pleasures that await. Lusty men and women from every stratum of Japanese society free themselves of all inhibitions...

MARTINE GLOWINSKI

POINT OF VIEW
$6.50/433-X
With the assistance of her new, unexpectedly kinky lover, she discovers and explores her exhibitionist tendencies—until there is virtually nothing she won't do before the horny audiences her man arranges! Unabashed acting out for the sophisticated voyeur.

RICHARD McGOWAN

A HARLOT OF VENUS
$6.50/425-9
A highly fanciful, epic tale of lust on Mars! Cavortia—the most famous and sought-after courtesan in the cosmopolitan city of Venus—finds love and much more during her adventures with some of the most remarkable characters in recent erotic fiction.

M. ORLANDO

THE ARCHITECTURE OF DESIRE
Introduction by Richard Manton.
$6.50/490-9
Two novels in one special volume! In The Hotel Justine, an elite clientele is afforded the opportunity to have any and all desires satisfied. The Villa Sin is inherited by a beautiful woman who soon realizes that the legacy of the ancestral estate includes bizarre erotic ceremonies. Two pieces of prime real estate.

CHET ROTHWELL

KISS ME, KATHERINE
$5.95/410-0
Beautiful Katherine can hardly believe her luck. Not only is she married to the charming and oh-so-agreeable Nelson, she's free to live out all her erotic fantasies with other men. Katherine has discovered Nelson to be far more devoted than the average spouse—and the duo soon begin exploring a relationship more demanding than marriage! Soon, Katherine's desires become more than any one man can handle.

MARCO VASSI

THE STONED APOCALYPSE
$5.95/401-1/mass market
"Marco Vassi is our champion sexual energist."—VLS
During his lifetime, Marco Vassi praised by writers as diverse as Gore Vidal and Norman Mailer, and his reputation was worldwide. The Stoned Apocalypse is Vassi's autobiography; chronicling a cross-country trip on America's erotic byways, it offers a rare glimpse of a generation's sexual imagination.

ROBIN WILDE

TABITHA'S TICKLE
$6.50/468-2
Tabitha's back! The story of this vicious vixen—and her torturously tantalizing cohorts—didn't end with Tabitha's Tease. Once again, men fall under the spell of scrumptious co-eds and find themselves enslaved to demands and desires they never dreamed existed. Think it's a man's world? Guess again. With Tabitha around, no man gets what he wants until she's completely satisfied—and, maybe, not even then....

TABITHA'S TEASE
$5.95/387-2
When poor Robin arrives at The Valentine Academy, he finds himself subject to the torturous teasing of Tabitha—the Academy's most notoriously domineering co-ed. But Tabitha is pledge-mistress of a secret sorority dedicated to enslaving young men. Robin finds himself the utterly helpless (and wildly excited) captive of Tabitha & Company's weird desires! A marathon of ticklish torture!

ERICA BRONTE

PIRATE'S SLAVE
$5.95/376-7
Lovely young Erica is stranded in a country where lust knows no bounds. Desperate to escape, she finds herself trading her firm, luscious body to any and all men willing and able to help her. Her adventure has its ups and downs, ins and outs—all to the undeniable pleasure of lusty Erica!

CHARLES G. WOOD

HELLFIRE
$5.95/358-9
A vicious murderer is running amok in New York's sexual underground—and Nick O'Shay, a virile detective with the NYPD, plunges deep into the case. He soon becomes embroiled in an elusive world of fleshly extremes, hunting a madman seeking to purge America with fire and blood sacrifices. Set in New York's infamous sexual underground.

CLAIRE BAEDER, EDITOR

LA DOMME: A DOMINATRIX ANTHOLOGY
$5.95/366-X
A steamy smorgasbord of female domination! Erotic literature has long been filled with heartstopping portraits of domineering women, and now the most memorable have been brought together in one beautifully brutal volume. A must for all fans of true Woman Power.

MASQUERADE BOOKS

CHARISSE VAN DER LYN
SEX ON THE NET
$5.95/399-6
Electrifying erotica from one of the Internet's hottest and most widely read authors. Encounters of all kinds—straight, lesbian, dominant/submissive and all sorts of extreme passions—are explored in thrilling detail.

STANLEY CARTEN
NAUGHTY MESSAGE
$5.95/333-3
Wesley Arthur discovers a lascivious message on his answering machine. Aroused beyond his wildest dreams by the acts described, Wesley becomes obsessed with tracking down the woman behind the seductive voice. His search takes him through strip clubs, sex parlors and no-tell motels—and finally to his randy reward....

AKBAR DEL PIOMBO
DUKE COSIMO
$4.95/3052-0
A kinky romp played out against the boudoirs, bathrooms and ballrooms of the European nobility, who seem to do nothing all day except each other. The lifestyles of the rich and licentious are revealed in all their glory.

A CRUMBLING FAÇADE
$4.95/3043-1
The return of that incorrigible rogue, Henry Pike, who continues his pursuit of sex, fair or otherwise, in the most elegant homes of the most debauched aristocrats.

CAROLE REMY
FANTASY IMPROMPTU
$6.50/513-1
A mystical, musical journey into the deepest recesses of a woman's soul. Kidnapped and held in a remote island retreat, Chantal—a renowned erotic writer—finds herself catering to every sexual whim of the mysterious and arousing Bran. Bran is determined to bring Chantal to a full embracing of her sensual nature, even while revealing himself to be something far more than human....

BEAUTY OF THE BEAST
$5.95/332-5
A shocking tell-all, written from the point-of-view of a prize-winning reporter. And what reporting she does! All the secrets of an uninhibited life are revealed, and each lusty tableau is painted in glowing colors.

DAVID AARON CLARK
THE MARQUIS DE SADE'S JULIETTE
$4.95/240-1
The Marquis de Sade's infamous Juliette returns—and emerges as the most perverse and destructive nightstalker modern New York will ever know. One by one, the innocent are drawn in by Juliette's empty promise of immortality, only to fall prey to her strange and deadly lusts.

ANONYMOUS
NADIA
$5.95/267-1
Follow the delicious but neglected Nadia as she works to wring every drop of pleasure out of life—despite an unhappy marriage. A classic title providing a peek into the secret sexual lives of another time and place.

NIGEL McPARR
THE STORY OF A VICTORIAN MAID
$5.95/241-8
What were the Victorians really like? Chances are, no one believes they were as stuffy as their Queen, but who would have imagined such unbridled libertines!

TITIAN BERESFORD
CINDERELLA
$6.50/500-X
Beresford triumphs again with this intoxicating tale, filled with castle dungeons and tightly corseted ladies-in-waiting, naughty viscounts and impossibly cruel masturbatrixes—nearly every conceivable method of erotic torture is explored and described in lush, vivid detail.

JUDITH BOSTON
$6.50/525-5
Young Edward would have been lucky to get the stodgy old companion he thought his parents had hired for him. Instead, an exquisite woman arrives at his door, and Edward finds his lewd behavior never goes unpunished by the unflinchingly severe Judith Boston! Together they take the downward path to perversion!

NINA FOXTON
$5.95/443-7
An aristocrat finds herself bored by run-of-the-mill amusements for "ladies of good breeding." Instead of taking tea with proper gentlemen, naughty Nina "milks" them of their most private essences. No man ever says "No" to Nina!

P. N. DEDEAUX
THE NOTHING THINGS
$5.95/404-6
Beta Beta Rho—highly exclusive and widely honored—has taken on a new group of pledges. The five women will be put through the most grueling of ordeals, and punished severely for any shortcomings—much to everyone's delight!

LYN DAVENPORT
THE GUARDIAN II
$6.50/505-0
The tale of Felicia Brookes—the lovely young woman held in submission by the demanding Sir Rodney Wentworth—continues in this volume of sensual surprises. No sooner has Felicia come to love Rodney than she discovers that she must now accustom herself to the guardianship of the debauched Duke of Smithton. How long will this last? Surely Rodney will rescue her from the domination of this stranger. Won't he?

DOVER ISLAND
$5.95/384-8

Dr. David Kelly has planted the seeds of his dream— a Corporal Punishment Resort. Soon, many people from varied walks of life descend upon this isolated retreat, intent on fulfilling their every desire. Including Marcy Harris, the perfect partner for the lustful Doctor....

THE GUARDIAN
$5.95/371-6

Felicia grew up under the tutelage of the lash—and she learned her lessons well. Sir Rodney Wentworth has long searched for a woman capable of fulfilling his cruel desires, and after learning of Felicia's talents, sends for her. Felicia discovers that the "position" offered her is delightfully different than anything she could have expected!

LIZBETH DUSSEAU
THE APPLICANT
$6.50/501-8

"Adventuresome young women who enjoys being submissive sought by married couple in early forties. Expect no limits." Hilary answers an ad, hoping to find someone who can meet her special needs. The beautiful Liza turns out to be a flawless mistress, and together with her husband, Oliver, she trains Hilary to be the perfect servant. Scandalous sexual servitude.

ANTHONY BOBARZYNSKI
STASI SLUT
$4.95/3050-4

Adina lives in East Germany, where she can only dream about the freedoms of the West. But then she meets a group of ruthless and corrupt STASI agents. They use her body for their own perverse gratification, while she opts to use her talents and attractions in a final bid for total freedom!

JOCELYN JOYCE
PRIVATE LIVES
$4.95/309-0

The lecherous habits of the illustrious make for a sizzling tale of French erotic life. A widow has a craving for a young busboy; he's sleeping with a rich businessman's wife; her husband is minding his sex business elsewhere! Scandalous sexual entanglements run through this tale of upper crust lust!

SARAH JACKSON
SANCTUARY
$5.95/318-X

Sanctuary explores both the unspeakable debauchery of court life and the unimaginable privations of monastic solitude, leading the voracious and the virtuous on a collision course that brings history to throbbing life.

THE WILD HEART
$4.95/3007-5

A luxury hotel is the setting for this artful web of sex, desire, and love. A newlywed sees sex as a duty, while her hungry husband tries to awaken her to its tender joys. A Parisian entertains wealthy guests for the love of money. Each episode provides a new variation in this lusty Grand Hotel!

LOUISE BELHAVEL
FRAGRANT ABUSES
$4.95/88-2

The saga of Clara and Iris continues as the now-experienced girls enjoy themselves with a new circle of worldly friends whose imaginations match their own. Perversity follows the lusty ladies around the globe!

SARA H. FRENCH
MASTER OF TIMBERLAND
$5.95/327-9

A tale of sexual slavery at the ultimate paradise resort. One of our bestselling titles, this trek to Timberland has ignited passions the world over—and stands poised to become one of modern erotica's legendary tales.

MARY LOVE
MASTERING MARY SUE
$5.95/351-1

Mary Sue is a rich nymphomaniac whose husband is determined to declare her mentally incompetent and gain control of her fortune. He brings her to a castle where, to Mary Sue's delight, she is unleashed for a veritable sex-fest!

THE BEST OF MARY LOVE
$4.95/3099-1

Mary Love leaves no coupling untried and no extreme unexplored in these scandalous selections from *Mastering Mary Sue, Ecstasy on Fire, Vice Park Place, Wanda,* and *Naughtier at Night.*

AMARANTHA KNIGHT
THE DARKER PASSIONS: THE PICTURE OF DORIAN GRAY
$6.50/342-0

Amarantha Knight takes on Oscar Wilde, resulting in a fabulously decadent tale of highly personal changes. One young man finds his most secret desires laid bare by a portrait far more revealing than he could have imagined....

THE DARKER PASSIONS READER
$6.50/432-1

The best moments from Knight's phenomenally popular Darker Passions series. Here are the most eerily erotic passages from her acclaimed sexual reworkings of *Dracula, Frankenstein, Dr. Jekyll & Mr. Hyde* and *The Fall of the House of Usher.*

THE DARKER PASSIONS: THE FALL OF THE HOUSE OF USHER
$6.50/528-X

The Master and Mistress of the house of Usher indulge in every form of decadence, and initiate their guests into the many pleasures to be found in utter submission.

THE DARKER PASSIONS: DR. JEKYLL AND MR. HYDE
$4.95/227-2

It is a story of incredible transformations achieved through mysterious experiments. Explore the steamy possibilities of a tale where no one is quite who—or what—they seem. Victorian bedrooms explode with hidden demons!

MASQUERADE BOOKS

THE DARKER PASSIONS: FRANKENSTEIN
$5.95/248-5

What if you could create a living human? What shocking acts could it be taught to perform, to desire? Find out what pleasures await those who play God....

THE DARKER PASSIONS: DRACULA
$5.95/326-0

The infamous erotic retelling of the Vampire legend. "Well-written and imaginative, Amarantha Knight gives fresh impetus to this myth, taking us through the sexual and sadistic scenes with details that keep us reading.... A classic in itself has been added to the shelves."   —Divinity

PAUL LITTLE

THE BEST OF PAUL LITTLE
$6.50/469-0

One of Masquerade's all-time best-selling authors. Known throughout the world for his fantastic portrayals of punishment and pleasure, Little never fails to push readers over the edge of sensual excitement.

ALL THE WAY
$6.95/509-3

Two excruciating novels from Paul Little in one hot volume! *Going All the Way* features an unhappy man who tries to purge himself of the memory of his lover with a series of quirky and uninhibited lovers. *Pushover* tells the story of a serial spanker and his celebrated exploits.

THE DISCIPLINE OF ODETTE
$5.95/334-1

Odette's was sure marriage would rescue her from her family's "corrections." To her horror, she discovers that her beloved has also been raised on discipline. A shocking erotic coupling!

THE PRISONER
$5.95/330-9

Judge Black has built a secret room below a penitentiary, where he sentences the prisoners to hours of exhibition and torment while his friends watch. Judge Black's House of Corrections is equipped with one purpose in mind: to administer his own brand of rough justice!

TEARS OF THE INQUISITION
$4.95/146-2

The incomparable Paul Little delivers a staggering account of pleasure and punishment. "There was a tickling inside her as her nervous system reminded her she was ready for sex. But before her was...the Inquisitor!" One of history's most infamous periods comes to throbbing life via the perverse imagination of Paul Little.

DOUBLE NOVEL
$4.95/86-6

The Metamorphosis of Lisette Joyaux tells the story of a young woman initiated into a new and incredible world world of lesbian lusts. *The Story of Monique* reveals the twisted sexual rituals that beckon the ripe and willing Monique.

CHINESE JUSTICE AND OTHER STORIES
$4.95/153-5

The story of the excruciating pleasures and delicious punishments inflicted on foreigners under the leaders of the Boxer Rebellion. Each foreign woman is brought before the authorities and grilled, much to the delight of their perverse captors. Scandalous deeds and shocking exploitation!

CAPTIVE MAIDENS
$5.95/440-2

Three beautiful young women find themselves powerless against the debauched landowners of 1824 England. They are banished to a sexual slave colony, and corrupted by every imaginable perversion. Soon, they come to crave the treatment of their unrelenting captors.

SLAVE ISLAND
$5.95/441-0

A leisure cruise is waylaid by Lord Henry Philbrock, a sadistic genius. The ship's passengers are kidnapped and spirited to his island prison, where the women are trained to accommodate the most bizarre sexual cravings of the rich, the famous, the pampered and the perverted.

ALIZARIN LAKE

SEX ON DOCTOR'S ORDERS
$5.95/402-X

Beth, a nubile young nurse, uses her considerable skills to further medical science by offering incomparable and insatiable assistance in the gathering of important specimens. Soon, an assortment of randy characters is lending a hand in this highly erotic work. No man leaves naughty Nurse Beth's station without surrendering what she needs!

THE EROTIC ADVENTURES OF HARRY TEMPLE
$4.95/127-6

Harry Temple's memoirs chronicle his amorous adventures from his initiation at the hands of insatiable sirens, through his stay at a house of hot repute, to his encounters with a chastity-belted nympho!

JOHN NORMAN

TARNSMAN OF GOR
$6.95/486-0

This controversial series returns! *Tarnsman* finds Tarl Cabot transported to Counter-Earth, better known as Gor. He must quickly accustom himself to the ways of this world, including the caste system which exalts some as Priest-Kings or Warriors, and debases others as slaves. A spectacular world unfolds in this first volume of John Norman's Gorean series.

OUTLAW OF GOR
$6.95/487-9

In this second volume, Tarl Cabot returns to Gor, where he might reclaim both his woman and his role of Warrior. But upon arriving, he discovers that his name, his city and the names of those he loves have become unspeakable. Cabot has become an outlaw, and must discover his new purpose on this strange planet, where danger stalks the outcast, and even simple answers have their price....

MASQUERADE BOOKS

PRIEST-KINGS OF GOR
$6.95/488-7

The third volume of John Norman's million-selling Gor series. Tarl Cabot searches for the truth about his lovely wife Talena. Does she live, or was she destroyed by the mysterious, all-powerful Priest-Kings? Cabot is determined to find out—even while knowing that no one who has approached the mountain stronghold of the Priest-Kings has ever returned alive....

NOMADS OF GOR
$6.95/527-1

Another provocative trip to the barbaric and mysterious world of Gor. Norman's heroic Tarnsman finds his way across this Counter-Earth, pledged to serve the Priest-Kings in their quest for survival. Unfortunately for Cabot, his mission leads him to the savage Wagon People—nomads who may very well kill before surrendering any secrets....

RACHEL PEREZ

AFFINITIES
$4.95/113-6

"Kelsy had a liking for cool upper-class blondes, the long-legged girls from Lake Forest and Winnetka who came into the city to cruise the lesbian bars on Halsted, looking for breathless ecstasies...." A scorching tale of lesbian libidos unleashed, from a writer more than capable of exploring every nuance of female passion in vivid detail.

SYDNEY ST. JAMES

RIVE GAUCHE
$5.95/317-1

The Latin Quarter, Paris, circa 1920. Expatriate bohemians couple with abandon—before eventually abandoning their ambitions amidst the intoxicating temptations waiting to be indulged in every bedroom.

GARDEN OF DELIGHT
$4.95/3058-X

A vivid account of sexual awakening that follows an innocent but insatiably curious young woman's journey from the furtive, forbidden joys of dormitory life to the unabashed carnality of the wild world.

DON WINSLOW

PRIVATE PLEASURES
$6.50/504-2

An assortment of sensual encounters designed to appeal to the most discerning reader. Frantic voyeurs, licentious exhibitionists, and everyday lovers are here displayed in all their wanton glory—proving again that fleshly pleasures have no more apt chronicler than Don Winslow.

THE INSATIABLE MISTRESS OF ROSEDALE
$6.50/494-1

The story of the perfect couple: Edward and Lady Penelope, who reside in beautiful and mysterious Rosedale manor. While Edward is a true connoisseur of sexual perversion, it is Lady Penelope whose mastery of complete sensual pleasure makes their home infamous. Indulging one another's bizarre whims is a way of life for this wicked couple, and none who encounter the extravagances of Rosedale will forget what they've learned....

SECRETS OF CHEATEM MANOR
$6.50/434-8

Edward returns to his late father's estate, to find it being run by the majestic Lady Amanda. Edward can hardly believe his luck—Lady Amanda is assisted by her two beautiful, lonely daughters, Catherine and Prudence. What the randy young man soon comes to realize is the love of discipline that all three beauties share.

KATERINA IN CHARGE
$5.95/409-7

When invited to a country retreat by a mysterious couple, two randy young ladies can hardly resist! But do they have any idea what they're in for? Whatever the case, the imperious Katerina will make her desires known very soon—and demand that they be fulfilled... Sexual innocence subjugated and defiled.

THE MANY PLEASURES OF IRONWOOD
$5.95/310-4

Seven lovely young women are employed by The Ironwood Sportsmen's Club, where their natural talents are put to creative use. A small and exclusive club with seven carefully selected sexual connoisseurs, Ironwood is dedicated to the relentless pursuit of sensual pleasure.

CLAIRE'S GIRLS
$5.95/442-9

You knew when she walked by that she was something special. She was one of Claire's girls, a woman carefully dressed and groomed to fill a role, to capture a look, to fit an image crafted by the sophisticated proprietress of an exclusive escort agency. High-class whores blow the roof off in this blow-by-blow account of life behind the closed doors of a sophisticated brothel.

TAU'TEVU   N. WHALLEN
$6.50/426-7

In a mysterious land, the statuesque and beautiful Vivian learns to subject herself to the hand of a mysterious man. He systematically helps her prove her own strength, and brings to life in her an unimagined sensual fire. But who is this man, who goes only by the name of Orpheo?

COMPLIANCE
$5.95/356-2

Fourteen stories exploring the pleasures of ultimate release. Characters from all walks of life learn to trust in the skills of others, hoping to experience the thrilling liberation of sexual submission. Here are the many joys to be found in some of the most forbidden sexual practices around....

THE CLASSIC COLLECTION
PROTESTS, PLEASURES, RAPTURES
$5.95/400-3

Invited for an allegedly quiet weekend at a country vicarage, a young woman is stunned to find herself surrounded by shocking acts of sexual sadism. Soon, her curiosity is piqued, and she begins to explore her own capacities for cruelty. The ultimate tale of an extraordinary woman's erotic awakening.

MASQUERADE BOOKS

THE YELLOW ROOM
$5.95/378-3
The "yellow room" holds the secrets of lust, lechery, and the lash. There, bare-bottomed, spread-eagled, and open to the world, demure Alice Darvell soon learns to love her lickings. In the second tale, hot heiress Rosa Coote and her lusty servants whip up numerous adventures in punishment and pleasure.

SCHOOL DAYS IN PARIS
$5.95/325-2
The rapturous chronicles of a well-spent youth! Few Universities provide the profound and pleasurable lessons one learns in after-hours study—particularly if one is young and available, and lucky enough to have Paris as a playground. A stimulating look at the pursuits of young adulthood, set in a glittering city notorious for its amorous excesses.

MAN WITH A MAID
$4.95/307-4
The adventures of Jack and Alice have delighted readers for eight decades! A classic of its genre, *Man with a Maid* tells an outrageous tale of desire, revenge, and submission. This tale qualifies as one of the world's most popular adult novels—with over 200,000 copies in print!

CONFESSIONS OF A CONCUBINE III: PLEASURE'S PRISONER
$5.95/357-0
Filled with pulse-pounding excitement—including a daring escape from the harem and an encounter with an unspeakable sadist—*Pleasure's Prisoner* adds an unforgettable chapter to this thrilling confessional.

CLASSIC EROTIC BIOGRAPHIES

JENNIFER
$4.95/107-1
The return of one of the Sexual Revolution's most notorious heroines. From the bedroom of a notoriously insatiable dancer to an uninhibited ashram, *Jennifer* traces the exploits of one thoroughly modern woman as she lustfully explores the limits of her own sexuality.

JENNIFER III
$5.95/292-2
The further adventures of erotica's most daring heroine. Jennifer, the quintessential beautiful blonde, has a photographer's eye for details—particularly of the masculine variety! One by one, her subjects submit to her demands for sensual pleasure, becoming part of her now-infamous gallery of erotic conquests.

RHINOCEROS

KATHLEEN K.

SWEET TALKERS
$6.95/516-6
Kathleen K. ran a phone-sex company in the late 80s, and she opens up her diary for a very thought provoking peek at the life of a phone-sex operator—and reveals a number of secrets and surprises. Transcripts of actual conversations are included.

"If you enjoy eavesdropping on explicit conversations about sex... this book is for you."   —Spectator

"Highly recommended."   —Shiny International
Trade /$12.95/192-6

THOMAS S. ROCHE

DARK MATTER
$6.95/484-4
"*Dark Matter* is sure to please gender outlaws, body-mod junkies, goth vampires, boys who wish they were dykes, and anybody who's not to sure where the fine line should be drawn between pleasure and pain. It's a handful."   —Pat Califia

"Here is the erotica of the cumming millenium: velvet-voiced but razor-tongued, tarted-up, but smart as a whip behind that smudged black eyeliner—encompassing every conceivable gender and several in between. You will be deliciously disturbed, but never disappointed." —Poppy Z. Brite

NOIROTICA: AN ANTHOLOGY OF EROTIC CRIME STORIES
$6.95/390-2
A collection of darkly sexy tales, taking place at the crossroads of the crime and erotic genres. Thomas S. Roche has gathered together some of today's finest writers of sexual fiction, all of whom explore the murky terrain where desire runs irrevocably afoul of the law.

ROMY ROSEN

SPUNK
$6.95/492-5
A tale of unearthly beauty, outrageous decadence, and brutal exploitation. Casey, a lovely model poised upon the verge of super-celebrity, falls for an insatiable young rock singer—not suspecting that his sexual appetite has led him to experiment with a dangerous new aphrodisiac. Casey becomes an addict, and her craving plunges her into a strange underworld, where bizarre sexual compulsions are indulged behind the most exclusive doors and the only chance for redemption lies with a shadowy young man with a secret of his own.

MOLLY WEATHERFIELD
CARRIE'S STORY
$6.95/485-2

"I had been Jonathan's slave for about a year when he told me he wanted to sell me at an auction. I wasn't in any condition to respond when he told me this..." Desire and depravity run rampant in this story of uncompromising mastery and irrevocable submission. A unique piece of erotica that is both thoughtful and hot!

"I was stunned by how well it was written and how intensely foreign I found its sexual world.... And, since this is a world I don't frequent... I thoroughly enjoyed the National Geo tour." —bOING bOING

"Hilarious and harrowing... just when you think things can't get any wilder, they do." —Black Sheets

CYBERSEX CONSORTIUM
CYBERSEX: THE PERV'S GUIDE TO FINDING SEX ON THE INTERNET
$6.95/471-2

You've heard the objections: cyberspace is soaked with sex. Okay—so where is it!? Tracking down the good stuff—the real good stuff—can waste an awful lot of expensive time, and frequently leave you high and dry. The Cybersex Consortium presents an easy-to-use guide for those intrepid adults who know what they want. No horny hacker can afford to pass up this map to the kinkiest rest stops on the Info Superhighway.

AMELIA G, EDITOR
BACKSTAGE PASSES
$6.95/438-0

Amelia G, editor of the goth-sex journal Blue Blood, has brought together some of today's most irreverant writers, each of whom has outdone themselves with an edgy, antic tale of modern lust. Punks, metalheads, and grunge-trash roam the pages of Backstage Passes, and no one knows their ways better...

GERI NETTICK WITH BETH ELLIOT
MIRRORS: PORTRAIT OF A LESBIAN TRANSSEXUAL
$6.95/435-6

The alternately heartbreaking and empowering story of one woman's long road to full selfhood. Born a male, Geri Nettick knew something just didn't fit. And even after coming to terms with her own gender dysphoria—and taking steps to correct it—she still fought to be accepted by the lesbian feminist community to which she felt she belonged. A fascinating, true tale of struggle and discovery.

DAVID MELTZER
UNDER
$6.95/290-6

The story of a 21st century sex professional living at the bottom of the social heap. After surgeries designed to increase his physical allure, corrupt government forces drive the cyber-gigolo underground—where even more bizarre cultures await him.

ORF
$6.95/110-1

He is the ultimate musician-hero—the idol of thousands, the fevered dream of many more. And like many musicians before him, he is misunderstood, misused—and totally out of control. Every last drop of feeling is squeezed from a modern-day troubadour and his lady love.

LAURA ANTONIOU, EDITOR
NO OTHER TRIBUTE
$6.95/294-9

A collection sure to challenge Political Correctness in a way few have before, with tales of women kept in bondage to their lovers by their deepest passions. Love pushes these women beyond acceptable limits, rendering them helpless to deny anything to the men and women they adore. A volume dedicated to all Slaves of Desire.

SOME WOMEN
$6.95/300-7

Over forty essays written by women actively involved in consensual dominance and submission. Professional mistresses, lifestyle leatherdykes, whipmakers, titleholders—women from every conceivable walk of life lay bare their true feelings about explosive issues.

BY HER SUBDUED
$6.95/281-7

These tales all involve women in control—of their lives, their loves, their men. So much in control that they can remorselessly break rules to become powerful goddesses of the men who sacrifice all to worship at their feet.

TRISTAN TAORMINO & DAVID AARON CLARK, EDITORS
RITUAL SEX
$6.95/391-0

While many people believe the body and soul to occupy almost completely independent realms, the many contributors to Ritual Sex know—and demonstrate—that the two share more common ground than society feels comfortable acknowledging. From personal memoirs of ecstatic revelation, to fictional quests to reconcile sex and spirit, Ritual Sex provides an unprecedented look at private life.

TAMMY JO ECKHART
PUNISHMENT FOR THE CRIME
$6.95/427-5

Peopled by characters of rare depth, these stories explore the true meaning of dominance and submission. From an encounter between two of society's most despised individuals, to the explorations of longtime friends, these tales take you where few others have ever dared....

AMARANTHA KNIGHT, EDITOR
SEDUCTIVE SPECTRES
$6.95/464-X

Breathtaking tours through the erotic supernatural via the macabre imaginations of today's best writers. Never before have ghostly encounters been so alluring, thanks to a cast of otherworldly characters well-acquainted with the pleasures of the flesh.

MASQUERADE BOOKS

SEX MACABRE
$6.95/392-9

Horror tales designed for dark and sexy nights. Amarantha Knight—the woman behind the Darker Passions series—has gathered together erotic stories sure to make your skin crawl, and heart beat faster.

FLESH FANTASTIC
$6.95/352-X

Humans have long toyed with the idea of "playing God": creating life from nothingness, bringing life to the inanimate. Now Amarantha Knight collects stories exploring not only the act of Creation, but the lust that follows....

GARY BOWEN
DIARY OF A VAMPIRE
$6.95/331-7

"Gifted with a darkly sensual vision and a fresh voice, [Bowen] is a writer to watch out for."
—Cecilia Tan

Rafael, a red-blooded male with an insatiable hunger for the same, is the perfect antidote to the effete malcontents haunting bookstores today. The emergence of a bold and brilliant vision, rooted in past and present.

RENÉ MAIZEROY
FLESHLY ATTRACTIONS
$6.95/299-X

Lucien was the son of the wantonly beautiful actress, Marie-Rose Hardanges. When she decides to let a "friend" introduce her son to the pleasures of love, Marie-Rose could not have foretold the excesses that would lead to her own ruin and that of her cherished son.

JEAN STINE
THRILL CITY
$6.95/411-9

Thrill City is the seat of the world's increasing depravity, and this classic novel transports you there with a vivid style you'd be hard pressed to ignore. No writer is better suited to describe the extremes of this modern Babylon.

SEASON OF THE WITCH
$6.95/268-X

"A future in which it is technically possible to transfer the total mind...of a rapist killer into the brain dead but physically living body of his female victim. Remarkable for intense psychological technique. There is eroticism but it is necessary to mark the differences between the sexes and the subtle altering of a man into a woman." —The Science Fiction Critic

GRANT ANTREWS
MY DARLING DOMINATRIX
$6.95/447-X

When a man and a woman fall in love, it's supposed to be simple and uncomplicated—unless that woman happens to be a dominatrix. Curiosity gives way to desire in this story of one man's awakening to the joys of willing slavery.

JOHN WARREN
THE TORQUEMADA KILLER
$6.95/367-8

Detective Eva Hernandez gets her first "big case": a string of vicious murders taking place within New York's SM community. Eva assembles the evidence, revealing a picture of a world misunderstood and under attack—and gradually comes to understand her own place within it.

THE LOVING DOMINANT
$6.95/218-3

Everything you need to know about an infamous sexual variation—and an unspoken type of love. Mentor—a longtime player in scene—guides readers through this world and reveals the too-often hidden basis of the D/S relationship: care, trust and love.

LAURA ANTONIOU WRITING AS "SARA ADAMSON"
THE TRAINER
$6.95/249-9

The Marketplace—the ultimate underground sexual realm includes not only willing slaves, but the exquisite trainers who take submissives firmly in hand. And now these mentors divulge the desires that led them to become the ultimate figures of authority.

THE SLAVE
$6.95/173-X

This second volume in the "Marketplace" trilogy further elaborates the world of slaves and masters. One talented submissive longs to join the ranks of those who have proven themselves worthy of entry into the Marketplace. But the delicious price is staggeringly high....

THE MARKETPLACE
$6.95/3096-2

"Merchandise does not come easily to the Marketplace.... They haunt the clubs and the organizations.... Some are so ripe that they intimidate the poseurs, the weekend sadists and the furtive dilettantes who are so endemic to that world. And they never stop asking where we may be found...."

DAVID AARON CLARK
SISTER RADIANCE
$6.95/215-9

Rife with Clark's trademark vivisections of contemporary desires, sacred and profane. The vicissitudes of lust and romance are examined against a backdrop of urban decay in this testament to the allure of the forbidden.

THE WET FOREVER
$6.95/117-9

The story of Janus and Madchen—a small-time hood and a beautiful sex worker on the run from one of the most dangerous men they have ever known—The Wet Forever examines themes of loyalty, sacrifice, redemption and obsession amidst Manhattan's sex parlors and underground S/M clubs. Its combination of sex and suspense led Terence Sellers to proclaim it "evocative and poetic."

MICHAEL PERKINS
EVIL COMPANIONS
$6.95/3067-9

Set in New York City during the tumultuous waning years of the Sixties, *Evil Companions* has been hailed as "a frightening classic." A young couple explores the nether reaches of the erotic unconscious in a shocking confrontation with the extremes of passion.

THE SECRET RECORD: MODERN EROTIC LITERATURE
$6.95/3039-3

Michael Perkins surveys the field with authority and unique insight. Updated and revised to include the latest trends, tastes, and developments in this misunderstood and maligned genre.

AN ANTHOLOGY OF CLASSIC ANONYMOUS EROTIC WRITING
$6.95/140-3

Michael Perkins has collected the very best passages from the world's erotic writing. "Anonymous" is one of the most infamous bylines in publishing history—and these steamy excerpts show why! Includes excerpts from some of the most famous titles in the history of erotic literature.

LIESEL KULIG
LOVE IN WARTIME
$6.95/3044-X

Madeleine knew that the handsome SS officer was a dangerous man, but she was just a cabaret singer in Nazi-occupied Paris, trying to survive in a perilous time. When Josef fell in love with her, he discovered that a beautiful woman can sometimes be as dangerous as any warrior.

HELEN HENLEY
ENTER WITH TRUMPETS
$6.95/197-7

Helen Henley was told that women just don't write about sex—much less the taboos she was so interested in exploring. So Henley did it alone, flying in the face of "tradition" by writing this touching tale of arousal and devotion in one couple's kinky relationship.

ALICE JOANOU
BLACK TONGUE
$6.95/258-2

"Joanou has created a series of sumptuous, brooding, dark visions of sexual obsession, and is undoubtedly a name to look out for in the future."
—Redeemer

Exploring lust at its most florid and unsparing, *Black Tongue* is a trove of baroque fantasies—each redolent of forbidden passions. Joanou creates some of erotica's most mesmerizing and unforgettable characters.

TOURNIQUET
$6.95/3060-1

A heady collection of stories and effusions from the pen of one our most dazzling young writers. Strange tales abound, from the story of the mysterious and cruel Cybele, to an encounter with the sadistic entertainment of a bizarre after-hours cafe. A complex and riveting series of meditations on desire.

CANNIBAL FLOWER
$4.95/72-6

The provocative debut volume from this acclaimed writer. "She is waiting in her darkened bedroom, as she has waited throughout history, to seduce the men who are foolish enough to be blinded by her irresistible charms.... She is the goddess of sexuality, and *Cannibal Flower* is her haunting siren song."
—Michael Perkins

PHILIP JOSÉ FARMER
A FEAST UNKNOWN
$6.95/276-0

"Sprawling, brawling, shocking, suspenseful, hilarious..."
—Theodore Sturgeon

Farmer's supreme anti-hero returns. "I was conceived and born in 1888." Slowly, Lord Grandrith—armed with the belief that he is the son of Jack the Ripper—tells the story of his remarkable and unbridled life. His story begins with his discovery of the secret of immortality—and progresses to encompass the furthest extremes of human behavior.

THE IMAGE OF THE BEAST
$6.95/166-7

Herald Childe has seen Hell, glimpsed its horror in an act of sexual mutilation. Childe must now find and destroy an inhuman predator through the streets of a polluted and decadent Los Angeles of the future. One clue after another leads Childe to an inescapable realization about the nature of sex and evil....

DANIEL VIAN
ILLUSIONS
$6.95/3074-1

Two tales of danger and desire in Berlin on the eve of WWII. From private homes to lurid cafés, passion is exposed in stark contrast to the brutal violence of the time, as desperate people explore their deepest, darkest sexual desires.

SAMUEL R. DELANY
THE MAD MAN
$8.99/408-9

"Reads like a pornographic reflection of Peter Ackroyd's *Chatterton* or A. S. Byatt's *Possession*.... Delany develops an insightful dichotomy between [his protagonist]'s two worlds: the one of cerebral philosophy and dry academia, the other of heedless, 'impersonal' obsessive sexual extremism. When these worlds finally collide...the novel achieves a surprisingly satisfying resolution...." —Publishers Weekly

For his thesis, graduate student John Marr researches the life of Timothy Hasler: a philosopher whose career was cut tragically short over a decade earlier. On another front, Marr finds himself increasingly drawn toward shocking, depraved sexual entanglements with the homeless men of his neighborhood, until it begins to seem that Hasler's death might hold some key to his own life as a gay man in the age of AIDS. Unquestionably one of Delany's most shocking works, *The Mad Man* is one of American erotic literature's most transgressive titles.

MASQUERADE BOOKS

EQUINOX
$6.95/157-8
The Scorpion has sailed the seas in a quest for every possible pleasure. Her crew is a collection of the young, the twisted, the insatiable. A drifter comes into their midst and is taken on a fantastic journey to the darkest, most dangerous sexual extremes—until he is finally a victim to their boundless appetites. An early title that set the way for the author's later explorations of extreme, forbidden sexual behaviors. Long out of print, this disturbing tale is finally available under the author's original title.

ANDREI CODRESCU
THE REPENTANCE OF LORRAINE
$6.95/329-5
"One of our most prodigiously talented and magical writers."
—*NYT Book Review*
By the acclaimed author of *The Hole in the Flag* and *The Blood Countess*. An aspiring writer, a professor's wife, a secretary, gold anklets, Maoists, Roman harlots—and more—swirl through this spicy tale of a harried quest for a mythic artifact. Written when the author was a young man, this lusty yarn was inspired by the heady days of the Sixties. Includes a new introduction by the author, detailing the events that inspired *Lorraine's* creation. A touching, arousing product from a more innocent time.

TUPPY OWENS
SENSATIONS
$6.95/3081-4
Tuppy Owens tells the unexpurgated story of the making of *Sensations*—the first big-budget sex flick. Originally commissioned to appear in book form after the release of the film in 1975, *Sensations* is finally released under Masquerade's stylish Rhino*ceros* imprint.

SOPHIE GALLEYMORE BIRD
MANEATER
$6.95/103-9
Through a bizarre act of creation, a man attains the "perfect" lover—by all appearances a beautiful, sensuous woman, but in reality something far darker. Once brought to life she will accept no mate, seeking instead the prey that will sate her hunger for vengeance.

LEOPOLD VON SACHER-MASOCH
VENUS IN FURS
$6.95/3089-X
This classic 19th century novel is the first uncompromising exploration of the dominant/submissive relationship in literature. The alliance of Severin and Wanda epitomizes Sacher-Masoch's dark obsession with a cruel, controlling goddess and the urges that drive the man held in her thrall. This special edition includes the letters exchanged between Sacher-Masoch and Emilie Mataja, an aspiring writer he sought to cast as the avatar of the forbidden desires expressed in his most famous work.

BADBOY

WILLIAM J. MANN, EDITOR
GRAVE PASSIONS
$6.50/405-4
A collection of the most chilling tales of passion currently being penned by today's most provocative gay writers. Unnatural transformations, otherworldly encounters, and deathless desires make for a collection sure to keep readers up late at night—for a variety of reasons!

J. A. GUERRA, EDITOR
COME QUICKLY: FOR BOYS ON THE GO
$6.50/413-5
Here are over sixty of the hottest fantasies around—all designed to get you going in less time than it takes to dial 976. Julian Anthony Guerra, the editor behind the phenomenally popular *Men at Work* and *Badboy Fantasies*, has put together this volume especially for you—a busy man on a modern schedule, who still appreciates a little old-fashioned action.

JOHN PRESTON
HUSTLING: A GENTLEMAN'S GUIDE TO THE FINE ART OF HOMOSEXUAL PROSTITUTION
$6.50/517-4
The very first guide to the gay world's most infamous profession. John Preston solicited the advice and opinions of "working boys" from across the country in his effort to produce the ultimate guide to the hustler's world. Hustling covers every practical aspect of the business, from clientele and payment options to "specialties," sidelines and drawbacks. No stone is left unturned—and no wrong turn left unadmonished—in this guidebook to the ins and outs of this much-mythologized trade.

"...Unrivalled. For any man even vaguely contemplating going into business this tome has got to be the first port of call."
—*Divinity*

"Fun and highly literary. What more could you expect form such an accomplished activist, author and editor?"
—*Drummer*
Trade $12.95/137-3
MR. BENSON
$4.95/3041-5
A classic erotic novel from a time when there was no limit to what a man could dream of doing.... Jamie is an aimless young man lucky enough to encounter Mr. Benson. He is soon led down the path of erotic enlightenment, learning to accept this man as his master. Jamie's incredible adventures never fail to excite—especially when the going gets rough! One of the first runaway bestsellers in gay erotic literature, *Mr. Benson* returns to capture the imagination of a new generation.

MASQUERADE BOOKS

TALES FROM THE DARK LORD
$5.95/323-6

A new collection of twelve stunning works from the man *Lambda Book Report* called "the Dark Lord of gay erotica." The relentless ritual of lust and surrender is explored in all its manifestations in this heart-stopping triumph of authority and vision from the Dark Lord!

TALES FROM THE DARK LORD II
$4.95/176-4

The second volume of John Preston's masterful short stories. Includes an interview with the author, and a sexy screenplay written for pornstar Scott O'Hara.

THE ARENA
$4.95/3083-0

There is a place on the edge of fantasy where every desire is indulged with abandon. Men go there to unleash beasts, to let demons roam free, to abolish all limits. At the center of each tale are the men who serve there, who offer themselves for the consummation of any passion, whose own bottomless urges compel their endless subservience. The thrilling tale of the ultimate erotic club, brought to vivid life by onw of gay erotica's masters.

THE HEIR•THE KING
$4.95/3048-2

The ground-breaking novel *The Heir*, written in the lyric voice of the ancient myths, tells the story of a world where slaves and masters create a new sexual society. This edition also includes a completely original work, *The King*, the story of a soldier who discovers his monarch's most secret desires. A special double volume, available only from Badboy.

....

THE MISSION OF ALEX KANE

SWEET DREAMS
$4.95/3062-0

It's the triumphant return of gay action hero Alex Kane! In *Sweet Dreams*, Alex travels to Boston where he takes on a street gang that stalks gay teenagers. Mighty Alex Kane wreaks a fierce and terrible vengeance on those who prey on gay people everywhere!

GOLDEN YEARS
$4.95/3069-5

When evil threatens the plans of a group of older gay men, Kane's got the muscle to take it head on. Along the way, he wins the support—and very specialized attentions—of a cowboy plucked right out of the Old West. But Kane and the Cowboy have a surprise waiting for them....

DEADLY LIES
$4.95/3076-8

Politics is a dirty business and the dirt becomes deadly when a political smear campaign targets gay men. Who better to clean things up than Alex Kane! Alex comes to protect the dreams, and lives, of gay men imperiled by lies and deceit.

STOLEN MOMENTS
$4.95/3098-9

Houston's evolving gay community is victimized by a malicious newspaper editor who is more than willing to sacrifice gays on the altar of circulation. He never counted on Alex Kane, fearless defender of gay dreams and desires.

SECRET DANGER
$4.95/111-X

Homophobia: a pernicious social ill not confined by America's borders. Alex Kane and the faithful Danny are called to a small European country, where a group of gay tourists is being held hostage by ruthless terrorists. Luckily, the Mission of Alex Kane stands as firm foreign policy.

LETHAL SILENCE
$4.95/125-X

The Mission of Alex Kane thunders to a conclusion. Chicago becomes the scene of the right-wing's most noxious plan—facilitated by unholy political alliances. Alex and Danny head to the Windy City to take up battle with the mercenaries who would squash gay men underfoot.

....

MATT TOWNSEND

SOLIDLY BUILT
$6.50/416-X

The tale of the tumultuous relationship between Jeff, a young photographer, and Mark, the butch electrician hired to wire Jeff's new home. For Jeff, it's love at first sight; Mark, however, has more than a few hang-ups. Soon, both are forced to reevaluate their outlooks, and are assisted by a variety of hot men....

....

JAY SHAFFER

SHOOTERS
$5.95/284-1

No mere catalog of random acts, *Shooters* tells the stories of a variety of stunning men and the ways they connect in sexual and non-sexual ways. A virtuoso storyteller, Shaffer always gets his man.

ANIMAL HANDLERS
$4.95/264-7

In Shaffer's world, each and every man finally succumbs to the animal urges deep inside. And if there's any creature that promises a wild time, it's a beast who's been caged for far too long. Shaffer has one of the keenest eyes for the nuances of male passion.

FULL SERVICE
$4.95/150-0

Wild men build up steam until they finally let loose. No-nonsense guys bear down hard on each other as they work their way toward release in this finely detailed assortment of masculine fantasies. One of gay erotica's most insightful chroniclers of male passion.

....

D. V. SADERO

IN THE ALLEY
$4.95/144-6

Hardworking men—from cops to carpenters—bring their own special skills and impressive tools to the most satisfying job of all: capturing and breaking the male sexual beast. Hot, incisive and way over the top, D.V. Sadero's imagination breathes fresh life into some of the genre's most traditional situations. One of the new generation's most exhilarating voices.

MASQUERADE BOOKS

SCOTT O'HARA
DO-IT-YOURSELF PISTON POLISHING
$6.50/489-5

Longtime sex-pro Scott O'Hara draws upon his acute powers of seduction to lure you into a world of hard, horny men long overdue for a tune-up. Pretty soon, you'll pop your own hood for the servicing you know you need....

SUTTER POWELL
EXECUTIVE PRIVILEGES
$6.50/383-X

No matter how serious or sexy a predicament his characters find themselves in, Powell conveys the sheer exuberance of their encounters with a warm humor rarely seen in contemporary gay erotica.

GARY BOWEN
WESTERN TRAILS
$6.50/477-1

A wild roundup of tales devoted to life on the lone prairie. Gary Bowen—a writer well-versed in the Western genre —has collected the very best contemporary cowboy stories. Some of gay literature's brightest stars tell the sexy truth about the many ways a rugged stud found to satisfy himself—and his buddy—in the Very Wild West.

MAN HUNGRY
$5.95/374-0

By the author of *Diary of a Vampire*. A riveting collection of stories from one of gay erotica's new stars. Dipping into a variety of genres, Bowen crafts tales of lust unlike anything being published today.

KYLE STONE
HOT BAUDS 2
$6.50/479-8

Another collection of cyberfantasies—compiled by the inimitable Kyle Stone. After the success of the original *Hot Bauds*, Stone conducted another heated search through the world's randiest bulletin boards, resulting in one of the most scalding follow-ups ever published. Here's all the scandalous stuff you've heard so much about—sexy, shameless, and eminently user-friendly.

FIRE & ICE
$5.95/297-3

A collection of stories from the author of the infamous adventures of PB 500. Randy, powerful, and just plain bad, Stone's characters always promise one thing: enough hot action to burn away your desire for anyone else....

HOT BAUDS
$5.95/285-X

The author of *Fantasy Board* and *The Initiation of PB 500* bombed cyberspace for the hottest fantasies of the world's horniest hackers. Stone has assembled the first collection of the raunchy erotica so many gay men cruise the Information Superhighway for.

FANTASY BOARD
$4.95/212-4

The author of the scalding sci-fi adventures of PB 500 explores the more foreseeable future—through the intertwined lives (and private parts) of a collection of randy computer hackers. On the Lambda Gate BBS, every hot and horny male is in search of a little virtual satisfaction—and is certain to find even more than he'd hoped for!

THE CITADEL
$4.95/198-5

The sequel to *The Initiation of PB 500*. Having proven himself worthy of his stunning master, Micah—now known only as '500'—will face new challenges and hardships after his entry into the forbidding Citadel. Only his master knows what awaits—and whether Micah will again distinguish himself as the perfect instrument of pleasure....

THE INITIATION OF PB 500
$4.95/141-1

He is a stranger on their planet, unschooled in their language, and ignorant of their customs. But this man, Micah—now known only by his number—will soon be trained in every last detail of erotic personal service. And, once nurtured and transformed into the perfect physical specimen, he must begin proving himself worthy of the master who has chosen him....

RITUALS
$4.95/168-3

Via a computer bulletin board, a young man finds himself drawn into a series of sexual rites that transform him into the willing slave of a mysterious stranger. Gradually, all vestiges of his former life are thrown off, and he learns to live for his Master's touch....

ROBERT BAHR
SEX SHOW
$4.95/225-6

Luscious dancing boys. Brazen, explicit acts. Unending stimulation. Take a seat, and get very comfortable, because the curtain's going up on a show no discriminating appetite can afford to miss.

JASON FURY
THE ROPE ABOVE, THE BED BELOW
$4.95/269-8

The irresistible Jason Fury returns—this time, telling the tale of a vicious murderer preying upon New York's go-go boy population. No one is who or what they seem, and in order to solve this mystery and save lives, each studly suspect must lay bare his soul—and more!

ERIC'S BODY
$4.95/151-9

Meet Jason Fury—blond, blue-eyed and up for anything. Fury's sexiest tales are collected in book form for the first time. Follow the irresistible Jason through sexual adventures unlike any you have ever read....

MASQUERADE BOOKS

LARS EIGHNER

WHISPERED IN THE DARK
$5.95/286-8
A volume demonstrating Eighner's unique combination of strengths: poetic descriptive power, an unfailing ear for dialogue, and a finely tuned feeling for the nuances of male passion.

AMERICAN PRELUDE
$4.95/170-5
Eighner is widely recognized as one of our best, most exciting gay writers. He is also one of gay erotica's true masters—and *American Prelude* shows why. Wonderfully written, blisteringly hot tales of all-American lust.

B.M.O.C.
$4.95/3077-6
In a college town known as "the Athens of the Southwest," studs of every stripe are up all night—studying, naturally. Relive university life the way it was supposed to be, with a cast of handsome honor students majoring in Human Homosexuality.

DAVID LAURENTS, EDITOR

SOUTHERN COMFORT
$6.50/466-6
Editor David Laurents now unleashes a collection of tales focusing on the American South—reflecting not only Southern literary tradition, but the many contributions the region has made to the iconography of the American Male.

WANDERLUST: HOMOEROTIC TALES OF TRAVEL
$5.95/395-3
A volume dedicated to the special pleasures of faraway places. Gay men have always had a special interest in travel—and not only for the scenic vistas. Wanderlust celebrates the freedom of the open road, and the allure of men who stray from the beaten path....

THE BADBOY BOOK OF EROTIC POETRY
$5.95/382-1
Over fifty of today's best poets. Erotic poetry has long been the problem child of the literary world—highly creative and provocative, but somehow too frank to be "literature." Both learned and stimulating, *The Badboy Book of Erotic Poetry* restores eros to its rightful place of honor in contemporary gay writing.

AARON TRAVIS

BIG SHOTS
$5.95/448-8
Two fierce tales in one electrifying volume. In *Beirut*, Travis tells the story of ultimate military power and erotic subjugation; *Kip*, Travis' hypersexed and sinister take on film noir, appears in unexpurgated form for the first time.

EXPOSED
$4.95/126-8
A volume of shorter Travis tales, each providing a unique glimpse of the horny gay male in his natural environment! Cops, college jocks, ancient Romans—even Sherlock Holmes and his loyal Watson—cruise these pages, fresh from the throbbing pen of one of our hottest authors.

BEAST OF BURDEN
$4.95/105-5
Five ferocious tales. Innocents surrender to the brutal sexual mastery of their superiors, as taboos are shattered and replaced with the unwritten rules of masculine conquest. Intense, extreme—and totally Travis.

IN THE BLOOD
$5.95/283-3
Written when Travis had just begun to explore the true power of the erotic imagination, these stories laid the groundwork for later masterpieces. Among the many rewarding rarities included in this volume: "In the Blood" —a heart-pounding descent into sexual vampirism, written with the furious erotic power that is Travis' trademark.

THE FLESH FABLES
$4.95/243-4
One of Travis' best collections. *The Flesh Fables* includes "Blue Light," his most famous story, as well as other masterpieces that established him as the erotic writer to watch. And watch carefully, because Travis always buries a surprise somewhere beneath his scorching detail....

SLAVES OF THE EMPIRE
$4.95/3054-7
"A wonderful mythic tale. Set against the backdrop of the exotic and powerful Roman Empire, this wonderfully written novel explores the timeless questions of light and dark in male sexuality. The locale may be the ancient world, but these are the slaves and masters of our time...." —John Prestor

BOB VICKERY

SKIN DEEP
$4.95/265-5
So many varied beauties no one will go away unsatisfied. No tantalizing morsel of manflesh is overlooked—or left unexplored! Beauty may be only skin deep, but a handful of beautiful skin is a tempting proposition.

JR

FRENCH QUARTER NIGHTS
$5.95/337-5
Sensual snapshots of the many places where men go down and dirty—from the steamy French Quarter to the steam room at the old Everard baths. These are nights you'll wish would go on forever....

TOM BACCHUS

RAHM
$5.95/315-5
The imagination of Tom Bacchus brings to life an extraordinary assortment of characters, from the Father of Us All the cowpoke next door, the early gay literati to rude queercore mosh rats. No one is better than Bacchus staking out sexual territory with a swagger and a sly grin

MASQUERADE BOOKS

BONE
$4.95/177-2

Queer musings from the pen of one of today's hottest young talents. A fresh outlook on fleshly indulgence yields more than a few pleasant surprises. Horny Tom Bacchus maps out the tricking ground of a new generation.

KEY LINCOLN
SUBMISSION HOLDS
$4.95/266-3

A bright young talent unleashes his first collection of gay erotica. From tough to tender, the men between these covers stop at nothing to get what they want. These sweat-soaked tales show just how bad boys can really get.

CALDWELL/EIGHNER
QSFX2
$5.95/278-7

The wickedest, wildest, other-worldliest yarns from two master storytellers—Clay Caldwell and Lars Eighner. Both eroticists take a trip to the furthest reaches of the sexual imagination, sending back ten stories proving that as much as things change, one thing will always remain the same....

CLAY CALDWELL
ASK OL' BUDDY
$5.95/346-5

Set in the underground SM world, Caldwell takes you on a journey of discovery—where men initiate one another into the secrets of the rawest sexual realm of all. And when each stud's initiation is complete, he takes his places among the masters—eager to take part in the training of another hungry soul...

STUD SHORTS
$5.95/320-T

"If anything, Caldwell's charm is more powerful, his nostalgia more poignant, the horniness he captures more sweetly, achingly acute than ever."
—Aaron Travis

A new collection of this legend's latest sex-fiction. With his customary candor, Caldwell tells all about cops, cadets, truckers, farmboys (and many more) in these dirty jewels.

TAILPIPE TRUCKER
$5.95/296-5

Trucker porn! In prose as free and unvarnished as a cross-country highway, Caldwell tells the truth about Trag and Curly—two men hot for the feeling of sweaty manflesh. Together, they pick up—and turn out—a couple of thrill-seeking punks.

SERVICE, STUD
$5.95/336-8

Another look at the gay future. The setting is the Los Angeles of a distant future. Here the all-male populace is divided between the served and the servants—guaranteeing the erotic satisfaction of all involved.

QUEERS LIKE US
$4.95/262-0

"Caldwell at his most charming." —Aaron Travis

For years the name Clay Caldwell has been synonymous with the hottest, most finely crafted gay tales available. *Queers Like Us* is one of his best: the story of a randy mailman's trek through a landscape of willing, available studs.

ALL-STUD
$4.95/104-7

This classic, sex-soaked tale takes place under the watchful eye of Number Ten: an omniscient figure who has decreed unabashed promiscuity as the law of his all-male land. One stud, however, takes it upon himself to challenge the social order, daring to fall in love. Finally, he is forced to fight for not only himself, but the man he loves.

CLAY CALDWELL AND AARON TRAVIS
TAG TEAM STUDS
$6.50/465-8

Thrilling tales from these two legendary eroticists. The wrestling world will never seem the same, once you've made your way through this assortment of sweaty, virile studs. But you'd better be wary—should one catch you off guard, you just might spend the rest of the night pinned to the mat....

LARRY TOWNSEND
LEATHER AD: S
$5.95/407-0

The second half of Townsend's acclaimed tale of lust through the personals—this time told from a Top's perspective. A simple ad generates many responses, and one man finds himself in the enviable position of putting these studly applicants through their paces......

LEATHER AD: M
$5.95/380-5

The first of this two-part classic. John's curious about what goes on between the leatherclad men he's fantasized about. He takes out a personal ad, and starts a journey of self-discovery that will leave no part of his life unchanged.

BEWARE THE GOD WHO SMILES
$5.95/321-X

Two lusty young Americans are transported to ancient Egypt—where they are embroiled in regional warfare and taken as slaves by marauding barbarians. The key to escape from this brutal bondage lies in their own rampant libidos, and urges as old as time itself.

MASQUERADE BOOKS

2069 TRILOGY
(This one-volume collection only $6.95) 244-2
For the first time, Larry Townsend's early science-fiction trilogy appears in one massive volume! Set in a future world, the 2069 Trilogy includes the tight plotting and shameless male sexual pleasure that established him as one of gay erotica's first masters.

MIND MASTER
$4.95/209-4
Who better to explore the territory of erotic dominance than an author who helped define the genre—and knows that ultimate mastery always transcends the physical. Another unrelenting Townsend tale.

THE LONG LEATHER CORD
$4.95/201-9
Chuck's stepfather never lacks money or clandestine male visitors with whom he enacts intense sexual rituals. As Chuck comes to terms with his own desires, he begins to unravel the mystery behind his stepfather's secret life.

MAN SWORD
$4.95/188-8
The très gai tale of France's King Henri III, who was unimaginably spoiled by his mother—the infamous Catherine de Medici—and groomed from a young age to assume the throne of France. Along the way, he encounters enough sexual schemers and politicos to alter one's picture of history forever!

THE FAUSTUS CONTRACT
$4.95/167-5
Two attractive young men desperately need $1000. Will do anything. Travel OK. Danger OK. Call anytime... Two cocky young hustlers get more than they bargained for in this story of lust and its discontents.

THE GAY ADVENTURES OF CAPTAIN GOOSE
$4.95/169-1
Hot young Jerome Gander is sentenced to serve aboard the H.M.S. Faerigold—a ship manned by the most hardened, unrepentant criminals. In no time, Gander becomes well-versed in the ways of horny men at sea, and the Faerigold becomes the most notorious vessel to ever set sail.

CHAINS
$4.95/158-6
Picking up street punks has always been risky, but in Larry Townsend's classic Chains, it sets off a string of events that must be read to be believed.

KISS OF LEATHER
$4.95/161-6
A look at the acts and attitudes of an earlier generation of gay leathermen, Kiss of Leather is full to bursting with the gritty, raw action that has distinguished Townsend's work for years. Sensual pain and pleasure mix in this tightly plotted tale.

RUN, LITTLE LEATHER BOY
$4.95/143-8
One young man's sexual awakening. A chronic underachiever, Wayne seems to be going nowhere fast. He finds himself bored with the everyday—and drawn to the masculine intensity of a dark and mysterious sexual underground, where he soon finds many goals worth pursuing....

RUN NO MORE
$4.95/152-7
The continuation of Larry Townsend's legendary Run, Little Leather Boy. This volume follows the further adventures of Townsend's leatherclad narrator as he travels every sexual byway available to the S/M male.

THE SCORPIUS EQUATION
$4.95/119-5
The story of a man caught between the demands of two galactic empires. Our randy hero must match wits—and more—with the incredible forces that rule his world.

THE SEXUAL ADVENTURES OF SHERLOCK HOLMES
$4.95/3097-0
A scandalously sexy take on this legendary sleuth. "A Study in Scarlet" is transformed to expose Mrs. Hudson as a man in drag, the Diogenes Club as an S/M arena, and clues only the redoubtable—and very horny—Sherlock Holmes could piece together. A baffling tale of sex and mystery.

....

DONALD VINING
CABIN FEVER AND OTHER STORIES
$5.95/338-4
Eighteen blistering stories in celebration of the most intimate of male bonding. Time after time, Donald Vining's men succumb to nature, and reaffirm both love and lust in modern gay life.

"Demonstrates the wisdom experience combined with insight and optimism can create."
—Bay Area Reporter

....

DEREK ADAMS
PRISONER OF DESIRE
$6.50/439-9
Scalding fiction from one of Badboy's most popular authors. The creator of horny P.I. Miles Diamond returns with this volume bursting with red-blooded, sweat-soaked excursions through the modern gay libido.

THE MARK OF THE WOLF
$5.95/361-9
I turned to look at the man who stared back at me from the mirror. The familiar outlines of my face seemed coarser, more sinister. An animal? The past comes back to haunt one well-off stud, whose unslakeable thirsts lead him into the arms of many men—and the midst of a perilous mystery.

MY DOUBLE LIFE
$5.95/314-7
Every man leads a double life, dividing his hours between the mundanities of the day and the outrageous pursuits of the night. The creator of sexy P.I. Miles Diamond shines a little light on the wicked things men do when no one's looking.

HEAT WAVE
$4.95/159-4
"His body was draped in baggy clothes, but there was hardly any doubt that they covered anything less than perfection.... His slacks were cinched tight around a narrow waist, and the rise of flesh pushing against the thin fabric promised a firm, melon-shaped ass...."

MASQUERADE BOOKS

MILES DIAMOND AND THE DEMON OF DEATH
$4.95/251-5
Derek Adams' gay gumshoe returns for further adventures. Miles always find himself in the stickiest situations—with any stud whose path he crosses! His adventures with "The Demon of Death" promise another carnal carnival.

THE ADVENTURES OF MILES DIAMOND
$4.95/118-7
The debut of Miles Diamond—Derek Adams' take on the classic American archetype of the hardboiled private eye. "The Case of the Missing Twin" promises to be a most rewarding case, packed as it is with randy studs. Miles sets about uncovering all as he tracks down the elusive and delectable Daniel Travis.

KELVIN BELIELE
IF THE SHOE FITS
$4.95/223-X
An essential and winning volume of tales exploring a world where randy boys can't help but do what comes naturally—as often as possible! Sweaty male bodies grapple in pleasure, proving the old adage: if the shoe fits, one might as well slip right in....

JAMES MEDLEY
THE REVOLUTIONARY & OTHER STORIES
$6.50/417-8
Billy, the son of the station chief of the American Embassy in Guatemala, is kidnapped and held for ransom. Frightened at first, Billy gradually develops an unimaginably close relationship with Juan, the revolutionary assigned to guard him.

HUCK AND BILLY
$4.95/245-0
Young love is always the sweetest, always the most sorrowful. Young lust, on the other hand, knows no bounds—and is often the hottest of one's life! Huck and Billy explore the desires that course through their young male bodies, determined to plumb the lusty depths of passion.

FLEDERMAUS
**FLEDERFICTION:
STORIES OF MEN AND TORTURE**
$5.95/355-4
Fifteen blistering paeans to men and their suffering. Fledermaus unleashes his most thrilling tales of punishment in this special volume designed with Badboy readers in mind.

VICTOR TERRY
MASTERS
$6.50/418-6
A powerhouse volume of boot-wearing, whip-wielding, bone-crunching bruisers who've got what it takes to make a grown man grovel. Between these covers lurk the most demanding of men—the imperious few to whom so many humbly offer themselves....

SM/SD
$6.50/406-2
Set around a South Dakota town called Prairie, these tales offer compelling evidence that the real rough stuff can still be found where men roam free of the restraints of "polite" society—and take what they want despite all rules.

WHiPs
$4.95/254-X
Connoisseurs of gay writing have known Victor Terry's work for some time. Cruising for a hot man? You'd better be, because one way or another, these WHiPs—officers of the Wyoming Highway Patrol—are gonna pull you over for a little impromptu interrogation....

MAX EXANDER
**DEEDS OF THE NIGHT:
TALES OF EROS AND PASSION**
$5.95/348-1
MAXimum porn! Exander's a writer who's seen it all—and is more than happy to describe every inch of it in pulsating detail. A whirlwind tour of the hypermasculine libido.

LEATHERSEX
$4.95/210-8
Hard-hitting tales from merciless Max Exander. This time he focuses on the leatherclad lust that draws together only the most willing and talented of tops and bottoms—for an all-out orgy of limitless surrender and control....

MANSEX
$4.95/160-8
"Mark was the classic leatherman: a huge, dark stud in chaps, with a big black moustache, hairy chest and enormous muscles. Exactly the kind of men Todd liked—strong, hunky, masculine, ready to take control...."

TOM CAFFREY
TALES FROM THE MEN'S ROOM
$5.95/364-3
From shameless cops on the beat to shy studs on stage, Caffrey explores male lust at its most elemental and arousing. And if there's a lesson to be learned, it's that the Men's Room is less a place than a state of mind—one that every man finds himself in, day after day....

HITTING HOME
$4.95/222-1
Titillating and compelling, the stories in *Hitting Home* make a strong case for there being only one thing on a man's mind.

TORSTEN BARRING
GUY TRAYNOR
$6.50/414-3
Another torturous *tour de force* from Torsten Barring. Some call Guy Traynor a theatrical genius; others say he was a madman. All anyone knows for certain is that his productions were the result of blood, sweat and tears—all extracted from his young, hung actors! Never have artists suffered so much for their craft!

BUY ANY 4 BOOKS & CHOOSE 1 ADDITIONAL BOOK, OF EQUAL OR LESSER VALUE, AS YOUR FREE GIFT

MASQUERADE BOOKS

PRISONERS OF TORQUEMADA
$5.95/252-3
Another volume sure to push you over the edge. How cruel is the "therapy" practiced at Casa Torquemada? Barring is just the writer to evoke such steamy sexual malevolence.

SHADOWMAN
$4.95/178-0
From spoiled Southern aristocrats to randy youths sowing wild oats at the local picture show, Barring's imagination works overtime in these vignettes of homolust—past, present and future.

PETER THORNWELL
$4.95/149-7
Follow the exploits of Peter Thornwell as he goes from misspent youth to scandalous stardom, all thanks to an insatiable libido and love for the lash. Peter and his sex-crazed sidekicks find themselves pursued by merciless men from all walks of life in this torrid take on Horatio Alger.

THE SWITCH
$4.95/3061-X
Sometimes a man needs a good whipping, and *The Switch* certainly makes a case! Packed with hot studs and unrelenting passions.

BERT McKENZIE

FRINGE BENEFITS
$5.95/354-6
From the pen of a widely published short story writer comes a volume of highly immodest tales. Not afraid of getting down and dirty, McKenzie produces some of today's most visceral sextales.

SONNY FORD

REUNION IN FLORENCE
$4.95/3070-9
Captured by Turks, Adrian and Tristan will do anything to save their heads. When Tristan is threatened by a Sultan's jealousy, Adrian begins his quest for the only man alive who can replace Tristan as the object of the Sultan's lust.

ROGER HARMAN

FIRST PERSON
$4.95/179-9
A highly personal collection. Each story takes the form of a confessional—told by men who've got plenty to confess! From the "first time ever" to firsts of different kinds, *First Person* tells truths too hot to be purely fiction.

J. A. GUERRA, ED.

SLOW BURN
$4.95/3042-3
Welcome to the Body Shoppe! Torsos get lean and hard, pecs widen, and stomachs ripple in these sexy stories of the power and perils of physical perfection.

DAVE KINNICK

SORRY I ASKED
$4.95/3090-3
Unexpurgated interviews with gay porn's rank and file. Get personal with the men behind (and under) the "stars," and discover the hot truth about the porn business.

SEAN MARTIN

SCRAPBOOK
$4.95/224-8
Imagine a book filled with only the best, most vivid remembrances…a book brimming with every hot, sexy encounter its pages can hold… Now you need only open up *Scrapbook* to know that such a volume really exists.…

CARO SOLES & STAN TAL, EDITORS

BIZARRE DREAMS
$4.95/187-X
An anthology of stirring voices dedicated to exploring the dark side of human fantasy. *Bizarre Dreams* brings together the most talented practitioners of "dark fantasy," the most forbidden sexual realm of all.

CHRISTOPHER MORGAN

STEAM GAUGE
$6.50/473-9
This volume abounds in manly men doing what they do best—to, with, or for any hot stud who crosses their paths. Frequently published to acclaim in the gay press, Christopher Morgan puts a fresh, contemporary spin on the very oldest of urges.

THE SPORTSMEN
$5.95/385-6
A collection of super-hot stories dedicated to that most popular of boys next door—the all-American athlete. Here are enough tales of carnal grand slams, sexy interceptions and highly personal bests to satisfy the hungers of the most ardent sports fan. Editor Christopher Morgan has gathered those writers who know just the type of guys that make up every red-blooded male's starting line-up.…

MUSCLE BOUND
$4.95/3028-8
In the New York City bodybuilding scene, country boy Tommy joins forces with sexy Will Rodriguez in a battle of wits and biceps at the hottest gym in town, where the weak are bound and crushed by iron-pumping gods.

MICHAEL LOWENTHAL, ED.

THE BADBOY EROTIC LIBRARY VOLUME I
$4.95/190-X
Excerpts from *A Secret Life*, *Imre*, *Sins of the Cities of the Plain*, *Teleny* and others demonstrate the uncanny gift for portraying sex between men that led to many of these titles being banned upon publication.

THE BADBOY EROTIC LIBRARY VOLUME II
$4.95/211-6
This time, selections are taken from *Mike and Me* and *Muscle Bound*, *Men at Work*, *Badboy Fantasies*, and *Slowburn*.

ERIC BOYD

MIKE AND ME
$5.95/419-4
Mike joined the gym squad to bulk up on muscle. Little did he know he'd be turning on every sexy muscle jock in Minnesota! Hard bodies collide in a series of workouts designed to generate a whole lot more than rips and cuts.

MASQUERADE BOOKS

MIKE AND THE MARINES
$6.50/497-1
Mike takes on America's most elite corps of studs—running into more than a few good men! Join in on the never-ending sexual escapades of this singularly lustful platoon!

ANONYMOUS

A SECRET LIFE
$4.95/3017-2
Meet Master Charles: only eighteen, and quite innocent, until his arrival at the Sir Percival's Royal Academy, where the daily lessons are supplemented with a crash course in pure, sweet sexual heat!

SINS OF THE CITIES OF THE PLAIN
$5.95/322-8
Indulge yourself in the scorching memoirs of young man-about-town Jack Saul. With his shocking dalliances with the lords and "ladies" of British high society, Jack's positively sinful escapades grow wilder with every chapter!

IMRE
$4.95/3019-1
What dark secrets, what fiery passions lay hidden behind strikingly beautiful Lieutenant Imre's emerald eyes? An extraordinary lost classic of fantasy, obsession, gay erotic desire, and romance in a small European town on the eve of WWI.

TELENY
$4.95/3020-2
Often attributed to Oscar Wilde, *Teleny* tells the story of one young man of independent means. He dedicates himself to a succession of forbidden pleasures, but instead finds love and tragedy when he becomes embroiled in a cult devoted to fulfilling only the very darkest of fantasies.

HARD CANDY

KEVIN KILLIAN

ARCTIC SUMMER
$6.95/514-X
Highly acclaimed author Kevin Killian's latest novel examines the many secrets lying beneath the placid exterior of America in the '50s. With the story of Liam Reilly—a young gay man of considerable means and numerous secrets—Killian exposes the contradictions of the American Dream, and the ramifications of the choices one is forced to make when hiding the truth.

STAN LEVENTHAL

BARBIE IN BONDAGE
$6.95/415-1
Widely regarded as one of the most refreshing, clear-eyed interpreters of big city gay male life, Leventhal here provides a series of explorations of love and desire between men. Uncompromising, but gentle and generous, *Barbie in Bondage* is a fitting tribute to the late author's unique talents.

SKYDIVING ON CHRISTOPHER STREET
$6.95/287-6
"Positively addictive."   —Dennis Cooper
Aside from a hateful job, a hateful apartment, a hateful world and an increasingly hateful lover, life seems, well, all right for the protagonist of Stan Leventhal's latest novel. Having already lost most of his friends to AIDS, how could things get any worse? But things soon do, and he's forced to endure much more....

PATRICK MOORE

IOWA
$6.95/423-2
"Moore is the Tennessee Williams of the nineties—profound intimacy freed in a compelling narrative."
                                          —Karen Finley
"Fresh and shiny and relevant to our time. *Iowa* is full of terrific characters etched in acid-sharp prose, soaked through with just enough ambivalence to make it thoroughly romantic."   —Felice Picano
A stunning novel about one gay man's journey into adulthood, and the roads that bring him home again.

PAUL T. ROGERS

SAUL'S BOOK
$7.95/462-3
Winner of the Editors' Book Award
"Exudes an almost narcotic power.... A masterpiece."   —*Village Voice Literary Supplement*
"A first novel of considerable power... Sinbad the Sailor, thanks to the sympathetic imagination of Paul T. Rogers, speaks to us all."   —*New York Times Book Review*
The story of a Times Square hustler called Sinbad the Sailor and Saul, a brilliant, self-destructive, alcoholic, thoroughly dominating character who may be the only love Sinbad will ever know.

WALTER R. HOLLAND

THE MARCH
$6.95/429-1
A moving testament to the power of friendship during even the worst of times. Beginning on a hot summer night in 1980, *The March* revolves around a circle of young gay men, and the many others their lives touch. Over time, each character changes in unexpected ways; lives and loves come together and fall apart, as society itself is horribly altered by the onslaught of AIDS.

RED JORDAN AROBATEAU

LUCY AND MICKEY
$6.95/311-2
The story of Mickey—an uncompromising butch—and her long affair with Lucy, the femme she loves. A raw tale of pre-Stonewall lesbian life.
"A necessary reminder to all who blissfully—some may say ignorantly—ride the wave of lesbian chic into the mainstream."   —Heather Findlay

MASQUERADE BOOKS

DIRTY PICTURES
$5.95/345-7

"Red Jordan Arobateau is the Thomas Wolfe of lesbian literature... She's a natural—raw talent that is seething, passionate, hard, remarkable."

—Lillian Faderman, editor of *Chloe Plus Olivia*

Dirty Pictures is the story of a lonely butch tending bar—and the femme she finally calls her own.

DONALD VINING
A GAY DIARY
$8.95/451-8

Donald Vining's *Diary* portrays a long-vanished age and the lifestyle of a gay generation all too frequently forgotten. "*A Gay Diary* is, unquestionably, the richest historical document of gay male life in the United States that I have ever encountered.... It illuminates a critical period in gay male American history."

—*Body Politic*

LARS EIGHNER
GAY COSMOS
$6.95/236-1

A title sure to appeal not only to Eighner's gay fans, but the many converts who first encountered his moving nonfiction work. Praised by the press, *Gay Cosmos* is an important contribution to the area of Gay and Lesbian Studies.

FELICE PICANO
THE LURE
$6.95/398-8

"The subject matter, plus the authenticity of Picano's research are, combined, explosive. Felice Picano is one hell of a writer."   —Stephen King

After witnessing a brutal murder, Noel is recruited by the police, to assist as a lure for the killer. Undercover, he moves deep into the freneticism of Manhattan's gay high-life—where he gradually becomes aware of the darker forces at work in his life. In addition to the mystery behind his mission, he begins to recognize changes: in his relationships with the men around him, in himself...

AMBIDEXTROUS
$6.95/275-2

"Deftly evokes those placid Eisenhower years of bicycles, boners, and book reports. Makes us remember what it feels like to be a child..."

—*The Advocate*

Picano's first "memoir in the form of a novel" tells all: home life, school face-offs, the ingenuous sophistications of his first sexual steps. In three years' time, he's had his first gay fling—and is on his way to becoming the widely praised writer he is today.

MEN WHO LOVED ME
$6.95/274-4

"Zesty...spiked with adventure and romance...a distinguished and humorous portrait of a vanished age."   —*Publishers Weekly*

In 1966, Picano abandoned New York, determined to find true love in Europe. Upon returning, he plunges into the city's thriving gay community of the 1970s.

WILLIAM TALSMAN
THE GAUDY IMAGE
$6.95/263-9

"To read *The Gaudy Image* now...it is to see firsthand the very issues of identity and positionality with which gay men were struggling in the decades before Stonewall. For what Talsman is dealing with...is the very question of how we conceive ourselves gay."

—from the introduction by Michael Bronski

ROSEBUD

THE ROSEBUD READER
$5.95/319-8

Rosebud has contributed greatly to the burgeoning genre of lesbian erotica—to the point that our authors are among the hottest and most closely watched names in lesbian and gay publishing. Here are the finest moments from Rosebud's contemporary classics.

LESLIE CAMERON
WHISPER OF FANS
$6.50/542-5

"Just looking into her eyes, she felt that she knew a lot about this woman. She could see strength, boldness, a fresh sense of aliveness that rocked her to the core. In turn she felt open, revealed under the woman's gaze—all her secrets already told. No need of shame or artifice...." A fresh tale of passion between women, from one of lesbian erotica's up-and-coming authors.

RACHEL PEREZ
ODD WOMEN
$6.50/526-3

These women are sexy, smart, tough—some even say odd. But who cares, when their combined ass-ets are so sweet! An assortment of Sapphic sirens proves once and for all that comely ladies come best in pairs.

RANDY TUROFF
LUST NEVER SLEEPS
$6.50/475-5

A rich volume of highly erotic, powerfully real fiction from the editor of *Lesbian Words*. Randy Turoff depicts a circle of modern women connected through the bonds of love, friendship, ambition, and lust with accuracy and compassion. Moving, tough, yet undeniably true, Turoff's stories create a stirring portrait of contemporary lesbian life and community.

RED JORDAN AROBATEAU
ROUGH TRADE
$6.50/470-4

Famous for her unflinching portrayal of lower-class dyke life and love, Arobateau outdoes herself with these tales of butch/femme affairs and unrelenting passions. Unapologetic and distinctly non-homogenized, *Rough Trade* is a must for all fans of challenging lesbian literature.

MASQUERADE BOOKS

BOYS NIGHT OUT
$6.50/463-1
A *Red*-hot volume of short fiction from this lesbian literary sensation. As always, Arobateau takes a good hard look at the lives of everyday women, noting well the struggles and triumphs each woman experiences.

ALISON TYLER
VENUS ONLINE
$6.50/521-2
What's my idea of paradise? Lovely Alexa spends her days in a boring bank job, not quite living up to her full potential—interested instead in saving her energies for her nocturnal pursuits. At night, Alexa goes online, living out virtual adventures that become more real with each session. Soon Alexa—aka Venus—feels her erotic imagination growing beyond anything she could have imagined.

DARK ROOM: AN ONLINE ADVENTURE
$6.50/455-0
Dani, a successful photographer, can't bring herself to face the death of her lover, Kate. An ambitious journalist, Kate was found mysteriously murdered, leaving her lover with only fond memories of a too-brief relationship. Determined to keep the memory of her lover alive, Dani goes online under Kate's screen alias—and begins to uncover the truth behind the crime that has torn her world apart.

BLUE SKY SIDEWAYS & OTHER STORIES
$6.50/394-5
A variety of women, and their many breathtaking experiences with lovers, friends—and even the occasional sexy stranger. From blossoming young beauties to fearless vixens, Tyler finds the sexy pleasures of everyday life.

DIAL "L" FOR LOVELESS
$5.95/386-4
Meet Katrina Loveless—a private eye talented enough to give Sam Spade a run for his money. In her first case, Katrina investigates a murder implicating a host of society's darlings. Loveless untangles the mess—while working herself into a variety of highly compromising knots with the many lovelies who cross her path!

THE VIRGIN
$5.95/379-1
Veronica answers a personal ad in the "Women Seeking Women" category—and discovers a whole sensual world she never knew existed! And she never dreamed she'd be prized as a virgin all over again, by someone who would deflower her with a passion no man could ever show....

K. T. BUTLER
TOOLS OF THE TRADE
$5.95/420-8
A sparkling mix of lesbian erotica and humor. An encounter with ice cream, cappuccino and chocolate cake; an affair with a complete stranger; a pair of faulty handcuffs; and love on a drafting table. Seventeen tales.

LOVECHILD
GAG
$5.95/369-4
From New York's poetry scene comes this explosive volume of work from one of the bravest, most cutting young writers you'll ever encounter. The poems in *Gag* take on American hypocrisy with uncommon energy, and announce Lovechild as a writer of unforgettable rage.

ELIZABETH OLIVER
PAGAN DREAMS
$5.95/295-7
Cassidy and Samantha plan a vacation at a secluded bed-and-breakfast, hoping for a little personal time alone. Their hostess, however, has different plans. The lovers are plunged into a world of dungeons and pagan rites, as Anastasia steals Samantha for her own.

SUSAN ANDERS
CITY OF WOMEN
$5.95/375-9
Stories dedicated to women and the passions that draw them together. Designed strictly for the sensual pleasure of women, these tales are set to ignite flames of passion from coast to coast.

PINK CHAMPAGNE
$5.95/282-5
Tasty, torrid tales of butch/femme couplings. Tough as nails or soft as silk, these women seek out their antitheses, intent on working out the details of their own personal theory of difference.

ANONYMOUS
LAVENDER ROSE
$4.95/208-6
From the writings of Sappho, Queen of the island Lesbos, to the turn-of-the-century *Black Book of Lesbianism*; from *Tips to Maidens* to *Crimson Hairs*, a recent lesbian saga—here are the great but little-known lesbian writings and revelations. A one volume survey of hot and historic lesbian writing.

LAURA ANTONIOU, EDITOR
LEATHERWOMEN
$4.95/3095-4
These fantasies, from the pens of new or emerging authors, break every rule imposed on women's sexuality. The hottest stories from some of today's newest and most outrageous writers make this an unforgettable exploration of the female libido.

LEATHERWOMEN II
$4.95/229-9
Another groundbreaking volume of writing from women on the edge, sure to ignite libidinal flames in any reader. Leave taboos behind, because these Leatherwomen know no limits....

MASQUERADE BOOKS

A.L. REINE
DISTANT LOVE & OTHER STORIES
$4.95/3056-3

In the title story, Leah Michaels and her lover, Ranelle, have had four years of blissful, smoldering passion together. When Ranelle is out of town, Leah records an audio "Valentine:" a cassette filled with erotic reminiscences....

A RICHARD KASAK BOOK

SIMON LEVAY
ALBRICK'S GOLD
$12.95/518-2

From the man behind the controversial "gay brain" studies comes a chilling tale of medical experimentation run amok. Roger Cavendish, a diligent researcher into the mysteries of the human mind, and Guy Albrick, a researcher who claims to know the secret to human sexual orientation, find themselves on opposite sides of the battle over experimental surgery. Has Dr. Albrick already begun to experiment on humans? What are the implications of his receiving support from ultra-conservative forces? Simon Levay fashions a classic medical thriller from today's cutting-edge science.

SHAR REDNOUR, EDITOR
VIRGIN TERRITORY 2
$12.95/506-9

The follow-up volume to the groundbreaking *Virgin Territory*, including the work of many women inspired by the success of *VT*. Focusing on the many "firsts" of a woman's erotic life, *Virgin Territory 2* provides one of the sole outlets for serious discussion of the myriad possibilities available to and chosen by many contemporary lesbians. A necessary addition to the library of any reader interested in the state of contemporary sexuality.

VIRGIN TERRITORY
$12.95/457-7

An anthology of writing by women about their first-time erotic experiences with other women. From the ecstasies of awakening dykes to the sometimes awkward pleasures of sexual experimentation on the edge, each of these true stories reveals a different, radical perspective on one of the most traditional subjects around: virginity.

MICHAEL FORD, EDITOR
ONCE UPON A TIME:
EROTIC FAIRY TALES FOR WOMEN
$12.95/449-6

How relevant to contemporary lesbians are the lessons of these age-old tales? The contributors to *Once Upon a Time*—some of the biggest names in contemporary lesbian literature—retell their favorite fairy tales, adding their own surprising—and sexy—twists. *Once Upon a Time* is sure to be one of contemporary lesbian literature's classic collections.

HAPPILY EVER AFTER:
EROTIC FAIRY TALES FOR MEN
$12.95/450-X

A hefty volume of bedtime stories Mother Goose never thought to write down. Adapting some of childhood's most beloved tales for the adult gay reader, the contributors to *Happily Ever After* dig up the subtext of these hitherto "innocent" diversions—adding some surprises of their own along the way.

MICHAEL BRONSKI, EDITOR
TAKING LIBERTIES: GAY MEN'S ESSAYS
ON POLITICS, CULTURE AND SEX
$12.95/456-9

"Offers undeniable proof of a heady, sophisticated, diverse new culture of gay intellectual debate. I cannot recommend it too highly."—Christopher Bram
A collection of some of the most divergent views on the state of contemporary gay male culture published in recent years. Michael Bronski here presents some of the community's foremost essayists weighing in on such slippery topics as outing, masculine identity, pornography, the pedophile movement, political strategy—and much more.

FLASHPOINT: GAY MALE SEXUAL WRITING
$12.95/424-0

A collection of the most provocative testaments to gay eros. Michael Bronski presents over twenty of the genre's best writers, exploring areas such as Enlightenment, True Life Adventures and more. Sure to be one of the most talked about and influential volumes ever dedicated to the exploration of gay sexuality.

HEATHER FINDLAY, EDITOR
A MOVEMENT OF EROS:
25 YEARS OF LESBIAN EROTICA
$12.95/421-6

One of the most scintillating overviews of lesbian erotic writing ever published. Heather Findlay has assembled a roster of stellar talents, each represented by their best work. Tracing the course of the genre from its pre-Stonewall roots to its current renaissance, Findlay examines each piece, placing it within the context of lesbian community and politics.

CHARLES HENRI FORD & PARKER TYLER
THE YOUNG AND EVIL
$12.95/431-3

"*The Young and Evil* creates [its] generation as *This Side of Paradise* by Fitzgerald created his generation."
　　　　　　　　　　　　　　—Gertrude Stein
Originally published in 1933, *The Young and Evil* was an immediate sensation due to its unprecedented portrayal of young gay artists living in New York's notorious Greenwich Village. From flamboyant drag balls to squalid bohemian flats, these characters followed love and art wherever it led them—with a frankness that had the novel banned for many years.

MASQUERADE BOOKS

BARRY HOFFMAN, EDITOR
THE BEST OF GAUNTLET
$12.95/202-7

Gauntlet has, with its semi-annual issues, always publishing the widest possible range of opinions, in the interest of challenging public opinion. The most provocative articles have been gathered by editor-in-chief Barry Hoffman, to make *The Best of Gauntlet* a riveting exploration of American society's limits.

MICHAEL ROWE
WRITING BELOW THE BELT:
CONVERSATIONS WITH EROTIC AUTHORS
$19.95/363-5

"An in-depth and enlightening tour of society's love/hate relationship with sex, morality, and censorship." —*James White Review*
Journalist Michael Rowe interviewed the best erotic writers and presents the collected wisdom in *Writing Below the Belt.* Rowe speaks frankly with cult favorites such as Pat Califia, crossover success stories like John Preston, and up-and-comers Michael Lowenthal and Will Leber. A volume dedicated to chronicling the insights of some of this overlooked genre's most renowned pratitioners.

LARRY TOWNSEND
ASK LARRY
$12.95/289-2

One of the leather community's most respected scribes here presents the best of his advice to leathermen worldwide. Starting just before the onslaught of AIDS, Townsend wrote the "Leather Notebook" column for *Drummer* magazine. Now, readers can avail themselves of Townsend's collected wisdom, as well as the author's contemporary commentary—a careful consideration of the way life has changed in the AIDS era. No man worth his leathers can afford to miss this volume of sage advice and considered opinion.

MICHAEL LASSELL
THE HARD WAY
$12.95/231-0

"Lassell is a master of the necessary word. In an age of tepid and whining verse, his bawdy and bitter-sweet songs are like a plunge in cold champagne." —Paul Monette
The first collection of renowned gay writer Michael Lassell's poetry, fiction and essays. As much a chronicle of post-Stonewall gay life as a compendium of a remarkable writer's work.

AMARANTHA KNIGHT, EDITOR
LOVE BITES
$12.95/234-5

A volume of tales dedicated to legend's sexiest demon—the Vampire. Not only the finest collection of erotic horror available—but a virtual who's who of promising new talent. A must-read for fans of both the horror and erotic genres.

RANDY TUROFF, EDITOR
LESBIAN WORDS: STATE OF THE ART
$10.95/340-6

"This is a terrific book that should be on every thinking lesbian's bookshelf." —Nisa Donnelly
One of the widest assortments of lesbian nonfiction writing in one revealing volume. Dorothy Allison, Jewelle Gomez, Judy Grahn, Eileen Myles, Robin Podolsky and many others are represented by some of their best work, looking at not only the current fashionability the media has brought to the lesbian "image," but considerations of the lesbian past via historical inquiry and personal recollections.

ASSOTTO SAINT
SPELLS OF A VOODOO DOLL
$12.95/393-7

"Angelic and brazen."—Jewelle Gomez
A fierce, spellbinding collection of the poetry, lyrics, essays and performance texts of Assotto Saint—one of the most important voices in the renaissance of black gay writing. Saint, aka Yves François Lubin, was the editor of two seminal anthologies: 1991 Lambda Literary Book Award winner, *The Road Before Us: 100 Gay Black Poets* and *Here to Dare: 10 Gay Black Poets.* He was also the author of two books of poetry, *Stations* and *Wishing for Wings.*

WILLIAM CARNEY
THE REAL THING
$10.95/280-9

"Carney gives us a good look at the mores and lifestyle of the first generation of gay leathermen. A chilling mystery/romance novel as well."—Pat Califia
With a new introduction by Michael Bronski. First published in 1968, this uncompromising story of American leathermen received instant acclaim. *The Real Thing* finally returns from exile, ready to thrill a new generation.

EURYDICE
F/32
$10.95/350-3

"It's wonderful to see a woman...celebrating her body and her sexuality by creating a fabulous and funny tale." —Kathy Acker
With the story of Ela, Eurydice won the National Fiction competition sponsored by Fiction Collective Two and Illinois State University. A funny, disturbing quest for unity, *f/32* prompted Frederic Tuten to proclaim "almost any page... redeems us from the anemic writing and banalities we have endured in the past decade..."

CHEA VILLANUEVA
JESSIE'S SONG
$9.95/235-3

"It conjures up the strobe-light confusion and excitement of urban dyke life.... Read about these dykes and you'll love them." —Rebecca Ripley
Based largely upon her own experience, Villanueva's work is remarkable for its frankness, and delightful in its iconoclasm. Unconcerned with political correctness, this writer has helped expand the boundaries of "serious" lesbian writing.

MASQUERADE BOOKS

SAMUEL R. DELANY

THE MOTION OF LIGHT IN WATER
$12.95/133-0

"A very moving, intensely fascinating literary biography from an extraordinary writer....The artist as a young man and a memorable picture of an age."—William Gibson

Award-winning author Samuel R. Delany's autobiography covers the early years of one of science fiction's most important voices. *The Motion of Light in Water* follows Delany from his early marriage to the poet Marilyn Hacker, through the publication of his first, groundbreaking work.

THE MAD MAN
$23.95/193-4/hardcover

Delany's fascinating examination of human desire. For his thesis, graduate student John Marr researches the life and work of the brilliant Timothy Hasler: a philosopher whose career was cut tragically short over a decade earlier. Marr soon begins to believe that Hasler's death might hold some key to his own life as a gay man in the age of AIDS.

"What Delany has done here is take the ideas of the Marquis de Sade one step further, by filtering extreme and obsessive sexual behavior through the sieve of post-modern experience...."

—*Lambda Book Report*

"Delany develops an insightful dichotomy between [his protagonist's] two worlds: the one of cerebral philosophy and dry academia, the other of heedless, 'impersonal' obsessive sexual extremism. When these worlds finally collide ... the novel achieves a surprisingly satisfying resolution...."

—*Publishers Weekly*

FELICE PICANO

DRYLAND'S END
$12.95/279-5

The science fiction debut of the highly acclaimed author of *Men Who Loved Me* and *Like People in History*. Set five thousand years in the future, *Dryland's End* takes place in a fabulous techno-empire ruled by intelligent, powerful women. While the Matriarchy has ruled for over two thousand years and altered human society, it is now unraveling. Military rivalries, religious fanaticism and economic competition threaten to destroy the mighty empire.

ROBERT PATRICK

TEMPLE SLAVE
$12.95/191-8

"You must read this book."   —Quentin Crisp

"This is nothing less than the secret history of the most theatrical of theaters, the most bohemian of Americans and the most knowing of queens.... *Temple Slave* is also one of the best ways to learn what it was like to be fabulous, gay, theatrical and loved in a time at once more and less dangerous to gay life than our own."   —*Genre*

GUILLERMO BOSCH

RAIN
$12.95/232-9

"Rain is a trip..."   —Timothy Leary

An adult fairy tale, *Rain* takes place in a time when the mysteries of Eros are played out against a background of uncommon deprivation. The tale begins on the 1,537th day of drought—when one man comes to know the true depths of thirst. In a quest to sate his hunger for some knowledge of the wide world, he is taken through a series of extraordinary, unearthly encounters that promise to change not only his life, but the course of civilization around him. A moving fable for our time.

LAURA ANTONIOU, EDITOR

LOOKING FOR MR. PRESTON
$23.95/288-4

Edited by Laura Antoniou, *Looking for Mr. Preston* includes work by Lars Eighner, Pat Califia, Michael Bronski, Joan Nestle, and others who contributed interviews, essays and personal reminiscences of John Preston—a man whose career spanned the industry. Preston was the author of over twenty books, and edited many more. Ten percent of the proceeds from sale of the book will go to the AIDS Project of Southern Maine, for which Preston served as President of the Board.

CECILIA TAN, EDITOR

SM VISIONS: THE BEST OF CIRCLET PRESS
$10.95/339-2

"Fabulous books! There's nothing else like them."

—Susie Bright,
Best American Erotica and *Herotica 3*

Circlet Press, devoted exclusively to the erotic science fiction and fantasy genre, is now represented by the best of its very best: *SM Visions*—sure to be one of the most thrilling and eye-opening rides through the erotic imagination ever published.

RUSS KICK

OUTPOSTS:
A CATALOG OF RARE AND DISTURBING ALTERNATIVE INFORMATION
$18.95/0202-8

A huge, authoritative guide to some of the most bizarre publications available today! Rather than simply summarize the plethora of opinions crowding the American scene, Kick has tracked down and compiled reviews of work penned by political extremists, conspiracy theorists, hallucinogenic pathfinders, sexual explorers, and others. Each review is followed by ordering information for the many readers sure to want these publications for themselves. An essential reference in this age of rapidly proliferating information systems and increasingly extremes political and cultural perspectives.

BUY ANY 4 BOOKS & CHOOSE 1 ADDITIONAL BOOK, OF EQUAL OR LESSER VALUE, AS YOUR FREE GIFT

MASQUERADE BOOKS

LUCY TAYLOR
UNNATURAL ACTS
$12.95/181-0

"A topnotch collection..." —*Science Fiction Chronicle*
Unnatural Acts plunges deep into the dark side of the psyche and brings to life a disturbing vision of erotic horror. Unrelenting angels and hungry gods play with souls and bodies in Taylor's murky cosmos: where heaven and hell are merely differences of perspective; where redemption and damnation lie behind the same shocking acts.

TIM WOODWARD, EDITOR
THE BEST OF SKIN TWO
$12.95/130-6

A groundbreaking journal from the crossroads of sexuality, fashion, and art, *Skin Two* specializes in provocative essays by the finest writers working in the "radical sex" scene. Collected here are the articles and interviews that established the magazine's reputation. Including interviews with cult figures Tim Burton, Clive Barker and Jean Paul Gaultier.

MICHAEL LOWENTHAL, EDITOR
THE BEST OF THE BADBOYS
$12.95/233-7

The very best of the leading Badboys is collected here, in this testament to the artistry that has catapulted these "outlaw" authors to bestselling status. John Preston, Aaron Travis, Larry Townsend, and others are here represented by their most provocative writing.

PAT CALIFIA
SENSUOUS MAGIC
$12.95/458-5

A new classic, destined to grace the shelves of anyone interested in contemporary sexuality.
"*Sensuous Magic* is clear, succinct and engaging even for the reader for whom S/M isn't the sexual behavior of choice.... When she is writing about the dynamics of sex and the technical aspects of it, Califia is the Dr. Ruth of the alternative sexuality set...." —*Lambda Book Report*
"Pat Califia's *Sensuous Magic* is a friendly, non-threatening, helpful guide and resource... She captures the power of what it means to enter forbidden terrain, and to do so safely with someone else, and to explore the healing potential, spiritual aspects and the depth of S/M."

—*Bay Area Reporter*
"Don't take a dangerous trip into the unknown—buy this book and know where you're going!"
—*SKIN TWO*

MICHAEL PERKINS
THE GOOD PARTS: AN UNCENSORED GUIDE TO LITERARY SEXUALITY
$12.95/186-1

Michael Perkins, one of America's only critics to regularly scrutinize sexual literature, presents sex as seen in the pages of over 100 major fiction and nonfiction volumes from the past twenty years.

COMING UP:
THE WORLD'S BEST EROTIC WRITING
$12.95/370-8

Author and critic Michael Perkins has scoured the field of erotic writing to produce this anthology sure to challenge the limits of even the most seasoned reader. Using the same sharp eye and transgressive instinct that have established him as America's leading commentator on sexually explicit fiction, Perkins here presents the cream of the current crop.

DAVID MELTZER
THE AGENCY TRILOGY
$12.95/216-7

"...The Agency' is clearly Meltzer's paradigm of society; a mindless machine of which we are all 'agents,' including those whom the machine supposedly serves...." —Norman Spinrad

When first published, *The Agency* explored issues of erotic dominance and submission with an immediacy and frankness previously unheard of in American literature, as well as presented a vision of an America consumed and dehumanized by a lust for power.

JOHN PRESTON
MY LIFE AS A PORNOGRAPHER AND OTHER INDECENT ACTS
$12.95/135-7

A collection of renowned author and social critic John Preston's essays, focusing on his work as an erotic writer and proponent of gay rights.
"...essential and enlightening... [*My Life as a Pornographer*] is a bridge from the sexually liberated 1970s to the more cautious 1990s, and Preston has walked much of that way as a standard-bearer to the cause for equal rights...." —*Library Journal*

"*My Life as a Pornographer*...is not pornography, but rather reflections upon the writing and production of it. In a deeply sex-phobic world, Preston has never shied away from a vision of the redemptive potential of the erotic drive. Better than perhaps anyone in our community, Preston knows how physical joy can bridge differences and make us well."
—*Lambda Book Report*

CARO SOLES, EDITOR
MELTDOWN! AN ANTHOLOGY OF EROTIC SCIENCE FICTION AND DARK FANTASY FOR GAY MEN
$12.95/203-5

Editor Caro Soles has put together one of the most explosive collections of gay erotic writing ever published. *Meltdown!* contains the very best examples of the increasingly popular sub-genre of erotic sci-fi/dark fantasy: stories meant to shock and delight, to send a shiver down the spine and start a fire down below.

MASQUERADE BOOKS

LARS EIGHNER
ELEMENTS OF AROUSAL
$12.95/230-2

A guideline for success with one of publishing's best kept secrets: the novice-friendly field of gay erotic writing. Eighner details his craft, providing the reader with sure advice. Because that's what *Elements of Arousal* is all about: the application and honing of the writer's craft, which brought Eighner fame with not only the steamy *Bayou Boy*, but the illuminating *Travels with Lizbeth*.

STAN TAL, EDITOR
BIZARRE SEX
AND OTHER CRIMES OF PASSION
$12.95/213-2

From the pages of *Bizarre Sex*. Over twenty small masterpieces of erotic shock make this one of the year's most unexpectedly alluring anthologies. This incredible volume, edited by Stan Tal, includes such masters of erotic horror and fantasy as Edward Lee, Lucy Taylor and Nancy Kilpatrick.

MARCO VASSI
A DRIVING PASSION
$12.95/134-9

Marco Vassi was famous not only for his groundbreaking writing, but for the many lectures he gave regarding sexuality and the complex erotic philosophy he had spent much of his life working out. *A Driving Passion* collects the wit and insight Vassi brought to these lectures, and distills the philosophy that made him an underground sensation.

"The most striking figure in present-day American erotic literature. Alone among modern erotic writers, Vassi is working out a philosophy of sexuality."
—Michael Perkins, *The Secret Record*

"Vintage Vassi." —*Future Sex*

"An intriguing artifact... His eclectic quest for eroticism is somewhat poignant, and his fervor rarely lapses into silliness." —*Publishers Weekly*

THE EROTIC COMEDIES
$12.95/136-5

Short stories designed to shock and transform attitudes about sex and sexuality, *The Erotic Comedies* is both entertaining and challenging—and garnered Vassi some of the most lavish praise of his career. Also includes his groundbreaking writings on the Erotic Experience, including the concept of Metasex—the premise of which was derived from the author's own unbelievable experiences.

"To describe Vassi's writing as pornography would be to deny his very serious underlying purposes.... The stories are good, the essays original and enlightening, and the language and subject-matter intended to shock the prudish."—*Sunday Times* (UK)

"The comparison to [Henry] Miller is high praise indeed.... But reading Vassi's work, the analogy holds—for he shares with Miller an unabashed joy in sensuality, and a questing after experience that is the root of all great literature, erotic or otherwise.... Vassi was, by all accounts, a fearless explorer, someone who jumped headfirst into the world of sex, and wrote about what he found. And as he himself was known to say on more than one occasion, 'The most erotic organ is the mind.'"
—David L. Ulin, *The Los Angeles Reader*

THE SALINE SOLUTION
$12.95/180-2

"I've always read Marco's work with interest and I have the highest opinion not only of his talent but his intellectual boldness." —Norman Mailer

The story of one couple's spiritual crises during an age of extraordinary freedom. While renowned for his sexual philosophy, Vassi also experienced success in with fiction; *The Saline Solution* was one of the high points of his career, while still addressing the issue of sexuality.

THE STONED APOCALYPSE
$12.95/132-2

"...Marco Vassi is our champion sexual energist."
—*VLS*

During his lifetime, Marco Vassi was hailed as America's premier erotic writer. His reputation was worldwide. *The Stoned Apocalypse* is Vassi's autobiography, financed by his other groundbreaking erotic writing. Chronicling a cross-country roadtrip, *The Stoned Apocalypse* is rife with Vassi's insight into the American character and libido. One of the most vital portraits of "the 60s," this volume is a fitting testament to the writer's talents, and the sexual imagination of his generation.

SINS
OF THE
CITIES
OF THE
PLAIN

ANONYMOUS

MASQUERADE

THE PARLOR

N.T. MORLEY

SISTER RADIANCE

DAVID AARON CLARK

$6.95 • RHINOCEROS BOOKS

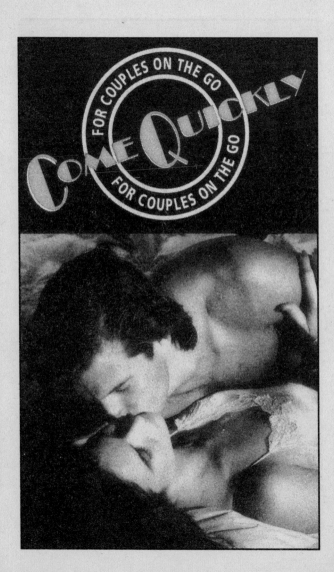

ODD
WOMEN

RACHEL PEREZ

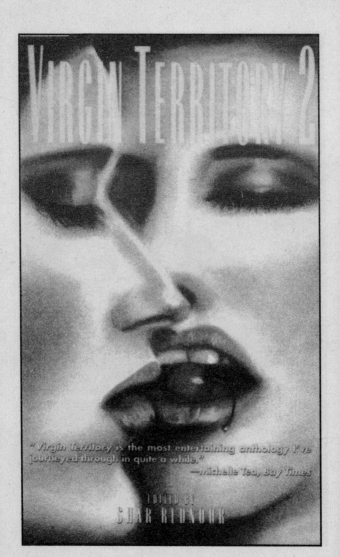

VIRGIN TERRITORY 2

"Virgin Territory is the most entertaining anthology I've journeyed through in quite a while."
—Michelle Tea, *Bay Times*

EDITED BY
CHAR REDNOUR

"Assotto Saint's words are the songs of America."
—Jewelle Gomez

ASSOTTO SAINT

SPELLS OF A VOODOO DOLL

PRISONER
OF DESIRE

DEREK ADAMS

lustneversleeps

Mindy turoff

SOLIDLY BUILT

MATT TOWNSEND

THE 50
BEST
PLAYGIRL
FANTASIES

EDITED BY
CHARLOTTE
ROSE

JUDITH BOSTON

TITIAN BERESFORD

Gynecocracy

VISCOUNT LADYWOOD

Three Volumes in One

A GAY DIARY

1 9 3 3 · 1 9 4 6

"A very pleasing chronicle of a life
clearly well and thoroughly lived." ·
—LIBRARY JOURNAL

DONALD VINING